NORMAL

Scott J. Holliday

Copyright 2017 Scott J. Holliday

All rights reserved.

ISBN-10: 0988555409

ISBN-13: 978-0988555402

This book is a work of fiction. The names, characters, places, and incidents are products of the writer's imagination or have been used fictitiously and are not to be construed as real. Any resemblance to persons living or dead is entirely coincidental.

All rights are reserved. With the exception of fair use excerpts for reviews and critical articles, no part of this book may be used or reproduced in any manner whatsoever without written permission from the author.

This is for my dad, who secretly believed his sons could do anything, and for my mom, who is the strongest person I know.

1

Redmine Prison, South Carolina — 1879

Roy Pellerin's cracked skin, patterned like a dry puddle, held no sweat glands, so his body's moisture was thrown off through the eyes, leaving them constantly swollen and dripping. The salty tears drew gnats and flies, but Roy refused to swat at them. He breathed evenly as he repeatedly punched the earthen wall of his solitary confinement cell, alternating between left and right fists, and counting to himself with each sodden thud.

Roy's cell was a hole in the ground. Four feet wide, eight feet long, and six feet deep. The same dimensions as a grave, he thought, and not by coincidence. The walls and floor were damp, packed clay stained with the blood and lust of those who had come before. The air was rank with a scent like dead birds. When the guards looked down on him they pinched their noses closed. Watching them grimace was one of the few pleasures Roy allowed himself.

The rest was work.

Roy did sit-ups and push-ups—a thousand of each. He did pull-ups by dangling bent-kneed from the iron bars above his head. He balanced on his hands and marched around the cell on them for hours. He ran back and forth across the cold floor, knees high, from morning to night, without growing tired. He counted out a double-number pattern as he punched the earthen wall—one one, two two, three three—up to five-hundred for each hand.

He was sickly thin, but physical pain no longer held sway, having been beaten into submission by methodical indifference. His muscles were like braided steel cables, his bones like the iron bars that had kept him prisoner for four-hundred-and-sixteen days.

Each day's passing was marked by the raising and lowering of a Confederate sponge bucket hanging from a rope in Roy's cell. Etched into a brass plate on the bucket's side was *C.S. ARSENAL, 12th, SOUTH CAROLINA, VOL ARTILLERY.* The bucket was once assigned to accompany a southern cannon during the war. It held the water for the sponge-head used to clean out and cool down the cannon's tube after each fired shot. Now the demoted bucket held Roy's urination and defecation. A guard came by each morning to bring it up and empty it, only to then refill it with the day's water supply. For Roy's first week the tainted water went untouched, but thirst, heat, and time conspired to crack his resolve.

Dysentery came and went. As did influenza, whooping cough, and pneumonia. They took their shots and failed.

Stale bread was Roy's daily meal, dropped into his cell through the iron bars overhead. He'd secretly made a game of catching the bread before it touched the ground, but when the guards caught on they made things difficult. Instead of dropping it straight down, as before, they tossed the bread this way or that, sending Roy sprawling for his catch. A missed catch would garner cackling, a made catch garnered silence. Roy hadn't missed his bread in forty-two days.

His teeth were loose in their sockets. At night he clenched his jaw for fear they might fall into his throat while he slept. A ragged wool blanket—another demoted Confederate issue, complete with Bull Run bullet holes and bloodstains—was both his clothing and bed, and all that stood between his body and the floor. At night he folded the blanket narrow and thick, and lay on top to get what little distance he could from the dampness. During the day he used the same blanket to block out the sun, bunching it between the bars above his head. Roy held no quarrel with the sun itself, but with the memories it threw like spears into his cell. When imprisoned and stripped of the few dignities that once made him human, memories were like weapons—useful only to inflict pain.

A sound stopped Roy's punching—the fluttering pages of a book falling through the air before clapping down inside his cell. Roy dropped his fists to his sides. "Thank you," he said aloud, knowing that the person, undoubtedly a guard with a Good Samaritan's soul, had once again gifted him a dime novel. He wished he knew the guard's name, or that he could for once see his face, but the man always arrived unexpectedly, and was gone before Roy could react.

Roy went over and picked up the book. It was a rare, first edition Beadle's Dime Novel. In the fading light of dusk he read the title—*Malaeska, the Indian Wife of the White Hunter.* Roy knew the story. He had read it some years ago while out on the sideshow circuit. It was good. He wished he could tell his benefactor how much he appreciated the gift. Moreover, he wished he could tell the kind stranger goodbye, for Roy Pellerin planned to die tonight.

It was the dead cart that had inspired Roy's plan. The wood-slatted, two-wheeled horse-drawn wagon on which the condemned rode in and the dead rode out of Redmine Prison. Roy imagined the cart a ferryboat, its driver Charon. The prison wall was the River

Styx, and for passage he only need pay the fatal fare.

But dying in his hole would be useless. He could lie there for hours or days without a guard taking notice. This wouldn't do. He must die in the prison yard, where his body would be immediately found. He must die during the mercy hour.

At eight p.m. every fourth Sunday, and after the other prisoners were returned to their cells or dropped back into their own solitary holes, Roy was given an hour to wander the empty yard alone, his shoulders covered with a burlap body bag so the guards would be spared the sight of his wretched skin. He'd overheard this above ground time called the mercy hour. It seemed the guards expected Roy to show his appreciation by running around the yard like a beast, grunting and squealing beneath the gas lamps, overjoyed at the time spent outside its cage. He obliged them, in part because he *was* overjoyed—the fresh air and open space were blessings, and the night sky somehow looked deeper, the stars brighter, when he was six feet closer to them—but his theatrics were mostly an act. He sucked in giant breaths and smiled like a pinhead for all to see. He talked to himself and stalked around the yard with animal steps. He howled like a dog. All as a means to show sharp contrast against his coming death.

Roy had practiced dying for months, each night willing his body into perfect stillness, his heart to an undetectable beat. In the hole he died for hours at a time, steadily lengthening his will to remain still. The arms and legs had come quickly, and the feet and hands followed suit. The chest had been stubborn, but a few weeks back he won it over. His eyelids held out the longest. They twitched, seemingly of their own accord, even in Roy's most solemn of states. The technique he found was to tear some lashes from each eye before dying. A dear price, for eyelashes were the only hair on his body. The pain seemed to paralyze the lids. Now they would no sooner twitch than hop off his face and dance a jig.

Having won the eyelids, Roy could now die during their mercy hour. He believed himself ready, save for one concern. He understood the guards wouldn't touch his skin to check for a pulse, but who knew their alternative methods for testing if he was still alive?

The question nagged him, but in the end it mattered not. Tonight would not be practice. Roy would not stir during his death, regardless of their technique. After four-hundred-and-sixteen days he would leave Redmine, either as a body believed dead or a body truly dead, for if he were caught he would fight until they killed him. With his final thought he would curse Samson. With his final breath he would tell Jesse he'd be waiting for her in the afterlife.

And what would she say if she could hear?

Roy knew precisely. She would spit in the dirt and tell him to steel up. She would throw her fists against her hips and say the afterlife is for goosecaps. "If you believe some god is up there waitin' for ya with tea and cakes, I've got a crate of snake oil to sell ya." Then she'd laugh crazily at her own wit, and her eyes would outshine the moon.

Roy beamed at the sound of Jesse's voice in his head, smiled at her remembered scent, the touch of her skin. He moved his hand over the scarred word on his chest, tracing each letter with his finger:

$$N \diamond R \wedge A L$$

The word was the only smooth part of his skin, the only part that actually looked like what it spelled. He often found himself absently tracing the word, particularly when Jesse invaded his mind. At first he cursed the hand that went to scar, but over time he came to accept that it was part of him now, one of the chapters in his volume.

As the sun fell away, Roy stacked his new book with the others against the far wall. He spread his wool blanket and folded it neatly. He smirked at his makeshift bed. It would be the last time he ever lay on the grimy thing. Later tonight he would lie amongst rotting bodies. Tomorrow night he would lie somewhere else, be it a real bed, a ditch, or a grave. It mattered not, so long as he was outside the wall. He closed his eyes hoping not to dream of the night he killed Jukey.

No dice.

Roy slept, and his dreaming hands still felt Jukey's body jerk against the pillow. His dreaming eyes still saw Jukey's lifeless face. His dreaming ears still heard the plinking notes of the failing music box.

❃

Paul Constantine snuck back toward the dead house. His hand was still sweaty from palming the dime novel he'd deftly dropped into Roy's cell. He wiped the palm against his leg before opening the dead house door and stepping inside.

Five bodies were stacked and waiting in the corner. Their final bowel movements filled the room with a cloying stench. Paul breathed through his mouth. He took a seat near the window and looked out.

The prison grounds were featureless, save for a few crabgrass patches and the solitary confinement holes that dotted the yard like tiger traps. Paul watched the dark spot of Roy's cell. He'd been watching the same spot every evening for over a year now. It'd been that long since the other guards had dragged his childhood friend through the prison gate, threw him in the hole, and closed the bars overhead. Paul hadn't seen Roy since. In all the passed time he hadn't allowed himself to be caught near his old friend's cell, or even to look down while making one of his secret drops. Whatever friendship they once shared had been erased by one hard fact—the boy he knew had grown into the killer of a helpless man.

Paul picked up a newspaper and twisted it in his hands, smearing ink on his fingers. The paper knotted tightly and tore. He shifted in the creaky chair. The sound echoed off the dead house walls and seemed to come back louder. He opened the tortured paper to the section he'd been reading prior to going out for his drop. The headline read *Malaria Outbreak Shuts Down Local Schools*. He turned to the *In Memoriam* section. A farmer named Kendall had dropped dead in his own tannery. A woman named Fitzgerald lost her husband to a stray bullet in a saloon shootout. A man named Smith had simply expired; the given cause of death was *God's will*.

Paul stopped reading and threw the newspaper aside. He dropped his forehead into his hands. How long until he found Roy's body stacked with these others, decomposing and stinking of shit? Most solitary confinement prisoners didn't last six months in the hole, much less the fourteen Roy was working on.

For his own sake, and maybe Roy's too, Paul prayed his old friend's death would come soon.

2

"Rise and shine, beast. You've got an hour."

Beast.

Four-hundred-and-seventeen days ago Roy had been *Scales, the Crying Lizard.* He was a feature act in Jack McLean's Congress of Curiosities, the sideshow with which he'd spent years traveling the country. The show was a pocket of mystery riding in the wake of The Top Tent Circus, the exotic element that clung strangely to the family friendly three-ring like a vestigial tail. It existed in the shadows, hiding in a place where men hesitated to go, and where they first peered long and hard, and pulled their loved ones close, before daring forward.

A vision of Jack McLean entered Roy's mind as he awakened beneath the prison guard's stare. McLean, the great man, stood impossibly tall behind the outside talker's podium, black top hat low on his brow. He pointed his riding crop toward the light and color of The Top Tent Circus and gazed as if seeing the big tents for the first time. "*There* is the light, my children," he called out, and then gestured toward the small tent behind him, "*here* the darkness. *There* is the spectacle, *here* the bizarre. *There* you will find what you have always found. But here?" A wink and a smirk. "*Here* there be monsters."

McLean's charm was no skill, Roy thought, but a gift imparted upon the man at birth. A blood right. He spoke not to people, but to the demons lurking in the corners of their souls. He pulled back the sideshow curtain to reveal a demented world where such demons roamed free. Inside his tent there was nothing more than a straw-thatched floor and a dimly lit stage, but Roy and the others—most of them just by emerging from the shadows and sitting down—would make good on McLean's promises. They were the stuff of children's nightmares and adult fascinations. They were contradiction—a drawing repulsion, a terrifying treat. People pointed and gasped. They covered their mouths. They laughed. They cried. They screamed.

Roy opened one eye to see the guard's bulldog face beyond the bars, lit by a shaft of moonlight. His teeth were like pebbles with dark slits between. He was fat and had a drunkard's nose, the vision of a man who passed too many things into his mouth.

Roy rose and stood beneath the iron door. The guard's face pulled away from the bars and moonlight reached down into the cell. Roy heard jingling keys. He looked over his hole to see what he always saw—the bucket, the blanket, and his stack of dime novels. More than a year of his life had been spent in this place, never with more than these three companions, and still there was a place called Hell? He felt no fear of it.

"Let's go, freak," the guard said as he keyed open the lock. "Up ya come."

The door's rusty joints shrieked like slaughterhouse pigs. Over time the sound had become a song in Roy's ears, signifying a mercy hour. Tonight the sound was a symphony. The guard lowered the same old rope for Roy to climb from the hole. Roy gripped it, the hemp like a spine in his fist. He thought to speed up like a spider, giving the guard a fright that might stop his heart and drop him dead.

No. Stick to the plan.

Roy fought adrenaline and climbed up painstakingly slow, the way a man near death might climb. His hands ached for action. His muscles tremored. He had entered solitary confinement with a vengeful seed in his guts, a dark embryo that had grown with each passing day. Inside him now was the full-grown vine, snaking its way through his chest, arms, and legs. It was alive and pulsating, ready to bloom in violent colors.

Roy emerged from the hole to feel a twilight breeze, the peppering of windblown sand. The guard stepped back and away—one thick hand extended out in warning, the other hovering at the thumper on his waist. The yard was hard earth and spotted grass. No trees. The prison itself took up the entire south wall like a giant skull. There were bars over windows and the door to the interior was as wide as Girda, the Heaviest Woman Alive, featured in Jack McLean's show. Girda's banner claimed that she weighed over five hundred pounds, and Roy guessed it wasn't far off. If the dog-faced guard could be accused of eating too much, Girda could be sent to Redmine for it. A former whorehouse madam, Jack McLean had picked up Girda at a saloon in Clarks Fork Bottom in the Montana Territory. The saloon's proprietor begged McLean to take her off his hands, said she was literally eating up all the profits the whores took in. McLean had been all too happy to help the man out.

Roy recalled Samson instructing Girda to sit on his legs while the other performers beat him about the head and upper body. They came with fists, pipes, chains, and finally his father's own knife to carve their sinister word into his chest. Their eyes had overflowed with malice; their ears had been deafened by rage. They never heard his protests, hadn't wanted to. After what he did they no longer saw him as one of their own, and they took the opportunity to give back some of the pain they'd endured throughout their lives.

Roy understood. He forgave them all.

All but Samson.

He turned his eyes toward the dead house. A man's face hovered in the small window. Roy felt a prickle of familiarity. No doubt he knew the man, but from where?

The man pulled back into the shadows.

A second guard came in and swung a burlap body bag over Roy's shoulders. It flitted down like a cape. If the fat guard was a bulldog, this one was an alley cat. His eyes were set far apart and there was a permanent squint to them. He kept a wispy mustache beneath his nose, and his lips always fidgeted like he was nibbling tiny things.

"Go do your thing, freak," the cat-faced guard said. He kicked Roy in the small of the back, sending him stumbling forward.

Roy could have stopped, spun, and cracked a fist across the cat guard's mouth, shattering his jaw before his squinty eyes had a chance to widen. He could twist the fat guard's neck, snapping the inner workings like celery stalks. But he didn't do those things. He shuffled toward the prison wall while scouring his memories, trying to place a name with the face he saw in the dead house window. How many faces had he seen in his life? Tens of thousands? How many farmers, blacksmiths, cobblers, whores, priests, and even prison guards? All walks of life had stared up or down at him with eyes as wide as boiled eggs. To single out one face among so many?

No dice.

The moon cast a white hue against the wall, exposing weathered wood divided by watchtower shadows. Roy ran his hand across the rough surface. One of the advantages to his skin was that no splinters could penetrate him. A cruel joke compared to the array of disadvantages. The top of the wall was laced with curled barbed-wire as thick as brambles. There were feathers caught up in the twisted metal, some still moving with the wind, appearing alive. He could smell the scents of men who'd spent their final days here, dripping sweat and tears. He envisioned a green field on the other side of the wall, an evening-red horizon. There was a farmhouse on the field, a barn, and a stable. He imagined himself walking in from a hard day's work, exhausted and hungry. Jesse would be there, cooking a meal. She would smile at him as he entered their home.

He recalled her in the sideshow tent, on the stage. A drumbeat played as she danced beneath the flickering fires. Slowly she peeled back layers of clothing to reveal the depths of her illustrations. A devil, a cracked heart, and a dragon that coiled for days. All were revealed to an audience of slack jaws and riveted eyes. When her dance was done she stood before them nearly naked, leaving all to wonder why that devil was grinning, whether that cracked heart could be mended, where that dragon's tail might finally end.

Like the stunned men in her audience, Roy had once dreamed answers to all three questions. Two answers still eluded him, but his chest swelled with the knowledge of where that dragon's tail ended. His mind's eye traced it down from her chest, around her back, and again around to her stomach. From there it-

Stop.

He inhaled deeply.

One.

Exhale.

Pause.

Inhale.

Two.

Exhale.

Pause.

After the third deep breath Roy came down to his knees and dropped his forehead against the wall. He relaxed his jaw, his neck, his shoulders, biceps, triceps, forearms, abdominals, thighs, calves, feet. He reached up, one hand on either side of his face, and ripped out some eyelashes. The pain clawed across his eyes, tunneled through his nose, and electrified his teeth.

He took a fourth long breath.

His blood flow slowed.

He took a fifth breath, maddeningly slow. The sound of his heartbeat fell to a hush. He thought of molasses in his veins, his heart struggling to pump it through.

He took a sixth long breath, watching that his chest and stomach did not move with the intake or out. There was no sound in his ears but a low hum. He thought of his brain as a rotten apple, useless to control his organs.

He took a seventh long breath. He recalled Jukey's dead face and forced his own to take the same limp position, rolling his eyes into his head and letting his tongue fall back into his throat.

With the eighth breath he imagined himself standing before a gunfighter donned in all black—a villain straight from a dime novel. The man's face was obscured by the brim of his black hat, but Roy sensed familiarity. The villain slowly lifted a revolver of blue-hued steel and took aim. He squeezed the trigger. A blaze of fire escaped the revolver's barrel. Heat bloomed in Roy's chest. He fell to the side, thumping down like a sack. His once fidgety eyelids were now iron caps. Each distant heartbeat was a stone touching down on the bottom of the ocean. His hands curled up and stiffened. His feet became ancient clay pots; kick them and they'd crack apart.

※

Paul waited in the dead house for Pops, his eight p.m. shift replacement. Pops had telegraphed he'd be late in arriving tonight, but Paul didn't mind. It was the day of Roy's mercy hour, and Paul had finally conceded to viewing the state of the murderer he'd first seen outside his schoolhouse so many years ago.

It was the first day of Paul's third year of school. Robert E. Lee was now with the south, and neither Paul nor any of his classmates were happy to be crammed into their hardback seats with summer still clinging to Louisiana's Bayou Rouge. The children sat listlessly, forward on their elbows, hands cupping chins, waiting for their teacher to finish a hushed conversation with a woman who'd interrupted attendance. The blackboard at the front of the room was still clean and dark, as it was yet to be touched by chalk or eraser this year, save for where Mr. Cairn had written his name in cursive script. The room smelled of ammonia and old wood. Paul sat along the far wall absently tracing where someone had carved *Elmer Gill is a lunger*, followed by the more recently added *so's your ma!*, into the desktop.

A sound from outside made Paul turn to the window. His heart rate increased when a scabby skinned, bald headed boy flashed into the schoolyard, running and shooting at imaginary things with imaginary pistols. The boy cocked his thumb and extended his fingers as he went, making *pow pow* noises and blowing false smoke away from scaly barrels.

Paul alone saw the strange boy, which made the boy his secret, a story he could hone and craft in his special way, drawing out the tension and suspense for his mother and father when he got home. Watching the boy, Paul imagined his parents reacting to the story he would tell—smirks would grow into smiles, smiles into astonishment, astonishment into approval.

But Paul couldn't hold the secret long. George Fickas, one of the older boys who was soon to graduate, stood and pointed. "Look!"

Everyone crowded the window. They gawked. Some laughed. Some said *eww* or *gross*. Jaws dropped open like wooden puppets.

The strange boy stopped and looked back at them.

Where most of the others were disgusted with the boy's appearance, Paul had been fascinated. The diamond pattern of red scabs, the bald head, the near lack of a nose, pebble-sized ears, and the shooting and barrel-rolling. Above the green grass, the boy looked like something escaped from a dream.

Back in the dead house a shiver washed over Paul's skin. If only he had gone straight home that day, Roy Pellerin might have been his only vivid memory from that first day of school. Now a different memory pounded against the door of Paul's mind. His hands went icy. The back of his neck tightened and throbbed. He breathed deeply and steepled his fingers before his face. He raised his eyes to look out the window.

Roy emerged from the hole.

The murderer was emaciated. He resembled nothing of the man they'd dragged through the gates over a year ago, and even less the boy Paul once knew. Still, it was unmistakably Roy. Despite his misgivings, Paul smiled as he watched Roy take in the night air and sky. His eyes filmed over and his chest ached.

His best good friend.

But when Roy looked toward him a coldness slivered into Paul's guts. He pushed back and away from the window, into shadow. From there he watched as Cyrus Lee strolled across the prison yard with a burlap bag under his arm. Lee threw the bag over Roy's shoulders, and then fell in line with the fat guard, Jeb Crittendon. There was a visual exchange between the two guards, and then Lee kicked Roy in the back.

Paul stood quickly, knocking over his chair. His hands became white-knuckled fists.

Roy stumbled across the yard, but did not fall. He straightened up and walked toward the wall.

The coldness in Paul's guts spread up into his heart and settled there. It burned as ice burns. He forced his hands back open and rubbed them together for warmth, telling himself Crittendon and Lee had good reason, and that Roy Pellerin—the murderer—deserved the torture and pain he received. But such thoughts didn't speak as loudly as Paul hoped they might. They couldn't drown out the loudest thought in his mind.

Goddammit, they're hurting my friend.

He stepped toward the dead house door.

3

Roy was concentrating on the Egyptian mummy he read about as a child. He imagined his own liver and lungs removed, just as the mummy's, and placed inside canopic jars alongside his intestines and stomach. The mummy's heart was left inside its chest to shrivel; it was the seat of the soul and should remain with its owner throughout the afterlife.

"Get up, beast," the dog guard said.

The voice seemed faint, a thousand miles away.

"I said get up!" the guard said. He kicked Roy's spine.

Roy felt the kick indifferently, the way a mountain feels a climber's footstep.

"I'm not asking again, freak," the guard said. "Get up now or you'll get up lumpy."

Roy heard a thumper slide from its holster. He pushed his mind into a well and swam it toward the unknown bottom.

The thumper cracked against the back of his head. It may have been a falling propeller seed.

The thumper connected again, this time across his ear and cheek. A cool touch of salve.

A boot-heel slammed into his ribcage. A butterfly.

Another boot to the spine. A raindrop.

The thumper crashed down across his lips, popping out teeth and sending them into the dirt. A kiss from his mother on the day he was born.

"Jesus," the cat guard said.

"The beast is finally dead," the dog guard said, breathing raggedly.

Lying beneath them, Roy searched for a vivid memory, something to keep his mind distanced from the pain in his body.

It came as no shock that he found Jesse.

She had come to Roy's wagon on the day that would prove to be his last with the sideshow. It was just past noon and the performance schedule had had not yet begun, the crowds had not yet rushed the circus and sideshow streets like so much blood filling veins. The camp was a din of indistinct voices occasionally cut through by the roars or bleats of animals. The air smelled of meat and corn over fires. Roy was inside his wagon, relaxing, mentally preparing for the judgment delivered from the audience's eyes when Jesse knocked softly on his door. Roy opened it to find her ready for her performance in an Indian headdress, moccasins, and a leather skirt and vest with hanging beads. Her smile became full as she climbed the steps to Roy's wagon, passed the threshold, and stood near the edge of his bed. "It's nice to see you."

"You look beautiful," Roy said.

Her eyes turned down. She scowled. "I asked you not to say that."

"I'm sorry," Roy said.

She glared at him. "I don't want you to be sorry."

"I'm so-" Roy said, catching himself. Then, "Why don't you have a seat?" He gestured toward the lone chair in his wagon.

"This was a mistake," Jesse said. "I shouldn't have come."

Roy searched desperately for something more to say, something that might stop her from leaving, but his words were dammed in his mouth. They just sat there stupidly, behind his teeth and riding his tongue.

Jesse moved back through his wagon door and pulled it nearly closed behind her, momentarily touching Roy's hand, which was still on the frame. She looked back at him through the slim crack, just one eye, and said, "He knows."

Roy's unsaid words slid back from his tongue and melted into his body, promising they'd come back when he was with her again, and that they'd be stronger. Stronger than Samson, even.

Lying battered on the prison yard hardpan, it came to Roy that he missed her touch. The body needs to be touched. After a year without a hug, a caress, or even a handshake, he had found find himself begging for touch, even in the form of a beating. Anything to feel the warmth of another human's skin against his own. Bruises and broken bones be damned.

Will she touch me again?

Roy pushed the question from his mind, just as Sisyphus pushes his stone back up the hill. There was nothing to be gained from a question without the possibility of an answer. It could wait until he found her. It could wait until he regained her love. It could wait until he put Samson in a grave of his own. Once he escaped he would move through society's back-alleys and forgotten paths to track the sideshow down. He would remain unseen and unheard until he was close enough to hear Samson's pumping heart, and then he would reach out and silence it.

❧

Paul's knees buckled when Jeb Crittendon's thumper came down on Roy's head. It was as if he, himself, had been hit. It dazed him, blurred his vision. He shook it off and took another step forward, but found he was punch drunk. The fight had left his body. Roy hadn't reacted to the blow, which surely meant he was dead. His body may be taking the abuse, but Paul's old friend was no longer there.

Relief came, and regret trailed. Paul could have at least said hello. Murderer or not, he could have at least let the man know he had an old friend nearby. He closed his eyes to the continued battering of Roy's lifeless body. "I'm sorry."

"What's that?"

Paul turned to find Pops Gildon had come up on him. He was a broad-shouldered man who wore a beard so thick you wondered if he had cheeks. "Looks like that freak finally died."

Paul said nothing.

"Always felt kinda sorry for him," Pops said. "You did, too. It ain't been hard to tell."

Neither man spoke for a moment. They watched as Jeb Crittendon and Cyrus Lee fussed over how to get Roy into the burlap body bag.

"Couple of shitheels," Pops said.

"They won't touch his skin," Paul said, "not even to bury him."

"They won't be burying him," Pops said. He clapped Paul's shoulder, gripped and squeezed. "You will. Think you can manage it?"

Along with standard guard duties, Paul was the dead house master at Redmine prison. The title meant two extra dollars a week, hours of hard labor in the blazing sun, and a measure of disdain from most of the other guards—as if he could buy and sell them with his extra change. Tomorrow he'd cart his old friend beyond the gate and bury him in a trench grave where hundreds of former prisoners already rested. Most had been lost to cholera or consumption, others had been murdered, and of course there were those who succumbed to the darkness and misery of solitary confinement.

"Of course," Paul said.

"I know you can physically do it," Pops said, "I mean to say, can you bury that man with a scrap of dignity?"

"I know what you mean to say," Paul said. He turned and went to the employee doorway at the prison wall. The sentry opened the locks to let him outside.

Paul walked a southern road home. The bad memory once again pounded at his mind. He couldn't help but let it in. Since Roy had returned to Paul's life, his mind flicked at the memory the way a tongue flicks at a canker sore.

When school let out on that first day of his third year, young Paul bounded from the door and hustled across the schoolyard. First day, worst day, and many more to come, but that didn't matter now; it was over and there was still plenty of daylight for fishing. That morning he'd hidden a cane fishing pole near his favorite river spot, and now he had a leftover strip of jerky for bait. He carried his good shoes and ran barefoot down the road, ignoring the rocks and sticks that stabbed at his feet.

He came to his fishing spot feeling high.

His pole was still there—line, cork bobber, and hook already tied on. He sat on a flat stump and wiped his palms against his good pants. His mother had instructed him home immediately after school, but there was time. His father would be out fishing, too, and he wouldn't be back until after dark. As long as Paul made it home before dad, the punishment would be worth the crime. Besides, when he told his parents the story about the strange boy he'd seen, they might be too swept up to punish him at all.

If there was one thing young Paul Constantine understood, it was that a good story was better than a cry or a lie, anytime.

In this spot the river was wide and slow. There were deep pockets everywhere, holes where trout liked to hide and keep cool, holes only Paul knew about. He laid the jerky across his knee and tore off a bit, carefully setting aside the rest. He pushed the meat on to the small hook and smiled.

Just then a big trout broke the water. It wiggled in the air and splashed down with a plop. Paul's body buzzed. He tossed out his line, aiming for the spot where the fish had landed. Direct hit. The cork bobber ducked under the ripples, popped back up, and wobbled to a stop as the water moved it along.

Paul's rear end complained about the hard stump, having been crammed into that crummy school seat all day. He moved down to the ground and leaned back to relax. He stretched out his legs and crossed one over the other, just like his father did on days when he drank whiskey. The bobber drifted with the water flow, dragging the tasty morsel of hooked meat behind it.

A twig snapped.

Paul looked up to see a gray dog standing on the opposite bank. A stray. It was gaunt with hunger and small enough to be confused for a possum. Its dark eyes bulged from its shrunken body. The dog watched Paul not with aggression, but with what Paul took as fascination. It lifted its nose and sniffed the air. It licked its chops with a pink tongue before letting its mouth hang open to display a dog's smile.

He can smell the jerky.

Paul smirked. It was an amazing thing, considering Paul himself couldn't smell the jerky and it'd just been in his own hands.

The dog took a tentative step toward the brown water. Its paw sank inches into the muck. It pulled back and tried again with its other foot, achieving the same result. Now it was wearing black socks. The dog looked curiously between its feet and the muck, seeming not to understand how the mushy ground had attached itself to him.

Paul laughed. The dog looked up and smiled again.

Paul twisted the handle of his fishing pole into the soft ground and produced his remaining jerky. "C'mere little fella," he said, motioning the salted meat toward the dog.

The dog ignored the muck and started into the water, but then it froze, looking past Paul.

"Looky here," a voice said from behind. "If it ain't Faggot Constantine."

Paul looked back to find his schoolmate, George Fickas. Adults would politely say he was *big for his age*. Paul would say *ogre*. George Fickas had a square head on top of no neck. His cantaloupe shoulders sloped down and away like they were just as scared of his face as everyone else. Following behind Fickas was his group of low-grade thugs, each one meaner and dumber than the next.

"Doing a little fishing, ladybird?" Fickas said.

Paul stood up and hid the jerky behind his back. If Fickas saw the meat he would bend Paul's arms backwards before having it for himself.

"Yeah," Paul said, "but I ain't got no bait. Just hoping for a miracle, really."

The dog mewled behind them. Paul closed his eyes; the damn thing would give him away. He could kill it for that.

"Well I'll be damned," Fickas said. He pointed at the dog. "If that ain't the mangiest thing I ever saw."

Paul slid the jerky into his back pocket and turned to the dog. It was now swimming across the river. The current wasn't strong. The dog's path was almost straight across as it hustled its little legs beneath the water.

A hand yanked the jerky from Paul's back pocket. He turned to see Fickas holding it up in front of his face.

"You lied to me, faggot," Fickas said. His Cro-Magnon eyebrows collided. "Not smart." He closed his fist around the jerky and socked Paul's guts. A cannon shot. Paul fell to the ground, his breath knocked away.

The dog arrived at the bank. It emerged from the river and shook off, spraying Paul with water. It trotted up and licked Paul's contorted face.

"Here boy," Fickas said. He was motioning the jerky toward the dog and backing away. His thugs all backed up with him. He made little whistling noises and the dog's ears perked up. It left Paul's side and followed Fickas with its tail whipping wildly.

"C'mere you little bastard," Fickas said. A sneer came to his lips.

The dog marched forward with its tongue flapping out. When it got within a foot of Fickas, the boy pulled the meat away and kicked the dog's ribs.

The dog yelped and rolled. It staggered to its feet with its tail now tucked between its legs. It looked between Paul and Fickas, confused.

George Fickas laughed with his hand flapped over his stomach. His thugs laughed, too, but Paul could see that most of them were faking it, too scared to defy their master's will.

Fickas held out the meat again. "Here you go, boy."

"Leave him alone," Paul tried to say, but his breath was still gone. All he managed was a hiss. He struggled to his knees.

The dog took a small step toward Fickas, lowered its head, and sniffed the ground. It raised its head again. It took another step, sniffing at the extended meat. It cocked its head one way, then the other. It looked back at Paul, who shook his head no, but of course the dog couldn't understand.

Paul closed his eyes when the dog opened its mouth to take the meat. He heard the dreadful crack of the dog's rib bones breaking, followed by Fickas' laughter.

The dog rolled and yelped again. It staggered to its feet but remained in a crouched position, whimpering and shivering.

George Fickas popped the jerky into his own mouth and laughed through slobbery chomps. He raised his fists above his head like a victorious boxer. The thugs clapped each other's backs and said false things.

Fickas crouched in front of the dog, level with its eyes. He breathed a gust of jerky into its face and giggled. The dog took a step back, still trembling, still whimpering. Fickas shot out a big hand and grabbed the dog by the scruff, lifting it off its feet.

"Everyone takes a turn," Fickas said, sweeping an arm toward his thugs.

The cowards exchanged horrified glances.

Paul came to his feet. He pushed through the crowd and tried to pull the dog from the bigger boy's grip.

Fickas socked Paul's mouth, sending him sprawling.

Paul's lips thumped. Thick and bloody. Loose teeth. He struggled back to his feet. "Please."

Fickas looked down at Paul. The dog hung limply from his clenched fist. "I'm not hurting him," he said, "you are." He nodded and the thugs were on Paul, corralling him in place. Fickas brandished a pot-roast-sized fist to show Paul what disobedience would bring. He dropped the dog from shoulder height. "Pick it up."

Paul looked down to see that the dog's eyes were glazed over from shock or pain. The gray fur around its mouth was clotted red. He picked it up and cradled it into his arms like a child.

Fickas clamped one big hand around Paul's throat and walked him backwards into the river. Paul squirmed, but the bigger boy's grip only tightened. Purple flashes across his eyes.

"Now," Fickas said, "you drown that dog or I drown you." He moved his hand to the back of Paul's neck and squeezed. The hand felt as big as Paul's father's. Bigger. Fickas pushed Paul's head down within a foot of the water. One thug cheered from the riverbank, but the rest had gone silent. The dog whimpered. It didn't seem to understand why these giant things were out to hurt it. It licked Paul's chin and reached a paw toward the boy's face as if to try and know.

Fickas punched Paul in the kidney, a stinging thump that nearly made him puke. "Do it."

"I can't," Paul screamed. "I ca-"

Another punch cut him off. Pain shot up his side and found his eye socket. Fickas pushed Paul's head underwater and held it there. The world went mute. The dog squirmed and scratched. The way Paul was holding it, they were now both drowning. He pushed the dog out to the side, hoping it could swim off faster than Fickas could catch it.

The pressure came off Paul's neck. He pulled his head from the water, gasping. He whirled around, searching. The dog was treading water. It couldn't rightly see which way to go. The thugs watched in silence as Fickas recovered it. He shoved it back into Paul's arms and again clamped Paul's neck. He brought his lips close to Paul's ear.

"The dog dies no matter what. Don't be stupid and die, too."

Paul moved the dog from his cradling arms into his hands. He looked into the confused, dark eyes to see the agony and confusion he would spend his days wishing he could unsee. He closed his own eyes and pushed the dog underwater, holding it there until its little paws finally stopped twitching.

4

The dead house stench was thick as butter. They had bagged Roy in dry-rotted burlap—the same body bag he'd worn like a cape in the yard. Through tiny holes in the bag he could see dots of flesh and hair, plus one dead eye staring down at him, not seeing. Roy imagined the man kneeling before some gates, more likely Hell's black than Heaven's pearly, his hands clamped together before him, begging. Roy longed to pinch the eyelid closed. He was lying face up with bodies beneath him and bodies atop, crushing down. He'd been tossed atop a stack of corpses in the night, but since the morning two more bodies had been added.

Blood dripped from a dead man's wound. Likely his penalty for a crime less severe than the one for which he was originally imprisoned. It seeped through Roy's burlap and was now dripping down on to his collarbone, adding a copper scent to the fetid air. Flies buzzed and swarmed the room like feasting Pagans. They touched down and launched, touched down and launched.

Overnight, Roy hadn't allowed himself to sleep in case his body shifted or he snored, but he'd been able to relax his mind in preparation for what might happen outside the wall. It couldn't have been later than eight a.m., but the day's heat had already swooped down and perched on South Carolina like the Phoenix returned to roost. Roy's muscles ached with the desire to flex and stretch out. The back of his head, his cheek, and mouth throbbed. The holes from his busted teeth dripped pus and blood. He held mouthfuls of the mixture until he absolutely must swallow. He closed his eyes and fought for some kind of rest. The *tick-tick* of dripping blood continued, each drip coming slower than the last.

He searched his mind for Jesse and found her. Just a girl, she stood shyly, head down, hands clasped before her waist, one ankle rolling nervously on her first day with the sideshow. She was eager then, not yet hewn and hardened by the entitled eyes of a thousand audiences. McLean announced he had picked her up at the Atlanta orphanage where they had just given a free performance. When he presented her to them he gave an impassioned speech about how she'd been abandoned by derelict parents and left to survive in an area torn by the Civil War battles of Peachtree Creek and Ezra Church.

Though McLean's speech was stirring, everyone thought the girl's presence was strange, for she wasn't one of them. She wasn't yet illustrated, wasn't yet a performer. It seemed McLean had welcomed the normal girl without reservation. There were whispered accusations of the old man's lust, of a slave girl, and worse.

Roy never fell into such gossip. In his estimation the girl was a freak in her own right—standing on the outside, just as they all were, only she stood on the opposite end of the scale. She had been treated differently, too, but because she was beautiful instead of ugly, desired instead of vilified. Women would naturally hate her. Men would either have her or hurt her. It was plain to see they already had.

That same night Jesse collected her first illustration. The tattoo artist thrust a leather bit into her mouth, telling her it was for the pain. She spat it out.

The dead house door creaked open. Roy heard shuffling footsteps and breathing. "Goddammit, Roy," a voice said, "how'd you hold on for so long?"

Roy nearly gasped when he felt the man's hand come down on the burlap over his shoulder. He put the voice together with the face he'd seen the night before. The mysterious man from the dead house window was Paul Constantine. His Cajun accent solidified it. On the road with the sideshow Roy rarely heard anyone speak with the same snipped words and Acadian lilt as he did. It was the voice of home.

"You were my best good friend," Paul said. "As close as a brother. I'm sorry I never came to you, but I…" Paul paused and breathed deeply. Shaky. When he spoke again his voice took on a dreamy quality. "I was thinking about the first time I saw you, outside the school. You were shooting and rolling in the grass. Do you remember?"

Roy recalled Paul as the freckle-faced kid in that schoolhouse classroom. His had been just one face amongst many, but the only one that hadn't pointed or laughed. It had been a muggy day in early September. The kind of day that made you wonder if the devil hadn't netted a piece of Hell and dragged it up to Louisiana for you to cook yourself on. That morning Roy's mother had walked him along the dusty road to the schoolhouse with a guarded posture. It was to be her son's first day. As they passed strangers on the road she stiffened and her hand tightened around his own. Roy watched the people. They made pinched faces and averted their eyes.

The schoolhouse was a one-room building. It was green with white trim around the windows. The roof was sound and the outer walls were long, knotty planks. It seemed out of place in the gnarled bayou, like a pretty stone in a muddy palm. As Roy and his mother came to the edge of the grass, she stopped and knelt to her son's level. "The world is full of fools, son. The idea is not to be one of them, understand?"

Roy didn't fully understand, but he nodded just the same. In his eight-year-old mind, the world was full of gators and snakes and gunfighters and Indians, but fools? The word sounded funny to him. He looked again at the schoolhouse, this time expecting to see circus clowns flying in and out of doors and windows.

He waited outside as his mother went in to talk with the teacher, saying she'd be back to get him in a moment.

Play time.

Roy produced two thumb-finger pistols and began shooting at shrubs and trees turned Indians. They attacked him from all sides. *Pow, pow, pow*, their bodies fell, their war cries were silenced. He rolled and flipped, dodging bullets and arrows. He was Roy Crockett, son of wild west hero Davy Crockett, and every bit as strong and accurate with a gun.

He turned the corner and came to the side of the schoolhouse where there was a window. It was split into four panes by white shafts. Inside there were children seated, their faces distorted by the hand-blown glass. Their skin appeared smooth, the color of milk. Roy continued shooting and running, picking off the school kids as he strafed past the window. He barrel-rolled and came up, pistols blazing. One by one they went down, until he leveled his sights on a freckle-faced boy staring at him.

Roy lowered his pistols. He turned his back to the window. Apart from his mother and father, the boy was the first person that'd looked at him without blinking or making a face. He felt a new feeling, but he wasn't sure where to put it.

"Look!"

There were the frenzied sounds of chairs scraping wood. The sounds hit Roy's back and made him cringe. He turned to see all the children smashed against the window now, their faces no longer distorted, but clear and sharp. Their eyes widened and their jaws unhinged. There were clean faces and dirty ones, tall kids and short ones, boys wearing suspenders, and girls with pretty things tied into their hair. Some laughed, and some shook their heads and said words he couldn't make out.

The feeling was fear, Roy decided. It welled up in him and made his heart kick his ribs. He backed away from the dozens of eyes, rounded the corner of the schoolhouse, and found some shade, a streak of shadow where he could hide. He leaned back against the wall and slid down to a curled position, his arms wrapped around his knees. His skin grew hot. His eyes threw water. He could hear a conversation inside the wall behind him. A man was speaking.

"This school is a place for people, not animals."

There was a silent moment and then a slapping sound.

Roy's mother burst from the schoolhouse with her spine broomhandle straight and her chin thrust out. She was trembling all over. She clasped Roy's hand and dragged him across the grass toward the road. Her skin felt hotter than his own.

"You mad bitch!" came a voice from behind. "Don't you bring that monster back here again, you hear?"

Roy looked back to see a man in clean clothes leaning out of the schoolhouse doorway. His collar was as white as the schoolhouse trim and high on his neck, pushing out reddish folds of skin. A blue tie was wrapped around his throat. It dropped down into a black jacket made to look like the man had square shoulders. He wore round spectacles that sat crookedly. There was a red handprint on his left cheek.

Was he *a fool?*

Roy looked again at the schoolhouse window. All the milky children were again seated and facing forward. All except the freckle-faced boy, who still watched him from close to the window, his eyes reading over Roy's scales.

More footsteps sounded off in the dead house. Paul's hand lifted from Roy's shoulder. There were new mouths breathing. Paul said, "Let's go, boys. They ain't gonna hop on that cart by themselves."

Roy felt one of the corpses above him slide away. He heard a thud as it slammed the floor. There was a dragging sound, a silent moment, and then another thud. He assumed the final sound was the body landing in the dead cart.

Roy was near the top of the pile now, but the cart would be loaded from top to bottom, meaning he would be beneath the majority of the pile on the way out. He steeled his aching spine, reminding himself he'd soon be free.

Another body slid off and was thrown into the cart.

Roy was next.

What if they could tell he wasn't dead? Were the others stiff with rigor mortis where he was not? Did he smell differently?

Two hands gripped his ankles over the burlap. Strong as C-clamps. He was pulled to the ground. Two more hands came under his armpits. He was carried for a moment and then tossed on top of the pile in the cart.

More thuds, more dragging. Then the other bodies came down on him, each one crashing down harder and heavier than the last. Eight in total, five above.

The weight was unbelievable. Worse was the lack of air. Had he been claustrophobic he might have screamed. He tried to push his mind away, back down into that deep well. No dice. The pressure was like hands squeezing his lungs, choking his throat, thumbs in his eyes.

The cart jerked into motion. The bodies above him jostled and settled into their traveling positions. Time stretch and slowed. No light and no sound. Roy couldn't steal a good breath. His chest trembled. He begged it to stop. His lungs fought to expand. He cursed them. His fingers curled and gripped the burlap on their own accord. His hands and feet ached to claw their way to freedom. He willed them still, imagining himself to be Henry, the Ossified Man, whose very muscles, tendons, and joints had grown into solid bone when he was a teen. McLean had picked up Henry at a sanatorium in The Indian Nation. He'd been left there by derelict parents to live out his days trapped in his own body. His Indian caretakers had been glad to rid themselves of a man they couldn't fix—either through medical or spiritual methods—but who wasn't soon to die. He was only to lie there eating their food and shitting himself for a lifetime. Henry's sideshow act had been simple. Behind closed curtains he was brought in and laid down on a table, sideways to the audience. The curtain would draw back, a minute of murmurs would pass, and then two stagehands would come out to pick Henry up—one at his head, the other at his feet—and carry him away like a board to the audience's gasps.

The cart stopped. It remained still for a moment, and then picked up pace again. The outer gate, Roy thought. The little air he could find was less acrid. He breathed in and out as slowly as he could. Controlling his organs was madness. They'd become lunatic inmates, now wardens in the asylum of his body.

The cart bumped along for fifteen minutes before stopping. The back gate fell open and slapped the ground, shaking the cart. A body slid off the top, relieving pressure. Another body slid off, and then another and another until Roy was no longer covered. He wanted to suck air like a landed fish. He wanted to tear free from the burlap, to get up and run.

No.

They'd cut him apart as he struggled within the bag. It would all be for naught. He remained still and cursed his mad heart and lungs, imagining their betrayals making waves on the burlap above him.

Two hands came to his ankles and pulled him off the cart. He hit the ground and felt rough gravel beneath his back. Through the burlap he could see tiny rays of sun. They were the same rays he'd seen all his life, but they were different now, somehow cleaner. Calmness washed over him. His mind regained some measure of control over his body. He breathed silently and evenly.

The guards working the corpses grunted and breathed heavily. More bodies came off the cart and piled up around him, blessedly not on top.

Then the shoveling began.

For hours Roy lay on the road, seeing the splintered sun move across the sky through his bag, hearing shovels chopping into dirt. Occasionally there was Paul's voice. He commanded two helpers to dig, stop, take a break, drink some water, and dig again.

Roy touched the burlap with his tongue, gauging its thickness and strength. If he were to rip his way out, he'd need to know how long it might take.

One by one the other bodies were dragged away, each one preceded and followed by more shoveling until finally it was Roy's turn.

"The freak," a voice said. It was a dumb voice, low and deliberate.

"Jesus," another voice said, equally as low, equally as dumb. "How long did he last?"

"Over a year, I think. More than anyone."

"Probably 'cause he's part animal."

"Let's go, boys," Paul said, "we ain't got all day." Paul was farther away than these other two, probably by the hole they'd been digging. "And get him out of that burlap."

It made no sense to remove him from the bag, so why would Paul order it? Maybe Paul knew he was alive? Maybe he wanted to help? Surely their childhood friendship meant something.

Hands on the burlap, untying the knot above Roy's head. Roy closed his eyes. He'd made no plan for what happened now. He hadn't allowed his hope to travel so far. He could let them bury him alive and try to dig out once they were gone, but how deep was the hole? No man, no matter how strong, could claw his way free from six feet of earth. Besides, there'd be no coffin around him to supply a little air. He wouldn't last two minutes before inhaling a lungful of dirt.

The bag came off of his head and down past his shoulders. His eyes remained closed. The insides of his eyelids turned red with the sun. New heat baked his arid skin. Another tug and the burlap slid entirely off.

Lying on the road, stiff and vulnerable, Roy felt reborn.

"Ugliest thing you ever did saw," one dumb voice said.

"I ain't touching it," said the other.

"Neither am I!"

"Fellas," Paul said.

There was a pause. Roy imagined Paul pleading with his eyes, the same way he did when they were boys. It was a look young Paul used to give his mother whenever he wanted more play time for himself and Roy, a second helping of supper, or to stay up late. Damn if it didn't work most every time. Roy fought the muscles on his face, which were threatening to smile.

"Tie a rope around his ankles," Paul said. "Drag him over and let's get this done."

Roy heard footsteps on gravel, then the sound of a rope zipping against wood as it came off the dead cart. If they bound his feet, he wouldn't be able to stand up and fight.

So now it was stand up or die.

❋

Paul was tired. He leaned on a shovel and pulled his hat down over his eyes. He hadn't slept last night. His wife was passed out from the drink and his son was fast asleep when he'd arrived home. He couldn't find a way to settle down and join them in slumber. With his nerves tingling, he sat on the stoop for hours, spinning a revolver chamber to an audience of crickets.

The revolver was his father's. When he was called to the Civil War he bought it and took it with him. Only the pistol came back. Paul, then only eleven years old, cleaned the gun and claimed it for his own.

He sat last night, thinking about Roy and their gunfighter games. He smiled to remember that Roy taught him how to use his thumb properly. "When you pull it back," young Roy said, taking his thumb into his hand like it was a pistol hammer, "it makes it a hair-trigger. Then all you do is graze it, and *bang*, bad guys are history."

They said that Roy had killed an armless man. Story had it the two men had been performers in a traveling sideshow, and one day Roy just got the notion to smother his friend under a goose-feather pillow, all for the bit of money in the man's wallet. As it was told, the rest of the freaks then turned against Roy, beating him nearly to death and carving up his chest.

Paul had been dismayed to find that Roy had grown up to become a murderer and a thief. He'd been disappointed to know the man in the hole was once his best good friend, but he told himself men reap what they sew, and if Roy's harvest was imprisonment and death then he'd orchestrated his own undoing. Still, the least Paul could do was inter his old friend with a scrap of dignity, as Pops had suggested. As it were, the burlap body bag was an item of shame and hatred. If their childhood friendship was worth anything, it was worth Paul's refusal to allow the man to be buried in it.

Paul sighed. The day was a scorcher. He wanted to close the hole, get back to Redmine, finish his shift, and get home to see his son before bed. Nothing could keep him awake tonight.

He looked up to see his twin gravediggers, John and Aaron Boyle, preparing to bring Roy's body over. John had pulled a rope from the cart and was leaning over Roy's scabby feet. Aaron had gloved his hands in burlap so he wouldn't have to touch Roy's skin as he picked up his ankles to help his brother along. Both men were giants capable of amazing feats of strength and long hours of hard labor in the sun. They were good for this kind of work—dumb and relatively harmless despite their size.

Paul yanked his shovel from the ground and stabbed it into a pile of fresh dirt, ready to cover Roy once the twins dragged him over. When Roy Pellerin's dead body sat up and opened its eyes Paul dropped the shovel, but it stayed stuck in the earth.

5

Roy's heart jumpstarted. The sun blinded him. Between blinks he saw the two prison guards, their heads cocked in confusion. They were twins. The left twin held a rope that looked like a shoelace in his huge hand. The right twin's hands were wrapped in the burlap bag. He was picking up Roy's ankles. Either one could be a strong man in McLean's show, Roy thought. Two for the price of one. Rubes would pay to see them wrestle each other.

The twins' confusion exploded into surprise. They backed away from Roy like they'd just stumbled upon a pit of cottonmouths.

Roy tried to leap to his feet, but his muscles barely responded and he fell to his side like a drunk. For so many hours his muscles ached to move, to be free from their prisons, but now they were worn-out toddlers after a tantrum. Along the road there was a dry field edged by a six-foot wide dirt line extending into the horizon. The ground was moist where new bodies were buried. Roy heard the click of a grasshopper's jump, followed by the buzz of its wings as it coasted back to the earth. He struggled to his knees, spitting out the mouthful of blood and pus he'd been holding. His tongue found the gap where Jeb Crittendon's thumper had knocked out two teeth.

"Sakes alive," a twin said.

Roy managed his way up from his knees, one leg and then the other. Pain shot from his ankles to his jaw. His arms and hands shivered with the wallops of his heart. The grasshopper clicked and buzzed again.

Roy turned to face the gravediggers.

The twins were standing catatonic with shock. Each wore a thumper, but no gun. The third guard was, of course, Paul. He came away from the hole he'd been digging and stopped between the twins, two feet behind them, his face pale and stricken. He was puny next to them, like a child king flanked by two monstrous eunuchs.

"Hello Paul," Roy said.

The twins looked at Paul between them.

"Hello Roy," Paul said.

"Thanks for the books."

"Sure thing."

There was a gun on Paul's waist—a six-shot revolver with a worn wooden handle. It had a black iron ring with a rawhide lace tied through it. Roy remembered it'd been Paul's father's, taken with him the day he went to the war. The gun seemed to say he hadn't come back. Roy was put in mind of the muggy afternoons when he and Paul had killed many a pretend Indian, and many a bad guy in a black hat with imaginary guns. They would cut them down while repeating the clever words the good guy's always used in Roy's books.

Funny; now Paul was wearing a black hat.

And his expression was blank. By now he probably had a wife and kids more important to him than a former friend accused of murder.

No. Not accused, *convicted*.

Paul pushed between the twins like they were saloon doors. "I'm sorry, Roy," he said. His hand moved toward the pistol on his waist.

Roy stepped forward and shot a fist at his old friend's face. Four-hundred-and-sixteen days of torture and pain were packed into his fingers and thumb. Each knuckle was a steel bearing, his arm a pile driver, his body an exploding furnace. Paul's facial bones were duck feathers compared to the packed-clay walls of his former cell. Roy could pulverize it all, but he held some back. The impact was at once exhilarating and empty.

Paul had managed to loose his revolver. As he fell his hand came up and the trigger was squeezed. The gun fired near Roy's ear, sending a bullet into the air.

High-pitched ringing was Roy's new and only sound.

The twin giants responded. The left one seemed to forget he was holding a rope, not a thumper, as he swung at Roy. The rope flopped harmlessly on Roy's bald head. The guard looked perplexed by the strange object in his hand.

Roy dove at the guard's exposed leg, driving hard with his shoulder. The knee cracked against its natural way. Roy thought of Camilla, the Camel Girl from Akron, Ohio. She was born with her knees working backwards, and she walked on all fours. Otherwise she was beautiful, and Roy felt it was a shame that her beauty would be used only to garner extra coins from rubes instead of buckling the knees of lovesick boys. McLean had managed to lure her away from a competing sideshow, banner and all, by offering the girl her own wagon. She snuck away from her previous show that same night, the banner draped over her shoulders. The first thing she did was set her makeup kit down in the middle of her own vanity and declare she'd never share her space again.

Both men toppled to the ground. Roy crawled up to the guard's chest to see a screaming mouth he couldn't hear due to the ringing gunshot in his ears. He drove down a fist, crushed bones, reloaded, and drove down again. The screaming mouth fell closed. The man's face was mashed. He and his twin would forever be different.

A fist impacted the back of Roy's head. His open eyes saw black. He fell to his hands, crawled forward, rolled to his side, and came to his feet, blinking and backing away. His vision came back hazy. The second twin moved toward him, tugging the thumper from his waist. He raised it above his head. Roy dodged the downward strike and rolled. Back up to his feet, he found the guard coming again, thumper aloft. Roy slipped to the side and punched the guard below the sternum. The guard doubled over and huffed out a breath. Roy grabbed a handful of greasy hair and brought up a knee to the guard's face once, twice. He let go. The guard toppled over.

Roy stood above the three downed men, his chest heaving as he sucked in maniac breaths. He threw back his head and laughed. This moment outside the wall, suddenly free, had been beyond his will to conceive.

But the guards were merely beaten, not dead.

Roy removed Paul's clothes. He found them a near perfect fit—dungarees and open neck shirt with a leather lace. Paul's boots were tight, but nevertheless they felt precious around Roy's hardened feet. Paul's black hat fit Roy's head nicely. Inside he found a leather bag full of coins. Roy cinched Paul's gun belt around his waist. The revolver's weight felt fine. On the cart he found a long leather duster and a nearly full waterskin. He slid on the jacket. It had been made comfortable through years of wear. He crisscrossed the waterskin strap, the rope, and the burlap bag—ends tied together—over his shoulders. He imagined he looked like a dime novel gunfighter, and with the black hat, a villain.

He considered riding out on the horse, but thought it smarter to go on foot. A reptilian man galloping through your town isn't the type of thing you wouldn't tell someone about. He unhooked the horse and gave it a hard slap on the backside, sending it down the road in a frenzy.

The twin guards slept and bled in the searing sun with their faces broken, one with a ruined knee. Roy considered dragging them under the cart for shade, but to Hell with them. Had they gotten the better of him, they'd have beaten him to death and buried him. They could burn. He dragged a naked Paul under the cart, close to the front where the shade would remain all afternoon. Paul's face might never be the same, either. If he had a wife she might cry. If he had children they might wonder if their father could still be called a man.

"I'm sorry, my friend," Roy said, placing a hand on Paul. "Look at you, huh?"

Roy patted his friend's chest and stood. A quick survey and he set out across the field, leaping over the burial line so as not to leave tracks. He raced toward a distant forest while moving away from the scene, away from the prison. When he came to the woods he stopped and looked back. The cart was a dot on the horizon, the road a thin line in the shimmering heat. Two more dots marked the twins. They had not yet begun to stir.

Roy entered the forest. If he was lucky enough to reach a town, his first purchase would be salve.

6

In Roy Pellerin's eight-year-old mind, the most dangerous and mystical predator in Lousiana's Bayou Rouge was the alligator. Sure, there were cottonmouths and bobcats, spiders and snapping turtles, and by combined number they were equally as dangerous as gators, but for Roy's money there was only the gator. Armor-bodied, quick, and with a million teeth like spits for human flesh, a gator could turn wrists and ankles into stumps, or living bodies into dead ones. The animals patrolled the river in front of Roy's childhood home like dinosaur sentinels, their eyes and snouts an inch above the water as they drifted in wait. Their exposed parts looked like harmless knobs, but Roy knew this was illusion. To the Pellerins, gators were more than deadly illusionists, but voodoo spellbinders with magic in their mouths; a gator's clapping jaw could turn an unborn human child into a son of its own.

Roy would know; he was such a son.

Roy must have liked the warm, dark pool of his mother's womb, because he stayed two weeks past his expected nine months. At the time Roy's mother, Verna, looked ready to split. Her husband, Thomas, wore a mask of worry. Roy was to be their first child, and his parents fretted his reluctance to enter their bayou home. Any advice would be welcome, so Thomas and Verna decided to visit an upriver neighbor whose wife had given birth to seven children, all on time and all healthy.

They set out from their home in the early morning haze, carefully picking their way to the water's edge. Thomas walked in front, reaching back to hold Verna's hand.

"Maybe there's a secret food or drink," Verna mused, breaking the morning silence, "or a way to stretch or bend."

"I reckon so," Thomas Pellerin said, eyes locked on the dangerous water.

The young couple would never reach their neighbor's home. Verna would later say there was something in the stillness of the dawn that gave her pause. She didn't like the shameful look of the Cypress trees, like they knew a secret but had sworn to keep it dry.

Thomas halted on their small dock, eyeing the water for rings pulling away from small shadows on the gleaming surface. He stayed in front of his wife, protecting her with knife in hand. He knelt down and scanned the still water diligently, but found nothing to cause alarm. He sheathed his knife and got on the skiff, turned back and held out his hand.

Verna came slowly to the dock's edge, cradling her gigantic belly. She gripped her husband's hand, stretched out a foot toward the skiff, and then stopped.

Thomas eyed her curiously.

Verna pulled back her foot just as a gator exploded from the water. Its massive jaws clacked together where her foot had just been. Thomas unsheathed his knife and slashed the gator's nose in one fluid motion. The gator growled and reeled. It snapped its jaws again, taking a chunk of the skiff before fleeing. An oily blood slick trailed away from its wound.

Verna's water broke. She would later say the sound of the gator's clapping jaw was what did it. She staggered backwards, dropped to her behind, and gave birth to her only son on a crooked, rotting dock above the Mississippi River.

Roy emerged from his mother's womb with rough scales all over his body. The diamond pattern covered his face, his hands, his feet, and his bald head. His father would say he wished he'd never given that gator a mark, because the goddamn thing returned the favor in folds upon his son.

❧

Roy's boyhood home was a wooden shack built into a hillside rising away from the riverbank. There were two bleached-out boulders on the hill above the roof. Young Roy saw the boulders as two eyes, fantasizing that a landslide had come down and tried to swallow his house but choked, died, and grew grass. The house's front and side walls were cypress planks weathered white from the constant burn of the sun. The roof was a puzzle of cedar shake shingles, pieced together in a let's-try-some-of-this kind of way. When the river rose the house would flood, so everything important was kept in old crawdad nets hung from pegs. Roy had one net dedicated strictly to his dime novels and newspapers. He hung the net high and tight to ensure their safety.

The house had one window that looked out over the marsh fields and muddy water. At night Roy would kneel on a stool under the window, watching his father hunt gators by moonlight. For work, Thomas was a coal passer on a bayou steamboat. He spent weeks and months traveling up and down the river system, shoveling coal into an inferno. On his off evenings, as on this evening, he hunted the river on their small skiff, his body hidden by the Spanish moss that dangled from the mighty Cypress trees and Live Oaks.

Young Roy watched from the window, eyes just above the sill as if a gator himself. Thomas had strapped his favorite knife to the end of a cypress pole and anchored the skiff on the far bank where there was generally more gator activity. He crouched and had been waiting for what seemed like hours. He didn't even twitch when mosquitoes sucked blood from his back. He'd just let them feed and go on their happy way, their fat bellies like rubies flying off into the twilight. He remained so still in the dusk that twice Roy lost sight of him and panicked. His little hands gripped the windowsill with force, his teeth left bite marks. But just before young Roy ran outside to save the day, his father's silhouette materialized against the trees, still alive and still motionless.

Thomas Pellerin was a legend in his son's eyes—strong, smart, and impervious. When Roy read stories of Davy Crockett, Indian fighter and war hero, he saw his father's face under Davy's coonskin cap. Davy Crockett didn't die at the Alamo. No sir, he changed his surname to Pellerin and was now here with his new family, hunting gators instead of Indians and Mexican army men.

And when Davy stabbed at a gator he never missed.

Now Roy's excitement grew as his father arced his spear upward in a silent motion. Roy could not see what his father saw in the black depths below, but there could be no doubt it was a gator. Thomas held his spear still for a chilling moment before violently driving it down. The knife cut deep into the gator's back, just behind the head, severing the spine, and Thomas twisted the pole hard before pulling the blade back out, leaving a wide and fatal wound.

In life the gator was feared and respected. In death it was revered. Willingly or not, the animal had given its life for the survival of others, and this point was not lost on Thomas Pellerin. Once the gator stopped thrashing, Roy's father knelt on the skiff and came down to its level. He lifted its great head into his arms and held it like a beloved child. He thanked the beast for its sacrifice before raising his eyes to God and thanking him, too. It was the alligator that provided the Pellerins with meat for eating and leather for shoes, belts, and laces. Selling the tanned leather also brought extra money into the home for milk, salt, books, and candles.

The crawdad, too, gave its life to the Pellerins. Young Roy was brought up on the sweet meat the crustacean provided, and in truth he enjoyed watching his father net crawdads more than watching him hunt gators. Netting was a dance. Against the backdrop of droning cicadas, Thomas casted and snapped his fingers for good luck as the net splashed down and sank into the muddy water. After a moment's pause, he jerked the net closed and slowly dragged it back toward the skiff. His muscles were mechanical and fibrous, like the working arms of a locomotive. His bumpy veins and bronze skin were drizzled in sweat. Roy would later be reminded of his father's netting dance when he first saw the Fero Brothers juggling act in New York. The motions were nearly the same, only his father possessed no flaming pins.

The Pellerins led a hidden life. For his first eight years Roy saw no other children. He never understood that he was different from other kids. The family's closest neighbor was either two miles downriver or a full mile up, and since Roy's father did most of the running it was rare that Roy or his mother had need to venture out. So isolated, Roy might have come out a monkey for all anyone in the Bayou Rouge knew. But this was before the schoolhouse.

There was tension in the house the day before Roy's first day of school. His father paced and his mother sat and stared through the window. They were saying nothing, which Roy knew meant they'd soon be saying everything. He decided it was best to be outside.

He crouched and dive-rolled through the marsh, shooting at cattails with his thumb-finger pistols. The cattails were Indians on the attack, and he was Davy Crockett's son, protecting his father's new identity and home. The adventure took him up to the hill above the house. He imagined he was on a saloon roof where he could better survey the town and make pick-off shots. He took a shooter's stance, surveying the land. His parents' voices came from beneath his feet.

"They won't understand," Thomas said.

"I don't care," Verna said. "No son of mine will go through life an uneducated fool."

"You can keep teaching him at home," Thomas said. "He's doing fine so far."

There was a pause. Roy imagined his mother steeling her spine and sticking out her chin. When her mind became stubborn about something, so did her body. "He's already passed most of what I can teach him, Tom. We can't keep him hidden his whole life."

Roy's father sighed.

"Facing adversity is good for a boy," she said. "It'll build him up. Look at yourself. My father hated you and was plain about it, but that didn't stop you."

Roy took aim at a tall cattail, seeing an Indian warrior, longbow drawn. His thumb went down, *pow*.

Thomas said, "Your father was just one man. Our son will be up against the entire world."

The next day, as Roy and his mother walked back from the schoolhouse, he noticed water crawling down her cheeks. In his eight years he'd never seen her throw water. He wondered if she was too hot.

"Want to find some shade, mama?"

"No," Verna said, "I'm fine."

They walked for several more minutes before Roy stopped again. His mother stopped just ahead of him and looked back.

"What is it, boy?"

"Do you wish I was more like the kids in the schoolhouse?"

Verna wiped a tear from her cheek.

Roy said, "More like milk and less like scabs?"

Verna picked her son up. She set him on her hip. He knew he was too heavy to carry for long, but it felt good to be there. She started walking again. Farther down the road she opened her mouth to speak, but in the end she said nothing.

7

Paul opened his eyes to darkness.

He blinked, but still the darkness.

A coffin?

Oh God.

He reached up but couldn't find the wooden top. His hands flailed in the dark space. Suddenly gravel ripped at his back as he was dragged into the light. One of the Boyle twins stood over him. The man's face was smashed and spattered with dry blood. Paul put a hand to his own throbbing jaw. Roy must have hit him. His mind had gone fuzzy at the sight of Roy coming alive. He recalled walking over, reaching for his gun, and seeing Roy step forward. Darkness followed. What had he intended to do, shoot him?

He sat up to see the other Boyle twin sitting at the roadside. He stared at his ruined knee like it was a dead pet. His face was just as destroyed as his brother's.

"What now?" the standing twin said.

Was it John or Aaron? Paul couldn't presently tell the difference. He looked at the horizon and then back at the cart. The horse was gone.

"He stole it," the standing twin said. "Probably miles away by now."

Paul looked between the speaking man and his brother. He decided Aaron had only a smashed face while John had both a smashed face and the reversible knee.

"Yeah, what're we gonna do?" John said. His eyes never moved from his leg.

Paul stood up. He searched the back of the cart and found a canvas tarpaulin to tie around his naked waist. He turned to see Aaron smirking beneath his crushed nose. By the depth of the man's sunburn Paul guessed a few hours had passed. He patted his hip in the spot where his holster had been. His father's gun was no longer there. Roy had it. He knew that. He also knew their jobs were lost unless he brought Roy back. That meant tracking him.

Paul imagined Roy running across the countryside wearing his clothes, his father's revolver in his scaly hand, a world of adventure spinning around him. He imagined himself chasing. The vision started a smile on his face, but it was quelled by a new thought— could he afford to leave his son alone with his wife, even for one day? Her drinking was well beyond control. Her blackout spells grew longer by the week. Dammit, he should have slapped that first bottle away from her. He should have knocked the depression clean out of her. He should have-

The image of his stillborn daughter appeared in Paul's mind, quieting his anger, as it often did. She had been a porcelain doll— eyes closed, fists clenched, not breathing. Never breathing. Her mother had held her close and rocked her. She had cried and pleaded with the midwife. She had blamed and screamed, had been full of fight, but when they took the dead child away Gloria went limp. She lay still, as beautiful and lifeless as the daughter she would never feed, never scold, and whose laughter they would never hear.

Soon after came the whiskey.

Paul, himself, had poured her first shot.

"Well?" Aaron said.

"You boys make your way back to Redmine," Paul said. "Let the warden know what happened."

John looked from his knee to his brother. They exchanged a fearful glance. "We don't have to tell him," Aaron said. "We can lie and say we buried him, just like the rest."

"Look at your faces and his knee," Paul said. "And that horse is worth more than a year of your pay."

They just stared.

Paul turned and headed down the road, away from the prison, barefoot and working his jaw up and down.

"What about you?" Aaron said.

"I'm going after him."

8

Cedar trees.

They smelled sweet and damp and reminded Roy of home. The limbs hung low, sweeping back and forth with the wind, their green leaves like little hands turning over and back, over and back. He could lie down and just breathe in and out for days, but he continued the pace he'd been on for hours. The gunshot had stopped ringing his ears. It was replaced by forest sounds. Everything was loud and vivid.

The clouds of mosquitoes and gnats had grown thick, which meant water nearby. Roy quickened his stride. His nostrils flared to detect moisture in the air. He came over a ridge to find a pond covered in algae. Holes in the slime dotted the water's surface and allowed the sun to sparkle against it. Tree trunks at the pond's edge were stripped of their bark. The pale wood was ringed in brown by the water's rising and falling. There were the split tracks of deer in the muck on the banks, along with turkey tracks, coon, and more. Roy's boot-heels squashed and erased the animal footprints as he approached the water's edge.

He finished what remained in his waterskin before carefully refilling it so as not to let in any green. He corked and threw back the full waterskin, undressed, and plunged into the pond without checking the depth.

The water was warm and thick. He tore off of a square of the dry-rotted burlap and used it to scour his skin. Dead scales came off him like cedar shavings. He scrubbed every inch of his body, watching the scabs float away and sink. His raw skin would dry out and scale over again in less than two hours, but for now he seemed merely a man with a splotchy sunburn.

After a final rinse he crawled from the muck as raw and exposed as a newborn child. The wind against his wet body made him shiver. Cold as a statue. He spread his arms and turned up his head. The canopy above rippled and shimmered like a green ocean. Blue pockets of sky winked down at him. His dirty clothes felt new as he slid them over his back. His black hat was a crown. He cinched the rope, burlap, and waterskin over his shoulders and buckled the gun-belt to his waist.

The undergrowth rustled. Roy's fresh skin tingled. Could they have tracked him down so quickly? He imagined the prison guards upon him, dragging him away. His mind went to Jesse, sitting in a room by herself, watching a door he would never come through. It was a room in the house he dreamed for them, on the farm they owned, in a place where they could be away from prison, away from the sideshow, away from the whole of society.

He waited for a voice telling him to ease the revolver from its holster and drop it. When the voice didn't come, Roy spun and pulled Paul's gun, drawing down the iron sights on a deer.

The deer stiffened, but stayed.

Roy lowered the gun. He released a breath and slowly moved to a tree where he sat down against the trunk. The deer's oily eyes tracked him along the way. Once Roy was still, the deer moved to the pond's edge to drink. It was either unafraid of Roy or too thirsty to care. After a quick drink it scampered off, showing its white tail.

Roy hefted the revolver. He turned it over in his hand. He spun the chamber and enjoyed the clicking sound. He aimed the gun at trees, rocks, and ferns. He clicked back the hammer, clicked it forward, and flipped the gun around his finger in an experienced fashion.

Jesse returned to his mind. She was no longer waiting in a farmhouse room, but a damsel in distress. In the fantasy she was tied to a wooden stake with villains all around, snickering and threatening. Roy busted in, revolver blazing. After the bandits were dispatched she kissed him deeply and wrapped herself around him, just like their first and only night together.

He closed his eyes to the divine memory.

He'd been drinking a little, her a lot. In small towns the sideshow would stay for a night or two and be gone, but in the cities they might stay for a week. It was in the cities that McLean's performers could find the kinds of back-alley saloons that would accept their money. They'd spend their nights laughing and clacking mugs just like regular society, and they'd wake up with regular society's same aching heads and swirling guts.

Roy and Jesse's special night had been in Raleigh at the Corktown Inn. The sideshow had passed through Raleigh many times over the years, and long-time performers knew the inn owner well. At the Corktown they were safe. It was a place where they could be loose and loud, and that night had been no exception. Their revelry went well past closing time. By then most of the others had gone back to the caravan, but a few stayed on. Jesse's job seemed to be picking up full shot glasses and putting them down empty. Roy's job was holding her upright. Such work he was more than pleased to do.

Jesse, no longer the shy new girl, no longer the outsider, was now The Illustrated Woman. She was equal parts exotic and untouchable, for she was Samson's girl, and the strong man ensured—with a stern look and the flexing of a variety of muscles—that all the male performers understood that painful results trailed their lingering eyes. A healthy fear of Samson had quelled Roy's advances, so he never figured he'd be close enough to breathe in her scent. He never dared believe he'd be touching her, or her him.

And yet here he was.

Samson had taken his leave earlier that evening, citing a meeting with McLean, and since then Jesse had moved closer and closer as the others turned in and the group got smaller. Soon it was down to Jesse, Roy, and Jukey. The Armless Marvel watched Jesse and Roy with bemused interest. There was one shot left on the table before him. Rum. The happy drink, he called it. Whiskey was for sadness.

"What?" Roy said, meeting Jukey's eyes, mimicking his bemused smirk.

"Nothing," Jukey said, shrugging his shoulders. "Just, you know, I like what I see."

"You're barking at a knot," Roy said.

"Am I?"

"Hold on," Jesse said, her words hampered by a drunken slur. She turned to Jukey. "What do you *think* you see?"

Jukey's smirk expanded into a wide smile. He leaned forward and down toward the table, placing his chin on the shot glass to hold up his head. "I see the future," he said, doing his best Madame Zora, fortune-teller impression. His eyes sparked over the sound of her false ethnic accent. "And it is *go-od*."

Jesse snorted. "You see what you choose."

Jukey released his chin from the shot glass. A drop of rum dangled from his skin. He tilted his head forward and picked up the glass between his lips. He lifted it off the table, threw back his head, and swallowed the liquid down. He spit the glass out and it bounced across the wooden tabletop, spinning like a coin. Roy caught it as it danced over the edge.

"I see all!" Jukey said, throwing up the stumps at the ends of his shoulders in proclamation. He suddenly stood and towered over them, wobbly.

"You're drunk," Roy said.

"Damn right," Jukey said. "I'm drunk and I'm in love. We should all be so lucky."

"That we should," Jesse said.

"Then luck is on our side," Jukey said. He bowed slowly but didn't come back up. He stayed bent at the waist for a long moment, his forehead hovering just above the tabletop.

Roy and Jesse exchanged a glance.

Roy reached toward The Armless Marvel, but Jukey shot back up before Roy could touch him. He stood straight and tall. "And now I shall take my leave." He nodded once at Roy, once and Jesse, and walked unsteadily away.

Jesse moved closer to Roy, so close they were sharing Roy's seat. Her scent was jasmine. She was with him publicly and openly. Mortal fear mixed with inordinate pleasure in Roy's guts. At any moment he expected a fist to the back of the head. He saw himself on the ground looking up at her and Samson, his head aching from the blow. It might be the last vision of his life.

When she turned to face him her hair graced his skin at the open collar. Against his scales it was more a sting, less a tickle. He closed his eyes to the sensation, letting it spill across him like water. When he opened them he saw the intricate tattooed patterns on her flesh. Skulls and flowers, devils and dragons. They came alive for him, shared their secrets with him.

"You're beautiful," he said.

Her eyes thinned down. "Don't say that."

"But you are," Roy said, "you're the most beaut-"

"Stop it," she said. She turned away. "It makes you just like the rest. Don't be like the rest."

This is not how it's supposed to go, Roy thought. The hero is supposed to tell the woman she's beautiful and the woman is supposed to swoon. After that they live happily ever after, right?

Jesse wasn't swooning. Roy was at a loss.

She picked up a used shot glass and turned it on an angle to well the few drops of whiskey that remained. She brought the glass to her lips and licked the inside clean.

Roy averted his eyes to the wet ring the shot glass had left behind. The circle was nearly perfect, save for a small break at the upper left side.

"Why do you say I'm beautiful?" Jesse said. She carefully set the shot glass back down, directly on the broken ring. "You don't see me like the rest do, so why do you say the same things they say?"

"I don't know how to say what I mean."

"Well," she said, turning to face him, her drunken eyes blinking slowly, "now's your chance to try."

Roy sighed. "You're with him."

"That's not what you want to say."

"Makes it no less true."

She studied Roy's face. Her chest began to heave with deep breaths. She appeared primal, intense. After a moment she said, "*He* thinks I'm beautiful."

Roy said, "I think you're in pain."

Her face contorted. He thought she might throw water. Instead she threw both arms around him and pulled herself in tight. She drew up her legs like a bride and nuzzled into his collarbone. Without looking up, she pointed to the rooms-for-rent upstairs. Inked in hard black lines from her shoulder to her hand was a spiraled snake.

Its split tongue extended to lick her fingertip.

Roy carried her upstairs, having forgotten a strong man named Samson ever existed.

In the room she moved quickly, turning Roy's dime novel romance into a rush job. Her experience unnerved him. He couldn't help but blurt that he was a virgin. The words just burst forth as she peeled down a dress strap. He stood there dumbly. She pulled him close.

Back in the forest, Roy holstered the gun and folded his arms over his chest. He stretched out his legs. Fatigue gripped his muscles and bones. Sleep came with no warning, and for once it was dreamless. They could have found him and killed him in that position, and when they pulled back his black hat they'd find the happiest man death had ever touched.

9

Roy Pellerin learned reading and handwriting at his mother's kitchen table. He learned all she knew about numbers by dragging Indian-head pennies and three-cent nickels across the battered wood, one pile to the other and back again. For six hours a day Roy kept his head down to the hard work, sliding the coins right for addition, left for subtraction, and up and down for multiplication and division. Handwriting was difficult and the math was misery, but reading was a joy and a reward for the day's effort.

Once he could read at a decent pace, Roy read aloud. His mother would listen while she cleaned and swept the house or prepared dinner. Roy would go on for hours this way, occasionally peeking up to catch the smile on her face, the dimples on her cheeks.

Roy read anything his father brought home—newspapers, dictionaries, encyclopedias, and even advertisements for yeast powder, toilet soaps, and billiard tables that wouldn't have fit through the door of their home. His mother made him read the clothing advertisements over and again, sighing to hear words like *overskirt* and *bustle* as she scowled and tugged at her stained apron. From the pictures Roy saw, he couldn't decipher why overskirts or bustles were an improvement over her current clothing, but he determined that he would one day go out into the world and bring some of them back to her.

Roy especially enjoyed the dime novels his father said were sweeping through cities and towns like plague. Besides his parents, dime novel characters were the only people Roy knew, and he loved them dearly. They lived on horseback or in frontier towns with saloons that had doors you could kick and no one would be upset. They were gunfighters and gold-rushers roaming the untamed west. They spent days on the trail, tracking Indians or villains in black hats. They panned for gold in rushing mountain streams. They did as they pleased and answered to no one. Some were on the right side of things, some were on the wrong, and those on the wrong always found their end.

Davy Crockett and all the other heroes wore his father's face, of course, and every bad guy—whether Indian or black-hatted scoundrel—wore the face of the schoolhouse teacher, Mr. Cairn. The face of a fool. Young Roy dreamed of one day going into the world to deal with such fools. He dreamed of a life in the west, a life on the trail, tracking scoundrels by day and camping by night. He dreamed of a hard life, a true life where good deeds were rewarded and bad deeds punished.

"I'm proud of you," his mother would say intermittently throughout his reading.

Her approval always made his stomach flutter. He knew she wanted him at the schoolhouse, but this was the best they could do. Later in life, Roy believed his mother would have been proud to learn that he painted the words on his own sideshow banner, counted money well enough to ensure that he wasn't getting railroaded, and had developed a signature with the swoops and whirls of a king.

A few months after Roy's tenth birthday, his father lost his coal passing job. He came home on a Friday with darkness on him. It looked like someone had softened his bones. He said, "Who needs the bastards, anyway? To Hell with 'em."

Roy didn't think his father's strong words agreed with how he really felt. He'd brought home no new dime novels or newspapers, only a brown jug.

"To freedom," Thomas Pellerin declared, yanking out the cork and holding the jug high before taking an impossibly long drink. He brought the bottle down and winced like he'd just swallowed embers. He shook his head and smiled. "To freedom," he said again, his voice now lowered to a whisper. The second drink was half that of the first.

That night Thomas Pellerin sat on the small dock in front of his bayou home, singing a slurry version of *I Wish I Was in Dixie* and yelling at things that weren't there. He sang praises to the crawdads and shook fists at the water and the stars.

When the singing and yelling was done, he stumbled back into the house and into bed, where he snored through the night and deep into the morning.

That next afternoon, a bleary-eyed Thomas set away from home. "I'll find work," he said, "don't worry."

A week later he came back with another jug. His eyes were reddened, his face was in need of a shave, and his shoulders were slumped, not just down, but forward, like he was a drying leaf curling in on itself.

Roy's mother looked her husband up and down, fists on her hips.

Thomas shrugged. "No dice."

The drunken days that followed worked very much like the first, but often times Thomas wouldn't make it back into the house. Roy and his mother would go out after dawn to find him sleeping on the dock or somewhere in the marsh. On the marsh days a worried look would come to Verna's face as they searched, and she would sigh with great relief when they discovered him face up instead of down.

As the days grew into weeks and months she'd less often sigh, more often kick her husband awake and leave him to come back on his own.

Thomas' hunting became fruitless. He declared the wretched river void of gators. Young Roy was no expert, but he believed his father's lack of success might have more to do with his stumbling and sour smell.

No gators meant no meat, no leather, and no extra money, which wasn't considered extra anymore. The Pellerin's survived on crawdads and water. Their shoes were run through and the nights were cold on their feet. There was no milk or salt. Worst of all, for Roy, there were no new books and no candles. He had to reread old material by the light and heat of day, which meant slow progress because he had to take breaks to wipe his watering eyes. They were down to pennies. Roy's mother sat at the window with her hands in her lap, whispering prayers.

Eventually God answered.

It was an exceptionally pretty morning on the bayou when the gray man arrived. Sunbeams reached through the trees to lift steam from the river and throw it into the sky. It was warm and animals were chattering. It was as though the gray man pushed daylight before him, but dragged the night behind. He was on a muscular white horse and wore a gray coat, a hat with a white feather stuck in it, and a yellow sash. There were gleaming metal parts all over his horse and his clothes. His mustache had loops on each end. Occasionally he'd pull and stretch the loops only to have them snap back into position.

Roy watched the man from the windowsill, wondering if God himself had come down from Heaven to grant his mother's requests.

Verna had to get Thomas out of bed. She did so by slapping him all over. Roy thought it was lucky it hadn't been a marsh morning, or they'd be dragging his father from the muck in front of Jesus' Dad.

Thomas Pellerin came out to meet the gray man with his hat in his hand. "Help you, sir?" he said with a froggy voice and squinted eyes.

"Will you join?" the gray man said.

"I don't rightly know what-"

"You know damn well what I mean, son."

The two men stared at each other. Roy thought it was like one of the gunfighter standoffs he'd read about, only without the guns. He guessed his dad lost when he blinked and looked down. "I never had any quarrel with the Federals," Thomas said, eyes on his worn-through shoes.

"It matters not. It is your duty."

"I ain't never owned a slave."

"A patriot would die for the cause," the gray man said, "and for his country. Are you a patriot, or a coward?"

Thomas clenched a fist. "I'm no coward."

"Seven dollars a week," the gray man said, "and a rifle you can keep." He looked at Verna and smiled. "His wages can be sent home."

Thomas stood for a long moment, eyes returning to his shoetops. Finally, he turned to his wife. "There's nothing for it. The gators are gone, the money's gone, and…"

"Take today to say your goodbyes," the gray man said. "Be at port tomorrow morning." He turned his great horse and trotted away.

The next morning Roy's father prepared to leave. He gave Verna a short smile and a long hug. She tried not to throw water, but no dice. After their embrace Thomas knelt down to Roy's height. He gripped his son's shoulders. "You've seen me hunt gators. Seen how it's done?"

Roy poked out his chin and nodded, yes.

Thomas put the knife into Roy's hand. Roy turned it over slowly. It had a long blade, sharpened so many times it seemed thin and brittle, but Roy knew it was strong. *T. Pellerin* was etched into the thickest part of the metal. The etching must have taken a long time because the letters were dead straight. The handle was wrapped in a leather strap, wound around many times. Roy gripped the handle. The knife seemed to pulsate in his hand.

"Did your mama ever tell you how you got your name, son?"

Roy shook his head.

"We named you after your great grandfather, *my* grandfather, Roy G. Pellerin, who served under Jackson in The War of 1812."

"He must be pretty old," Roy said.

Thomas snickered. "I reckon so. Did I ever tell you he fought in the Battle of New Orleans alongside five thousand men? They went up against fourteen thousand Brits. Grandpap said the battle lasted less than an hour, and he reckoned the Brits lost two thousand that day, while our side only lost seven." Thomas looked back at Verna, who was wiping water from her cheeks. "Funny thing is, neither side knew that the war was already over. All those men died for nothing."

"How come they didn't know?" Roy said.

"I reckon that's the way God wanted it."

Thomas stood and wiped his hands over his face, put on his hat. "I'll be back as soon as I can, and I'll make sure they send the money every week." He slung a sack over his shoulder and walked across their small yard to the road. When he got to the bend he turned and looked back. Roy waved and his father tipped his hat. Then he was gone.

Every day for the next three weeks Roy hunted gators while his mother netted for crawdads. Roy tied his father's knife to a straight pole he'd carved from a cypress branch. All day and night he crouched and scanned the water for bumpy eyes or snouts drifting behind the reeds. He tried to remain still like his father would, but his back and leg muscles throbbed and quivered. Mosquitoes ravaged any exposed skin. In most places the bugs couldn't pierce their needle-noses through his scales, but eventually they found the cracks and gaps. He couldn't help but slap at them, and then curse himself for moving. He figured all his fidgeting must have scared off every gator in the bayou.

His mother's luck was no better.

Their food supply dwindled and his mother spent the last of their savings. "We'll figure something out," she said, "we always do." She prayed by the window more often than before.

One morning Roy woke to find his mother out in the marsh. He watched at the window as she boarded the skiff and launched into the water. She began casting. By now she had the motions down perfectly. If not for her motherly shape Roy would swear he was looking at his father.

As day broke, Roy climbed the hill beside the house and moved up to the roof to watch her. Verna saw him. "Watch this, Roy!" she said, tossing out the net and snapping her fingers as it splash landed. She'd grown strong over the weeks. Her arms moved mechanically as she dragged the net in, and by God if she didn't drag in one of the biggest bundles of crawdads Roy had ever seen.

Verna Pellerin looked at the writhing bundle in shock. After a moment she thrust up the bundle proudly, turning toward Roy to display her bounty. Roy jumped up and down, cheering, until his eyes caught the knobs that had appeared near his mother's feet.

Roy's knees gave out. The world slowed. The only sound was droning cicadas. A thousand pounds of death slid beneath the surface toward his mother's exposed flesh, and she was just standing there, smiling. One crawdad had wriggled free of the net and was falling in slow motion, circling through the air, both claws open.

The gator exploded forth in flash of green scales and white water. It clamped its jaws on Verna's ankle. Her smile transformed into terror. Her hands opened. The net hung in mid air.

The gator rolled. Roy saw the scar that tracked across its nose, heard the crack of his mother's shinbone. The netted crawdads fell as Verna came down to one knee. They bounced across the skiff and skidded over the gator's yellow belly as it turned.

Roy leapt down from the roof, breaking both ankles on impact with the ground. He bit back a scream. His mother did not. Her shrieks pierced Roy's ears and drove him forward. She turned to her backside and strained against the gator's weight, but the effort was in vain. The gator pulled her to the skiff's edge, tilting the opposite end up like a dinner plate to a starving mouth.

Roy crawled toward the riverbank, where his pole-knife leaned against a dock post. He snatched it up. His mother struggled against the beast, but the gator flipped her over and over. Roy kept crawling. The brown water turned red. The gator flipped her again and pulled her off the skiff. Roy called for her. She disappeared under the water and came back up, gasping. Roy came to the end of the dock. He stuck out the blunt end of his pole for her to grab. It fell short. She went under once more. He stretched the pole out to the extent of his reach. It quivered under his muscle strain.

But she never came back up.

Roy stayed in place, pole outstretched, while the skiff spun in a lazy circle, splattered with blood and crawdads struggling in the stickiness.

An hour passed.

Still lying on the dock, Roy looked at his reflection in the still water. His eyes were swollen to the size of walnuts. His ankles thumped. She was gone. There was nothing for it.

Roy slid into the water and swam out to the skiff using one hand to propel himself while the other held the pole-knife. He climbed aboard the skiff to see the gator resting along the bank on the other side. Its nose was painted red with his mother's blood, much of it pooled and congealing in the scar his father had once given it. There was a patch of his mother's apron caught in its teeth. The beast had a fat, satisfied look in its eyes.

Roy rose to his knees.

The gator didn't move. Having taken its revenge, maybe it no longer cared to live. Or maybe it saw Roy as a son, a being that would never harm it.

Roy lifted the pole high above his head, held it for a chilling moment, and then plunged his father's knife between the gator's eyes, breaking through the stony skull.

The gator's body jerked. Its eyes searched in different directions.

Roy twisted hard before pulling back the pole. The gator thrashed for a second and then stopped. Its claws relaxed and opened.

Roy cut the rope that anchored the skiff. He pushed away from the bank. The slow current began to carry him downriver. He rolled to his back and looked up at the sun. He sucked heavy breaths of the sulfuric swamp air. His lungs felt like fire. He untied his father's knife, discarded the cypress pole, and held the blade flat against his chest.

10

Paul pulled a pair of old, square-toed boots on to his aching feet. Walking several miles barefoot and nearly naked from the dead cart left him limping with blisters. He felt fortunate that most of his walk had been after dusk, else this morning he'd be sunburned top to bottom. He worked his jaw and pain shot down his neck, emanating from the point where Roy had apparently punched him. He took an old hat, waistcoat, and duster from his closet and put on a new shirt, pants, and belt. He hefted a new coin bag to test its weight before dropping it into the hat, which he deftly slid on to his head.

He looked at his reflection in the glass shadow box nailed to the wall. The box contained the ornate Colt Dragoon revolver his father-in-law had given him on his wedding day. The piece was beautiful, and in the shadow box, useless. In the top dresser drawer were the black-powder cap and ball setups Paul had purchased separately from the gun.

"Don't you dare," Gloria Constantine said.

Paul's wife stood in their bedroom doorway with one arm wrapped around her mid-section, her hand cupping her thin frame at the waist. Though the morning sun was barely shedding light, her other hand already held a whiskey tumbler, two fingers full. Likely another blackout was on its way.

As a young woman, Gloria's face had been full of laughter and light. Now Paul could only see traces of that young face beneath her grim resolution. It was the same look she wore in the weeks that led up to their daughter's stillbirth. The baby had stopped kicking in her belly, and although the midwife was certain the child had been lost, Gloria was determined. At home she talked to the dead daughter inside her, sang to her, and asked Paul to lay his head down and listen for the girl's heartbeat. Paul obliged, placing his left ear down against his wife's belly.

He heard his wife's sniffles in his open ear, but only silence on the other side.

Last night Paul had told Gloria of what happened with Roy, referring to him as *the prisoner* during the story. He also told her of Roy's skin. He didn't mention their childhood friendship, and never had before.

She was as drunk then as she would soon be, and she had laughed at his story, chiding him for being too weak to contain a mere animal.

He told her he'd go after the prisoner and bring him back. It was either that or lose his job.

"You don't need that job, anyway," she said, "you should be clerking for my father."

Paul's father-in-law, Delmont Graves, was a prominent local attorney. Working for such a man would reduce Paul to brewing coffee and sweeping up around the office. But there would be hope; if he were a good boy, and he worked real hard for five short years, he could ascend to taking dictations. However, these things were not at the heart of the reason why Paul refused the job. As a prison guard he could work odd shifts—afternoons, overnights, and doubles— which meant he could be there for his son when his wife couldn't, or more appropriately, when she wouldn't. The job paid far less than what Paul felt he was worth, but point in fact the boy needed someone to look after him.

"My daddy gave you that gun," Gloria said. "It'll be over his dead body you use it to hunt down some *freak*." She spat the last word out like poison, and then took a drink. Paul couldn't remember the last time she winced at the liquor's harshness.

"What else would you have me do?" Paul said.

"It doesn't matter what you do." She looked away from him. "You're good for nothing. Always will be."

The last time he reached for her she recoiled from him, and he'd be a liar if he said he hadn't been relieved. She'd become skeletal and unattractive. Not fit, in body or mind. He looked past her now, through the doorway and down the hall. Their son, Jacob, leaned against a doorjamb. His eyes were remarkably big and blue, just like Paul's father's had been. The boy's little hand gripped the doorjamb hard, turning the tips of his fingers white.

"You loved me once," Paul said, speaking to Gloria but keeping his eyes on his son.

When no reply came he looked at her.

A shelf of tears had appeared on her lower eyelids. Her tightened lips had gone as white as her son's fingers.

"I did," she said.

"Ask me and I'll stay."

Gloria gave him her eyes for a moment, then she looked away again. "Don't bend your honor for me."

"Honor is nothing without love."

Gloria finished the whiskey in her glass. "Take him to my father when you go." She started out of the room.

Paul smashed the shadow box.

Gloria paused in the doorway. Down the hallway Jacob flinched, his face took on confusion.

Gloria looked back over her shoulder. Her cliffhanging tears had spilled down over her cheeks. She left the room, passing her son without notice.

Paul holstered the ornate gun and grabbed the gear from the top drawer. Jacob ran to meet his father in the bedroom doorway. He was still confused, seemingly ready to cry.

"Shhh," Paul said. He picked Jacob up and carried him out to the porch and down the steps. He tickled Jacob's exposed calf as he walked the dirt path from their small home to the road.

Jacob whimpered. He allowed the beginnings of a smile. "Where we going, daddy?"

"Pop-pop's house," Paul said.

"Pop-pop's house!" Jacob echoed, throwing a triumphant fist in the air.

Delmont Graves sat on his front porch smoking an ivory pipe. One leg was crossed over the other in a relaxed fashion reserved for women and men of station. A newspaper sat on a marble-topped end table, held down by a thick tumbler halfway emptied of rare bourbon. His waistcoat was silken and his beard was long, but trimmed to perfection over a black bowtie, which he wore despite the fact that it was Tuesday, his weekly day off.

From a distance Paul could smell the pipe's smoky aroma—Jamestown vanilla. The scent would be pleasant, if not for consideration of the smoker. Jacob squirmed and kicked in Paul's arms, itching to go to his grandfather. Paul set the boy down.

"Pop-pop!" Jacob said, scampering away.

Delmont Graves set down his pipe. He rose from his chair as the boy approached, and was standing just in time for Jacob to slam into his leg and grip tightly. One hand came down on the boy's head to tousle his hair. Apart from an array of gifts, this was the extent of the man's affection.

Paul walked up the lane at a moderate pace. The tobacco scent intensified as he drew closer. His father-in-law's house was well-built, albeit modest. It belied the depth of the man's wealth. He'd made a name for himself expanding the claims of rich landowners in the area, bringing any greedy, white-collar criminal with a scant land claim to his doorstep. Graves took his pound of flesh at thirty-three percent, a fee the prosperous men for whom he prosecuted were more than happy to pay.

Graves smiled wanly as Paul approached. The smile was a lie. It came to his face reluctantly, like a dog to an abusive master. "To what do I owe the pleasure?"

Paul stopped at the porch steps. He took off his hat, slid his coin bag into a pocket, and squeezed the hat with both hands. "I need a favor."

The old man's face hardened. It was a practiced, disinterested look. Contrived. Built for the courtroom.

"I need to leave town for a bit," Paul said. "And I'd very much appreciate it if you—that is to say, one of your hands—could look after the boy while I'm gone."

"His mother is unfit?" Graves said.

Paul wrung the bill of his hat. "You know she's unfit, sir."

Jacob decided one hug was enough. He ran across the porch and back down the steps, on to the green grass. He started a series of somersaults, laughing as he went and picking up grass stains on his knickerbockers. His laughter was music in Paul's ears, but he could see the stone-faced Graves struggling not to show irritation at the sound. The man could stand before judge and jury boldly telling lies to put money into pockets already overflowing, but drop an unwieldy boy into his presence and watch the stone come unseated.

Delmont put two hands on the porch railing and leaned forward. His *deep in thought* pose. Paul wanted to rap the old man's knuckles just to get one honest reaction from him, to see his face involuntarily move for once in his miserable life.

"And what do you plan to do with the weapon on your waist?" Graves said. He gave a small nod to the Colt Dragoon.

Paul cringed. He had intended to button his jacket and hide the gun before arriving. "Whatever's necessary."

"A drunken mother and a thug father," Graves said. "Seems as though the boy is set for life."

"Your gift," Paul said.

"An ornament."

Paul didn't respond. He knew how such a line of speaking with a lawyer would go. Might as well try to out-hiss a copperhead.

Graves released the railing and picked up the tumbler. A breeze lifted the corner of his newspaper. He straightened his back and towered for a moment, as if to impress upon Paul the strength of his station. "Send him in once you've said your good-bye." He turned and opened the screen door behind him. The spring sounded off—*ting-ting-ting*—as he passed through the doorway into his home.

Paul snatched up Jacob as he ran toward the porch. He carried his son up the stairs. "I'll be back soon. Mind your grandfather."

Jacob nodded.

Paul set Jacob on the porch, turning the boy to face him. He knelt to look into the boy's eyes, but Jacob was looking at the Colt. He reached out to it. Paul pulled back. "It's not a toy."

Jacob smiled. It made Paul ache with pride. If that smile would one day be as effective with young women as it was with his dad, it would land the boy in a heap of trouble with plenty of other fathers.

Jacob made a thumb-finger pistol and pointed it. His blue eyes twinkled when he dropped his thumb, *pow*.

Paul made like he'd been shot. "You got me," he said, clapping a hand over the false wound on his chest.

Jacob giggled. He took aim at Paul's feet.

Paul stood.

"Dance!" Jacob said, shooting imaginary bullets into the floor.

Paul kicked up his feet and jumped around, dodging and dancing. "I didn't do nothin', sheriff. I swear!"

Jacob stopped shooting. He blew pretend smoke away from his forefinger and holstered the pretend gun at this waist. Paul couldn't help but see a boyhood version of Roy in his son. The two shared the same love of conflict, heroes, and villains. He recalled the day his father carried Roy into their home so many years ago.

"What is this?" Paul's mother had said, wiping her floured hands on an apron. Winny Marie Constantine stood barely five feet tall, but she had the presence of a giant. "You're leaving tomorrow, Harold. You can't bring some boy here and leave him to my ca-"

She was going to say *care*, young Paul figured, but she saw Roy's skin and paused. Her hand went to her mouth.

"He's burned pretty bad," Harold said. He swept aside dishes and silverware as he lay the boy down on the kitchen table. "It's a miracle he's still breathing. Must've been out there for days."

Winny opened a cupboard and brought out a tin of salve. She'd used it on Paul's youthful cuts and burns over the years. Paul wondered if there would be enough, for it would have to cover the boy's entire body.

"Both his ankles are broken," Harold said. "He must've taken one hell of a tumble."

Paul's father had been out fishing. Tomorrow he was to head to the front lines of the war, and as he put it, he'd be damned if he wouldn't spend his last free day on the river.

"This boy came floating by on a skiff. I slung my line out and hooked his craft, pulled him in as he floated past. I reckoned he was dead, to be sure. Ain't nobody alive could suffer that much burning and just lay there. But then I saw his ankles and figured he couldn't stand. I wouldn't even have checked for a pulse, except I could see his little chest heaving. It's the damndest thing."

While his father told the tale, Paul felt growing shame. He knew the boy's skin was not a burn, but that it was… well, whatever it was. He'd seen the same boy outside the schoolhouse two years earlier, and yet he'd never told his parents the story. After what happened that day with George Fickas, young Paul had shrunken into himself. He stopped telling stories, and all but stopped talking. His fishing pole collected dust. He went to school, came home, ate his supper, and sulked off somewhere to sit and stare. He often found himself crying for no reason. His mother and father expressed their worry, but their concerns had been shelved by the war.

"We don't have the means to care for this boy," Winny said. "You're leaving and who knows when you'll be back, God forgive me, *if* you'll be back. Where will we get medicine and extra food?"

"I'll go fishing!" Paul said.

His parents both looked at him, surprised.

"I mean, I can help," Paul said, hands clasped behind his back, up on his tip-toes. "It's summer now. I can fish everyday and we can get medicine in town."

Harold put a hand on his son's head and smiled. "I'm sure you'd catch as many fish as any healthy boy would need."

Paul nodded.

Harold turned to his wife. "But this boy is sick. I've never seen a burn so bad. The least we can do is ease his passing."

A month later Paul Constantine had a new best friend. While his ankles recovered, Paul had learned the boy's name was Roy. He learned that Roy was homeschooled, that he carried a knife, and that his hero was Davy Crockett. He learned that Roy's father had gone off to the war, too, and that his mother was, as Roy put it, *just gone*.

Paul opened his mouth to ask what that meant, but he caught his mother's stern glance and left it alone. Instead he said, "Have you ever heard the story of Mrs. Patterson's hatpin?"

Winny rolled her eyes. "Now, Paul, I'm not sure that's an appropriate tale."

Paul kept his attention on Roy.

Roy's eyes moved back and forth between Paul and his mother. Finally, and quietly, he said, "No, I've never heard it."

Paul gave his mother a sidelong glance with pleading eyes.

Winny sighed. "All right then. Go ahead, but I won't bear witness to your blasphemy." She left the room.

Paul drew a deep breath. He closed his eyes and released the breath slowly through his nose. When his air ran out he took a second, quicker breath, and began. "Mrs. Patterson," he said, "was a frightfully mean woman."

Roy smiled.

"And her husband was bored. Bored with his job, bored with his wife, bored with his entire life. So bored was Mr. Patterson, that it was all he could do to stay awake, both at work and at home. It was said the man could even fall asleep while eating."

Roy giggled.

"Mrs. Patterson could abide all the sleeping," Paul said, growing more animated with the telling, "save for one thing. She wouldn't tolerate her husband sleeping in church. But sleep in church Mr. Patterson did, and soon Mrs. Patterson came to her wit's end. She went to see the pastor. 'What do I do?' she moaned. 'How do I stop the oaf from sleeping in church?'

"'There there, Mrs. Patterson,' the pastor said. 'I've got your solution in hand.' He opened a drawer, rummaged around, and finally produced a hatpin topped with Calvary's cross. 'Take this hatpin with you. During the sermon I'll be able to tell when your husband is sleeping, and I'll motion to you. When I do, just give him a poke in the leg.'

"The following Sunday, just as expected, Mr. Patterson dozed off during the pastor's sermon. Seeing this, the pastor put his plan into action. He called loudly from his pulpit, 'And who was it that made the ultimate sacrifice for your sins?' He then nodded to Mrs. Patterson. She jabbed the hatpin into her husband's leg.

"'Jesus Christ!' Mr. Patterson cried out."

Roy threw his head back with laughter.

"Soon Mr. Patterson dozed off again," Paul said, "and again the pastor noticed. He said, 'And what is the price of a man's transgression?' He nodded to Mrs. Patterson. She jabbed her husband's leg a second time.

"'Damnation!' Mr. Patterson wailed."

Roy's mouth fell open at the curse word. He looked around with his shoulders hunched, expecting Paul's mother to come flying in and start swatting her blasphemous son.

"Before long Mr. Patterson dozed off again," Paul said, "but this time the pastor didn't notice. His sermon was nearing its end, and he had picked up great steam. He was gesturing wildly to his congregation, all of which Mrs. Patterson took as signs she should jab her husband's leg. As she drove the hatpin deep into Mr. Patterson's tender flesh, the pastor said, 'And what did Eve say to Adam after their very first union?'

"Mr. Patterson screamed, 'You stick that thing in me again and I'll break it in half!'"

Roy exploded into laughter. Paul laughed right along with him. They bent and slapped knees. They wailed and hooted.

When they were done Paul's cheeks and ribs were sore. His eyes were wet, just as Roy's always seemed to be, and through his blurry vision he could swear the boy before him was as ordinary as any other.

"That's a humdinger," Roy said.

11

Roy heard movement in the woods. His eyes popped open. He pushed back his hat. It was well past dawn. He cursed himself for sleeping so late. The forest was still cool and his eyes threw no water. He slid the revolver from his waist and clicked back the hammer loudly, hoping to scare off a timid intruder.

No dice.

Leaves rustled. Whatever it was, it was getting closer. Roy turned an ear to the sound. He came up to one knee and leaned against the tree. He shivered with the chill that had set into his bones during the night.

The sound was orderly, something at a trot. Roy scanned back and forth, his eyes still adjusting to the light. Shapes formed from shadow. Tree trunks, a boulder, some ferns... and hustling left to right across the forest there was a cattle dog. It sniffed the ground furiously as it went by, hot on a trail.

"Dip!" A child's voice.

The dog stopped. Roy looked left, behind it. Between the trees there was a girl. She was dressed in boy's bib trousers and a white, button-down shirt. A red ribbon was tied in her blonde hair. She moved closer to the dog, taking the silent steps of a hunter. She bit her lower lip in concentration.

Roy felt absurd in hiding. This little girl couldn't be hunting him, could she?

"C'mon boy," she said, "find him. He can't hide forever."

Roy hunched lower to stay out of sight. He watched as the dog started again. It took two steps before stopping and pointing. The girl stopped, too.

"What is it, boy? Did you get him?"

Roy aimed his revolver at the dog. Moving only his eyes he tracked the dog's stare to a thick patch of bushes and small trees. The girl approached the dog and patted its head. The dog stayed rigid, eyes locked on target.

"Okay, boy," the girl said. "Go!"

The dog bolted forward. Leaves and branches crashed as a sheep burst forth from the undergrowth ahead. The dog gave chase and so did the girl. The sheep started out directly away from Roy, but it circled back through the woods, darting left and right as it avoided trees and rocks. The dog kept pace. The girl followed behind, laughing.

The sheep continued to circle until it was aimed straight at Roy. It thrashed through the trees, barely escaping the dog biting at its heels. It leapt over a boulder and skidded to a stop ten feet from Roy, startled by his presence. The dog hopped the boulder and skidded too, slamming into the sheep's backside. It nipped at the sheep's heels, causing the sheep to kick and spin around. They circled each other, playing like two boys. If they could laugh, they'd be laughing. If they had fists they'd be punching shoulders. They leapt back and forth, parrying and dodging, swiping and yelping.

The girl caught up to the scene, running hard. "Get him, Dip!" she said. "Get him, Dandy!"

Roy kept the revolver's sights on the dog, his eyes on the girl. Her smile fell away when she saw him. She stepped back as if to run, but then she composed herself.

"Mister, why are you pointing a gun at my dog?"

The dog and sheep stopped playing. They looked at the girl, both panting. Roy holstered the gun. He drew up his collar and pulled down his hat. "What're you doing out here?"

"What're *you* doing out here?" the girl said. "This is St. Luke's property, which means I'm the one that gets to ask the questions." She crossed her arms over her tiny frame.

"Then I best be on my way," Roy said. He began collecting his things. "It wouldn't do to have St. Luke upset by a trespasser."

The girl remained stoic. Roy moved past her, heading the same direction he'd been going the night before.

"Wait," the girl said.

Roy kept walking.

"You don't have to leave," she said. And then louder, "St. Luke's ain't a person."

"Figured that," Roy said without looking back.

"It's a place," the girl said.

"Good for St. Luke's."

"An orphanage."

Roy stopped. He looked back.

The little girl smiled. "I live there," she said. "They own these here woods, far as I know."

"What's the nearest town?" Roy said.

"Bracken. It's a good day's walk up the road from here." She pointed in a westerly direction. "My name is Sandra MacGillicutty Rae." She thumbed the center of her chest. "You can call me Sandy."

Roy tipped his hat to the girl. "Nice to meet you, Sandy," he said. He started in the direction she'd pointed.

"Don't be impolite," Sandy said.

Roy stopped again.

"When someone tells you their name, you're supposed to tell them yours back."

Roy smirked. "My apologies. The name's Roy."

"This here's Dip," Sandy said, pointing at the dog, "and that's Dandy." She pointed at the sheep. The two animals looked at Roy.

"Dip," Roy said, first nodding at the dog and then at the sheep. "Dandy."

"Sister McKinnon gave Dip his name," Sandy said, "God knows where she came up with it. We won Dandy at the churchyard fair. Father Klein said not to name him because once he grew up we'd eat him, but I named him anyway. I rhymed his name with mine. Do you like rhymes?"

Roy thought of his mother's face, glowing in candlelight as she recited his favorite poem each night of his youth. The poem was *My Star* by Robert Browning.

> *Now a dart of red,*
> *Now a dart of blue,*
> *Til my friends have said,*
> *They would fain see, too…*

"I suppose I do," he said.

"We're not really going to eat Dandy," Sandy said. At the sound of its name, the sheep looked at her. She patted its head. "You can't eat a thing that has a name."

Roy's stomach ached with idea of Dandy's legs on a plate. He would eat a named sheep or a nameless sheep just the same. "Well, I best be on my way." He started away again.

"Or maybe you could *stay?*" Sandy said.

Roy looked back to see delight in the girl's eyes. He continued walking, but over his shoulder he said, "If I do, there'll be Hell to *pay*." .

"That's not a nice word to *say*."

"Well, I'll make sure I *pray*."

Roy walked and listened, not looking back. After awhile he wondered if he'd gotten out of earshot. Just before he turned back again, Sandy yelled, "We'll meet again *someday!*"

Paul hopped over the burial line and inspected the ground. If Roy was wearing his boots and had crossed this way, there'd be a *PC* imprint from where Paul had carved his initials into the soles at the heels. He'd picked up the habit from his mother, who carved his initials into the soles of his new shoes before each new school year. When class got rowdy Mr. Cairn would have everyone remove their shoes and line them against the wall. Some of the children had no shoes to begin with, and Paul's mother refused to let some scallywag claim her son's good shoes as their own. When she made the carvings, the prints on the ground came out backwards, so when Paul started to do it himself, he carved the letters backwards so that the prints would read forward on the ground. This was infinitely more satisfying.

He found a print—the letters *PC* faintly depressed into the hard earth. Just as he thought, the horse had been sent away unburdened and Roy had set off on foot. He looked down the length of the burial line. It thinned into the horizon and would surely one day extend for miles in the opposite direction. His shovel was still stuck in the earth next to the empty hole in which Roy Pellerin was supposed to have been interred.

Paul started across the field. It would be impossible to follow

Roy's tracks in the field, and even if he could it would take too long. Roy needed supplies and food, and the closest westward town was Bracken. Paul would have to take his chances and head straight there. If he was lucky he could cut Roy off. At worst he could pick up his trail. In any case, if Roy wasn't headed to Bracken, Paul would have to come to terms with being a clerk.

He quickened his pace.

Passing hours in the forest, Paul thought of what he'd said to Gloria before he left. *Honor is nothing without love.* The words had fallen from his mouth before he'd had a chance to think on them, before he could change them into words that would hurt her. Instead he had exposed himself, had shown he still held feelings, and in return she dismissed him. The boy, too. *Take him to my father when you go.* Him. Not Jacob, but *him*. An object. A nuisance. When he was born she'd called him a gift from God.

He stopped at the edge of an algae-covered pond, squatted down to inspect the footprints. His heart climbed a rope when he found the letters *PC* riddling the ground around the water's edge. By providence he seemed to have taken Roy's precise path. He reached down to one of the prints and dragged his finger through the mud, adding a line to the *P* to make it an *R*. He closed the *C* to make it an *O* and added a *Y* to spell *ROY*.

A breeze blew across the forest. Paul sat down on the pond bank as he imagined Roy had done when he was here, maybe only hours before. He thought of Roy in this place, free and on the run. Scared? No. The boy he had known was a fearless spirit with a mind for adventure. If Roy Pellerin the man was anything like Roy Pellerin the boy, a life on the run was to his liking. He was headed west, of course, toward the frontier world he'd always wanted to see.

But wouldn't he already have seen it? In all the passed years of traveling with the sideshow, hadn't he gotten his fill of adventure?

God, Paul thought, the stories his old friend could tell. He drew in a breath. The pond's damp smell reminded him of his bayou home. He allowed his mind to return to the summer he and Roy had spent together, specifically the day of the storm.

School was coming soon, and Roy's ankles had long since healed. They were sitting on the riverbank at dusk, waiting for the nor'easter Paul's mother's arthritic elbow told her was coming. She said if they saw lightning they should start counting until they heard thunder. If they only got to three they should come in.

"Last year we learned math," young Paul said, explaining to Roy about school. "Adding and subtracting and multiplying. Like three times three equals nine. This year we're supposed to learn something called fractions."

"I know about numbers," Roy said, "but I know reading." He paused, and then said, "Is your teacher a fool?"

"Mr. Cairn? I don't think so. He knows about science and history. Why?"

Roy shrugged his shoulders. He tossed a stone and it skittered across the water.

"What is it?" Paul said. He searched his friend's scaly face.

Roy looked out over the water. He threw another stone. It skipped almost to the far bank before sinking. The ripples spread lazily out. "He thinks I'm a monster."

Paul skipped a stone. It made it halfway across and sank.

Roy skipped one.

Paul skipped one.

Roy skipped one.

"Because of your skin?" Paul said.

Roy nodded.

"Why is it like that?" Paul said, daring for the first time to ask about his friend's affliction. The question had danced on his tongue in the months since Roy had been adopted into their home, in the years since he'd seen him in the schoolyard.

"Depends on who you ask," Roy said.

"I'm asking you."

Roy picked up a stone. He looked at it, flipped it around in his hand. "My father says I was cursed by a magic gator." He skipped the stone. "But there's no magic in gators."

"And what do you say?"

"I say it's something called Ichthyosis. Some call it Harlequin. I read about it."

Paul felt excited by the mysterious words Roy used.

"The book said I probably shouldn't have lived but two days. It was written by a reverend."

"Well, what do they know?" Paul said. He punched Roy's shoulder and smiled.

"They know enough," Roy said. He looked straight into the water and focused on something beneath the surface. His eyes glazed over as he spoke. "On Thursday, April the fifth, seventeen-fifty, I went to see a most deplorable object of a child, born the night before of one Mary Evans in Charlestown. It was surprising to all who beheld it, and I scarcely know how to describe it. The skin was dry and hard and seemed to be cracked in many places, somewhat resembling the scales of a fish. The mouth was large and round and open. It had no external nose, but two holes where the nose should have been. The eyes appeared to be lumps of coagulated blood, turned out, about the bigness of a plum, ghastly to behold. It had no external ears, but holes where the ears should be. The hands and feet appeared to be swollen, were cramped up and felt quite hard. The back part of the head was much open. It made a strange kind of noise, very low, which I cannot describe. It lived about forty-eight hours and was alive when I saw it."

The two boys sat for a long while. The silence stretched between them like a tightening piano wire.

"You're not a monster," Paul said. He threw a stone straight into the water without skipping it. It clanged hollowly against an underwater log. "George Fickas is a monster."

"Who's George Fickas?" Roy said.

Paul shrugged. "Just a big, stupid kid. You won't have to worry about him at school, though. He already graduated."

"Does that mean he doesn't go to school anymore?"

"Yep. He was one of the older kids. Once you get old enough you don't get to come back."

"And then what?"

"Then I reckon you get a job."

Lightning flashed and the boys started counting out loud. They made it to nine before they heard thunder.

"Looks like we're all right for awhile," Paul said.

Roy smiled. He stood up and hopped into the river, cannonball style, making a huge splash.

His friend followed after.

Another lightning flash lit up the bayou as Paul emerged from the river. Roy was still swimming in, so Paul counted out loud by himself. The thunder clapped at the count of four. Paul sat down on the riverbank, dripping and waiting for Roy. He scooped up a handful of muck and squeezed it, letting it squish and fall from the slots between his fingers.

Roy climbed from the muck and howled like a dog. Paul dutifully joined him. The sound reverberated in his ears. Together they held the keening note for as long as their lungs held out. Once the howl was over they laughed breathlessly. It was their wild call, a bond that came to be one day as they played. Paul couldn't remember which one of them had started it.

Roy sat next to Paul and opened his mouth to speak, but he was distracted by a faraway sound. Both boys turned an ear to it. The sound was faint in the rising storm, but there could be no doubt it was a returning howl.

"A wolf?" Roy said.

"I reckon not," Paul said. "Somebody's bloodhound."

"We should go see." Roy turned to Paul with delight in his eyes.

"I just got to four," Paul said. "There's no time."

"Come on. Let's at least go see. We'll be back in plenty of time."

"Four." Paul held up four fingers. He understood his friend's love for adventure, but Winny Constantine was not Roy's mother. Paul could be scolded and punished for disobedience, and still he'd have a bed and a place at the table. Roy's risk was higher.

Roy stood. He looked in the direction from which the howl had come. For a moment the woods were quiet, and then the mournful howl began again.

"Four is not yet three," Roy said. He took a few steps, paused for a moment to listen, and then ran.

The path was well worn to this point at the river. They'd come here every day since Roy's ankles had healed. Where Roy was headed there was no path. The woods were overgrown and gnarled. Paul imagined the red bumps and scratches that would rise on his skin if he were to foray into such tangles, but Roy was fighting his way through the thick, unaffected.

"Wait up," Paul said.

The boys battled their way through the woods until they came to a small clearing. The storm had grown in intensity. Wind blew tree limbs around like the frantic arms of worried parents. Leaves and pine needles spun helplessly in the air. Paul wasn't sure they were headed in the direction of the howl anymore. Roy must have sensed the same. He howled loudly against the wind. They stopped and waited for the echoing call, but Roy's effort went unrewarded.

"Whatever it was," Paul said, "it's gone now."

"It's not gone," Roy said. "It's just this damn wind."

Lightning flashed. Paul counted out loud. At three the thunder clapped, shaking the ground beneath their feet. Roy raised a bald eyebrow to his friend. Through a smirk he said, "You count too slow." He took a few more steps and howled again.

This time the sound was reported back. It was close. It made Paul's skin tingle.

Roy dropped down to his haunches and scanned left and right across the clearing. He moved forward into the open. Paul stayed back at the wood line.

"What's that?" Roy said. He pointed.

Paul followed Roy's point to an object on the far side of the clearing. It was pale against the darkening woods and half-moon shaped at the top. It stuck out a couple feet from the ground. A headstone.

Still in a crouch, Roy made his way toward the headstone. The storm had quickly covered the sky, and the woods were turning black.

Though he'd seen it just a moment ago, Paul lost sight of the headstone. Soon Roy was swallowed in darkness, as well. Paul resisted following. He told himself Roy had to come back this way no matter what. He could just wait him out. He stood his ground.

A minute passed.

Paul began to shake from the cold. The clouds came on like God had thrown down a wet blanket. The first drops of rain hit the trees above his head.

Aw, hell.

Paul broke across the clearing in the remembered direction of the headstone. He ran possessed, crossing the clearing in seconds. He nearly tripped over Roy on the other side.

Roy was on his knees before a small grave plot. Paul knelt beside him. The rain was like a shower of stones. Lightning split the sky and the headstone lit up. Paul read the inscription.

SNIFFY

The boys turned to each other, eyes wide.

There came another howl. The sound was stronger than the wind, stronger than the storm.

A thunderclap shook the ground.

The boys ran back across the clearing the way they came. Paul fell behind. He pumped his legs hard to keep up, but as he reached the center of the clearing he went down with searing pain in his ankle.

Now at the pond bank, Paul reached for his left ankle as he recalled the pain of the small animal trap that had clamped on his leg that stormy day. His memory of what happened next was fuzzy. He recalled that Roy had come back to him, knelt over him, and over the noise of the rain had screamed, "Hold still."

But young Paul couldn't hold still. He was writhing against the trap, kicking and bucking. Roy's hands came to his shoulders and pinned him to the ground. He drew back a fist.

A moment later Paul was waking up. They were still in the clearing. The downpour had slowed, leaving the forest quiet and dripping. The left side of Paul's face thumped in pain. He blinked the rainwater from his eyes. "What happened?"

"Old Sniffy's having a good laugh at this," Roy said. He held up the small animal trap. It looked ridiculous and pathetic without any teeth. "This little guy had you kicking raindrops."

Paul sat up and rubbed his ankle as Roy tossed the trap aside. The pain wasn't bad. In fact, Paul felt embarrassed to see how little damage the animal trap had done.

"Sorry about that," Roy said.

"Sorry about what?"

"I had to hit you to stop your squirming. Only way to get a hold of that trap and pull it off."

Paul put a hand to his jaw. He worked it up and down. "Doesn't seem too bad."

"Want me to try again?"

Paul smiled. "I'd rather you helped me up."

Roy stood and offered his hand.

12

Roy came out of the forest to a two-track road heading north. Looking south he saw more forest with the road cutting through like a saw blade's path. To the north there was a sign. He stayed off the road, twenty feet inside the wood line until he reached it.

Bracken — 5 miles
pop 550

With such a population there would be a general store and a saloon. The coin bag weighed heavily on his head. His skin ached for want of salve, and his mouth wept for meat and ale. He crossed the road and walked along the western shoulder, no longer pushing through the forest, but ready to duck into cover at the sight of any horses or carts. It was nearing dusk. He reckoned it would be dark by the time he reached Bracken.

The forest turned over to cornfields with red barns and silos as he neared the town. Society. Closer still he heard a blacksmith hammering in the distance. He smelled kerosene and smoke. The farms turned over to smaller lots with houses near the road. He passed homes with oil lamps set on dinner tables—steaming plates of food, families praying for grace. The lots were divided by split-rail fences and lined by rock walls.

The glow of the town's gas lamps pierced the darkening sky.

Roy stopped short of town and looked it over. There was one main street with a few squat buildings on either side. Two silhouetted men crossed the thoroughfare. Three horses were tethered to a boardwalk rail. There was another sign.

Peace to All Who Enter Bracken

Roy passed the sign and moved into the town proper, picking his way through alleys and staying in shadow. He passed the blacksmith's shop. A blast of heat came from the open door. Orange sparks flew as the smith pounded and flipped hot iron. The intended object appeared to be a long dagger or a sword. Peace to *some* who enter Bracken. The blacksmith never looked up as Roy passed.

Ahead and to the right was a row of shops fronted by a long boardwalk. At the far end a sign marked the *Imperial Inn and Saloon*. To the left were a few ramshackle huts with no signs above them. Between them was the Bracken Bank and Loan, fronted by its own short boardwalk. The two men that had crossed the street were walking along the opposite boardwalk toward the Imperial. Their boot heels knocked hollowly as they went. They stopped for a moment to exchange something, and then continued through the saloon doors. Roy heard faint laughter and tinkling piano notes of *Home on the Range* from inside.

He came upon a signboard with years of paper layered on its

face. Tacked in with bright new nails was a wanted poster. Roy squinted, expecting to see a gator's likeness—dead or alive, a few dollars reward—but the face on the poster wasn't his own. Drawn in black ink was the face of a severe man. His beard was thick, his eyes blank. If the artist had meant to capture what this man would look like in his own coffin, it was dot on.

GENTLEMAN MURDERER!
a
REWARD of $500

will be provided to anyone who can capture and retain the outlaw, Frank Ledger. Though Ledger is a polite and cultured man—in fact a former judge presiding over Hale County—he is extremely dangerous, always armed, and may be found in the company of his three younger brothers. He is wanted for the VIGILANTE JUSTICE MURDER of one Waylon Fremont, gunned down on the streets of Bracken on May 29th, 1879. If you have any information on this man or his whereabouts, please report it to-

At that point the poster had been overlaid by a business card for William F. Brandson, Sexton and Undertaker. Either a prophetic coincidence or someone's idea of a hoot. Apart from the wanted poster there were town announcements, more business cards, and items for sale. Roy peeled back layers until he found a familiar yellow placard.

Jack McLean's Congress of Curiosities
Together with the Top Tent Circus
is Coming to Bracken April 20th at 6 p.m.!
Come see the spectacle! The ten-in-one tent featuring
Camilla, the Camel Girl
Girda, the Heaviest Woman Alive

Strong Man Samson
Scales, the Crying Lizard
and many more!

The placard was yellow, meaning it was put up in 1878. 1877 had been green, '76 was blue, and '75 was red.

The placards were the work of Jack McLean's advance man, Sully. It was an advance man's job to keep a day or two ahead of the circus and sideshow, nailing up these placards in upcoming towns. Sully was a small man with a fast horse and penchant for theatre, or theat-*ar*, as he would pronounce it. He'd put up placards by the dark of night and spend the next morning whispering to townsfolk how they must've magically appeared. By evening he'd visit saloons, hop on top of a bar or a table, and preach mightily of the show's barbaric acts, their appalling nature, and never mind the illustrated beauty who crossed the line by showing too much flesh.

By the next morning he'd be gone, the seeds of morbid fascination successfully planted.

The placards were colored with plant dye. They faded badly against the sun. The color rotated every four years, so this year's placard would be red again. No red placard on this signboard meant the show hadn't been through Bracken in over a year. Must have been too small a take for McLean to warrant a trip back through.

Roy moved past the signboard and up the boardwalk. A heavyset, balding man in suspenders sat outside a shop at the near end. He had a wild mustache and the beginnings of a beard on his cheeks and chin. His chair was tilted back against the wall and his hands were locked over his stomach. Fast asleep. The sign above the shop read *Earl's Goods*. Roy tipped his hat low and pushed up the collar on his duster. Satisfied his face was hidden, he approached the heavy man and knocked on the wall above his head.

The man awakened with a snort. His chair fell forward and

cracked down against the boardwalk. "Jesus Hell!" His was voice like that of a bullfrog. "You scared the shit right out of me!"

"You Earl?" Roy said, speaking into his collar.

The man's eyes squinted as he examined Roy's face. A meaty hand came up to rub his fuzzy chin and scratch his neck. "Whatever you're trying to hide, son, it ain't working."

Roy backed up a step. He'd sworn to himself he'd stay in the shadows, avoiding society altogether, and yet here he was, barely a day removed from prison, already breaking his promises. Damn his hunger. Damn his thirst. He might have to kill this man. His hand moved toward the revolver on his waist.

"I can see you been beat up something bad," the man said. He nodded toward the distance. "You been up in them hills?"

Roy's hand stopped. He looked over his shoulder. Past the buildings there were dark, forested hills just short of qualifying as mountains. Even at night you could see the gray veins of logging trails snaking through the pines.

Roy nodded. Better a victim than a freak.

"Well don't go up there again. Though I reckon you don't need me to tell you that."

"Shop open?" Roy said. "I could use something." His right hand went to the spot on his left arm where he habitually started the application of salve.

The man looked at the gun on Roy's hip. "Been closed a couple hours."

"You won't be robbed. I mean you no harm."

"Ain't worried about being robbed. Just ain't open."

Roy nodded and moved past the man, down the boardwalk.

"Now hold on a second," the man said.

Roy stopped, waited.

"How badly you needin' something?"

"Depends on what you got."

The man sighed. "All right, then. Come on back here and I'll let you in."

Roy turned and came back.

"Earl Walker's the name." He stuck out his hand to shake.

Roy paused. His muscles tensed. Just because this man couldn't see his affliction didn't mean he couldn't feel it. He watched Earl's eyes as they clasped hands.

"New in town?" Earl said as they shook.

If he felt Roy's scaly skin, it didn't register on his face. "Yes."

"You should call on the Imperial," Earl said, gesturing down the boardwalk. "They got booze, beds, and beauties."

All three sounded like pie slices to Roy, but salve sounded better. "I need something for what ails me."

"If one of those ain't for what ails ya," Earl said, "there ain't nothing that is!" He clapped Roy's shoulder.

The sensation of the man's touch shot down to Roy's toes and weakened his legs. Earl Walker was completely unknown to him, but any touch was an extraordinary kindness. A gust of wind could have knocked him over.

Earl produced an iron key ring and stabbed one into the lock. The door rattled a chain of bells overhead as it opened.

"Stay out of them hills," Earl said, crossing the threshold of his shop. "Once them Ledger boys get after you, they don't quit. But I reckon you met them already."

Roy followed Earl into the store. He breathed in cedar and spice like a sailor might take in the mighty sea. "Ledger boys?" His mind's eye traveled back to the wanted poster on the town signboard.

"I assume they're the ones that did that to your face? A bad lot, those fellas. They hide behind religion like it's a license to thieve and kill." He lit some candles on the countertop. "Shoulda used that smoker on your waist."

Roy looked around the small shop. Though it was poorly lit, he could see hammers, nails, flour, rock candy, medicine. He wished he had ten dollars.

"So what can I do you for?" Earl said.

"Salve," Roy said. "Got a couple wounds I need to cool down." He laid a hand on his waterskin and found it flat. "And might there be a well?"

"Well's in the alley past the Imperial." Earl turned to examine the wall of square cubbyholes behind him. He plucked out a small tin can. "Just one?"

"How many you got?"

Earl reached deep into the hole and pulled out five more small cans. "Total of six."

"I'll take them all."

Roy's stomach soured as he realized he'd have to take off his hat to get to the coin bag. His skin grew hot. Water rolled down his cheek and he wiped it away.

Earl came back to the counter with the six cans of salve stacked like a tiny totem pole. "Good stuff this salve. Ten cents a can, which makes a total of sixty. Anything else?"

"Jerky?" Roy said, hoping the jerky was far down the counter so he could remove and replace his hat while Earl's back was turned.

No dice.

Earl's hands flicked beneath the countertop and an open box of jerky touched down between them. "As much as you need. Penny a strip. Buy ten and I'll throw in a square of hardtack." He reached under the counter and produced a decently-sized chunk of bricklike biscuit.

Roy leaned forward and removed his hat, cupping the coin bag inside to keep it from falling. He plucked out the bag and slid the hat back on. "Then I'll take ten." He watched Earl's eyes.

Earl's expression didn't change. He pulled out ten strips of jerky and put them in a neat stack, using the hardtack as a base. He wrapped it all in brown paper, swiftly tied the bundle with twine, and slid the package next to the salve totem. "Seventy cents."

Roy opened the coin bag and poured the contents into his hand. All Indian-heads. Jesus, he hadn't expected that. Should have checked the bag before now. He spread them on the counter and counted out seventy. He gave Earl the money and put the rest back in the bag.

Earl dropped the pennies into his register and slid the drawer closed.

Roy packaged his new goods into the burlap bag and tied it over his shoulder. "Much obliged."

Earl nodded.

Roy saw something behind Earl's eyes. The man had something on his mind and was yet to express himself on it. Best to be gone by the time he got around to it. Roy turned toward the door.

"I saw you," Earl said.

Roy stopped. His heart gave a single hard pump before fluttering madly. The gun on his waist suddenly weighed fifty pounds.

"Pardon?" Roy said, not looking back.

"In Charleston," Earl said. "I saw you there."

Roy heard a drawer open. Heard something slide out. Heard the drawer close again. Something metallic clacked down on the countertop. He didn't want to kill this man, but want and need were separate things.

"You were with the sideshow. You're Scales, ain't ya?"

"That's not my name." Roy turned and drew his gun, sighting Earl's chest. He clicked back the hammer.

Earl Walker stood there holding a cigar. A copper tinderbox sat on the counter in front of him, emitting a yellow flame.

"Fair enough," Earl said, unfazed by the threat.

Roy lowered the revolver, eased back the hammer.

"I used to have a life there," Earl said, "in Charleston. Even had a wife." He studied the cigar as he rolled it between his index finger and thumb. "We had a son, too. I reckon he was supposed to be a twin, but his brother never grew quite right, and my son was born with little parts of his twin all over him." He touched his cigar to the flame. The end turned orange as he rolled it back and forth. He lifted it to his mouth and dragged in, brightening the cherry. "Doctor called him a *parasitic*. He died within a week. My wife, rest her soul, ended herself over it."

Roy slid the revolver back into its holster.

Earl pulled open a drawer, drew out another thin cigar, and offered it to Roy.

Roy hated cigars. Hated their look, their scent. Samson smoked them. Rather, he chewed them like an animal, and sometimes he liked to extinguish the cherry on the perfect flesh of an illustrated woman. Still, there was no payoff in insulting this man. He took the cigar.

Earl nodded toward the flaming tinderbox.

Roy lit up.

"Not but a week after they were gone, your show came to town," Earl said. "I'd been spending my time at the bottom of a bottle. Didn't know what was next for me. One day I found myself in your sideshow tent, watching y'all cross the stage. The fat lady, the girl who walked on all fours, the armless guy, and a bunch of others. It left me to wonder what he'd be like."

The man wanted to know what might have been for his son, had he lived. Straight from the freak's mouth, as it were. Roy considered offering the truth, but what good would it do to tell it? How could this man benefit from knowing his son's life would have been nothing but judgment and pain?

"Your son would've led a fine life," Roy said. "We all bear crosses."

Earl Walker continued to hold Roy's gaze.

Roy tasted the thin cigar, dragged in the smoke. It burned his throat but he didn't cough. His head lightened. His neck and shoulder muscles relaxed. He conjured a scene where Samson pinned Jesse down with his giant hands. His mind's eye saw Samson search for a good spot, somewhere along her ribs and up near her chest. He heard her scream when the embers found her flesh.

His jaw clenched, his neck and shoulders tensed back up. The taste of smoke turned bitter in his mouth. He crushed out the cherry and laid the cigar down. If Earl Walker felt insulted, he could say so.

"Crosses," Earl said, "is what them Ledger's boys will be wearing if you run into them, ya hear? You see a silver cross on a man's chest anywhere near these parts, you turn and run, understand?"

Roy nodded.

"The eldest one." Earl gestured in the direction of the signboard outside, the wanted poster. "Frank. Water runs deep and cold with him. You take a wide berth you see his likeness."

"Fair enough," Roy said.

Earl crushed out his own cigar and laid it next to Roy's. "My son was lucky to die, wasn't he?"

Roy thought of Jukey as he walked away.

13

When the caravan started away from Charleston in 1878, James Corr had been with the sideshow for just under a year. Like the other performers, he'd had a strange and difficult childhood because of his deformity, and by the time he reached a working age he'd found no decent way to make a living. He approached Jack McLean one night after a show in a Kansas cowtown, and didn't have to say a word. His lack of arms did the talking. The next day James Corr was Jukey, The Armless Marvel.

Jukey's act was more complicated than most of the others. He used his feet and powerful legs to perform the intricate daily tasks those with arms took for granted. He could light and smoke a cigarette, comb his hair, and even juggle. Audiences *oohed* and *ahhed*, and Jukey was a man reborn. He had come to the show with a slouch and shifty eyes—remnants of a youth spent in terror and shame—but after so many audiences had given him ovations he had begun to walk taller, had begun to believe he'd awakened from a decades-long nightmare.

The caravan moved toward the small town of Bracken for a one-nighter. They'd never been to the town before, and McLean thought it might be worth a stopover. It was a two-day trip from Charleston, and overnight they camped in Hale County.

After camp was set up, Jukey played poker on an ox cart with Scales and the two pinheads, Randy and Miriam. He held his cards between his toes just as easily as a regular man might do the same, fanning them out like peacock feathers above his toes. With his other foot he pinched a brass flask. To look quickly, you would swear the man playing cards had arms.

The pinheads played poorly because they had the brains of children. Their sideshow act was mostly to be observed, much like Scales, though they performed comedic antics and simple sleight-of-hand to those standing in line or walking the midway. The current the game was five-card stud. All bets had been made and Randy had been called. He laid down his hand and smiled strangely. A pair of threes, though they weren't placed together in his hand. Miriam laid down her hand. King high. Jukey laid down three tens. He offered a supreme smile. Scales snickered. "Lady luck has cursed you tonight, my friend." He laid down three jacks.

Jukey's smile flattened out. He watched as Scales drew in his jackpot pile of pennies, and he followed Scales's sightline to Randy's stake, which was down to one Indian-head.

"Who's that over there?" Scales said, looking off over Randy's shoulder. Jukey didn't look, but the easily distracted pinheads did. While their heads were turned, Scales moved half his jackpot to Randy's pile.

"Hey," Miriam said, turning back to the game. "There was no one there!"

"Yeaaah!" Randy said.

"I'm sorry," Scales said, shrugging. "I could have sworn I saw someone."

"I see someone," Jukey said. He lifted the flask to his lips, tipped it, and swallowed. In the distance walked Cecil Darton, the *someone* Jukey's eyes always seemed to find. Darton was the show's inside talker, the man who presented the performers, one by one, to the bug-eyed rubes Jack McLean corralled into the tent. Cecil's slick hair was only outmatched by his impeccable clothing, his gleaming black shoes. Legend held that he had never once stuttered on stage, never once missed a line. Cecil's every movement had a showman's purpose. There was a story in the way he tipped his hat or rubbed his hands, like all the time he was preparing for grand events.

"Witness, ladies and gentlemen," he'd said in Charleston, "the amazing feats of Jukey, The Armless Marvel." When he said *feats* it was with a wink and a wry smile, and audience ate him up like sugared cream.

Backstage Jukey basked in the light of Cecil's introductions. His ears soaked up the showman's voice, his eyes urgent to every gesture. Some of the performers found it cute. Others sneered; Cecil was a vision of what none of them could admit they wished to be. Coveting him was coveting society. To a sideshow performer on a traveling circuit, loving Cecil Darton was hating yourself.

"I can't do this anymore," Jukey said. "I can't keep hiding." The nubs at his shoulders moved as though the boy were throwing up phantom arms in despair.

Scales smirked. He picked up the cards and stacked them for shuffling. "Trust me," he said, "your feelings are well in the open."

The pinheads looked back and forth between the two men, uncomprehending this new conversation.

Jukey rolled his eyes. "You know what I mean." He laid his chin and cheek down against his collarbone. "I never knew anything like this. I never-"

"Reckoned how bad it would hurt?"

"Don't do that."

"Well," Scales said, "how many times we been over it?"

Jukey sighed. The answer was in the dozens, and Scales's advice was always the same. *Do something about the way you feel.* Though he had left the Corktown Inn drunk, and with a spotty memory, Jukey was aware of the night Scales had shared with Jesse. Scales had confided in him the secret, and Jukey had sworn to keep it dry. He'd done a pretty good job of it, too, save for the fact that he'd told Camilla. In any case, he knew Scales could stand behind his advice, as he had taken great risk when he accepted Jesse's advances.

"I'm not as brave as you are," Jukey said.

"Plenty of bravery in that copper," Scales said, nodding toward Jukey's flask while tapping the playing cards into a stack.

Jukey pretended not to listen. He looked around for prying eyes or listening ears, found none. He leaned close to Scales. The pinheads mimicked him, bringing all four together in conspiracy. He whispered, "You had the benefit of *knowing* you were wanted."

"Wanted by *Samson's* girl, need I remind." Scales said. He dealt a new hand.

As they picked up their cards Cecil Darton paraded by the game, his tilted head lolling gracefully with each proud step, his nose level with his eyes. It was Jukey's turn to bet, but he was no longer paying attention. Again he lifted the flask and drank.

"Time to play!" Miriam said.

"Yeaaah!" Randy said. It was his response to everything. You could tell him you were going to feed him worms and he'd gleefully cheer, *yeaaah!*

Both pinheads started clapping and chanting, "Time to play! Time to play!"

Jukey slammed a powerful heel on the ox cart floor. "Quiet, you fools!"

The pinheads hung their heads in shame. In a moment they would forget what they were ashamed about. It was a glorious existence.

Scales said, "We should all be so lucky."

"I thought Lady Luck had cursed me tonight?"

Scales shrugged.

Jukey drew in a breath. He laid down his cards, face up. He'd been dealt a flush. He used both feet to close the cap on his flask and set it atop his cards. He stood and followed Cecil to his wagon, catching up with the inside talker just as Cecil was coming to his door. "Excuse me, Mr. Cecil?"

Cecil Darton stopped. He held Jukey in thinly veiled contempt.

"Could we talk for a minute?" Jukey said.

Cecil closed his eyes. He released a long, exaggerated sigh. It was said he didn't like to use his voice when he wasn't performing. Had to save it. Had to preserve it.

"In private?" Jukey said.

Cecil scowled. Allowing a performer into his wagon was beyond his tolerance, but it seemed he knew better than to say no. The sideshow's performers were just as much his livelihood as their own. He pushed open the wagon door and theatrically waved Jukey inside.

Jukey climbed the steps and scanned the inside of Cecil's wagon. Immaculate. Clothes were pressed and hung, drawers were closed, the bed was two-bits tight. There were velvet curtains and an exotic scent, not quite cinnamon. He locked his eyes on a music box on the desk. It was carved from dark wood, and intricately designed with silver inlays. The seam between the top and bottom was almost undetectable.

"May I?" Jukey said.

Darton shrugged.

Jukey reached up with one toe and gently flipped the box open.

The inside was green velvet, folded around the centerpiece in a beautiful presentation. The figurine was mother of pearl, a banjo player in a straw hat. The machinery clicked alive and played *Oh Susanna* with plinking, metallic notes. Jukey closed his eyes to the music. He hummed along with the tune and moved his muscular legs in a slow, awkward dance.

Cecil removed his cufflinks and carefully placed them in a black, wooden jewelry case atop the dresser. He set an elbow on the dresser and leaned on it. He watched Jukey dance for a moment, and then clacked the jewelry case closed.

The sound pulled Jukey out of his trance. He spun to face Darton. "I'm sorry," he said. "It's just… being in here with you… I-"

"You *what*?"

Jukey smiled. His eyes found the oriental rug beneath his feet. He cocked his head and looked up at Cecil with a sidelong glance. "I love you, fella. That's what."

Neither man moved. The music box's tinging notes pierced holes in the expanding silence.

Oh Susanna…

Cecil's tilted head came forward. A smile opened up on his face.

…now don't you cry for me…

Jukey held his breath.

…for I come from Alabama…

Cecil tried to stifle his laughter, but could not. His chuckles burst forth one at a time, each following closer than the last until he was in an all out, belly gripping fit.

… with a banjo on my knee.

A single vein pulsated on Jukey's forehead. His risk was not rewarded, but punished. His love would not be full, but empty. He closed his eyes and fell to his knees, head down.

Cecil laughed to the point of tears while Jukey knelt before him. Once he was able to compose himself, Cecil wiped his cheeks and patted Jukey's head. He made that *ohh* sound people can't help but make after laughing so hard.

"You pet me as though I were an animal," Jukey said.

Cecil waved him off. He opened his mouth to reply, but lost the chance. Jukey sprung up and kicked the showman's sternum. The performer's cue-ball heel on the end of a fire piston leg dropped the inside talker to the floor.

※

Roy turned the handle on Bracken's town well, pulling up a bucket of water. He recalled Jukey running from Cecil's wagon, tripping and terrified. Jukey came to him and begged him to follow, blubbering something about Cecil being hurt. Roy followed him. As they went he caught a glimpse of Samson standing in the shadows between the wagons. At the time it merely seemed strange to Roy that Samson was there, but in hindsight he wished he'd paid more heed.

They stepped inside the wagon to find Cecil lying on his back in his perfect white suit, cuffs unlinked, not breathing. A music box struggled to plink out the notes of *Oh Susanna*. It needed winding. Roy dropped to a knee and felt Cecil's neck for a heartbeat, noting that the man would have been repulsed by his touch had he been conscious.

There was no heartbeat. He checked Cecil's wrist. Again, nothing. He slapped Cecil's face. Hard. He enjoyed the sound, the sting on his palm, but there was no response.

He slapped again.

Nothing.

Cecil was dead. He had been pretty and he didn't stutter or miss any lines, but he met the great equalizer all the same.

"Kill me," Jukey said.

Roy looked into the boy's eyes. He saw familiar pain. The look of a man who wanted nothing more from this world. Roy knew the look. He'd seen it in his own reflection more times than he cared to recall.

"We're animals to them," Jukey said, searching Roy's face. "And now I'm a murderer? You know what they'll do."

Roy thought to tell Jukey it would be okay, but he couldn't let the lie pass his lips. Jail for Jukey was as certain as the sunrise, and it would be nothing more than a torture chamber before death.

Jukey deftly plucked a goose feather pillow from Cecil's bed with his foot. He pushed the pillow into Roy's hands. He lay himself down next to Cecil and closed his eyes.

Roy clutched the pillow in trembling hands. "It doesn't have to be like this. There's time. We can find a way."

Jukey opened his eyes. He picked up his head and looked serenely at Roy. He moved a foot to touch Roy's shoulder. "You poor man."

Roy raised his bald eyebrows.

"Don't you know?"

"Apparently I don't," Roy said.

Jukey closed his eyes and let his head fall back softly to the floor. "Your skin will never be forgiven."

"But you can run," Roy said, "you can hide."

"I can survive?" Jukey said, his eyes still closed.

"Yes."

"I can continue to exist?"

"You can *live*."

"My sweet friend," Jukey said, "existing is not living."

The music box plinked slowly on.

now... don't... you...

Roy sat down on top of Jukey's muscular legs. He pressed the pillow over his friend's head. He clamped his right hand over Jukey's face like a spider. Beneath the pillow he could feel the boy's eye sockets. At first Jukey remained calm, but soon he began to buck and squirm. Roy held hard, thankful that Jukey had no arms to pry him from his task. It occurred to him if Jukey had arms there would be no task. James Corr might have been a New York lawyer or a Virginia farmer, maybe the first mate on a big ship. He'd at least be somewhere else. He'd at least be using his real name.

At length Jukey's body stopped bucking. His chest rose and fell for the last time, shuddering before it came to rest. Roy released the pillow. It stayed on Jukey's face. He lifted his hands up to his eyes.

The music box struggled on.

for... I... come.

Cecil Darton jolted into a sitting position, coughing and hacking. He gripped his chest and winced. Alive.

Roy pulled the pillow from Jukey's face, revealing the horror.

The bucket reached the top of the well. Roy dipped in his waterskin and filled it. He dumped the rest of the bucket over his head. Music and conversation wafted from inside the Imperial, along with the scent of ale and roasted pork. Two strips of jerky and a quarter of the crunchy hardtack had helped his shrunken stomach, but the scents remained tantalizing. He found an alley corner and sat down against the wall. Feeling safe in the shadows, he opened a tin of salve. The scent was clinical and sweet. He peeled off his shirt and began at his left elbow, rubbing in the ointment. He worked his way across his chest, over the word carved there, and to his other arm, liberally coating his skin while a conversation spilled from the window above his head.

"I'm gonna pick up the train in Colfax," a voice said. The word *train* piqued Roy's interest. "From there it's overnight to Chicago."

The sideshow generally passed through Chicago twice a year, once for the north side, once for the south. If Roy could make it to Chicago he'd certainly find a red placard. And then he'd be, at most, six months behind, probably less. He could continue to chase, or he could await them there.

"You really think people in Chicago will want these spoons?" a second voice said.

"Oh yes, sir," the first voice said, "and not just the spoons, but the forks and knives, too. I'd be surprised if I didn't sell them all within a week." His voice dropped in volume. "No one around here has any interest in anything so fine, but in Chicago, sir, in Chicago they know a thing or two about-"

"We've been at this long enough," the second voice said. "Where are the rest?"

There was a silent moment, and then the first voice said, "They're safe."

Roy continued with his salve, reaching across his back and then down his legs. The silence above him lingered. Roy slowed his hands and eventually stopped.

The second voice said, "I can get you to Chicago and back, but the loan is due in a month. Ten percent interest."

"Thank you, Mr. Dillon," the first voice said. "You won't regret it."

"Just be careful," Dillon said. "And don't be late. I'll have your money in the morning. Come by the bank."

"Yes sir," the first voice said. Roy heard a chair scrape wood. "Again, I thank you."

Roy pulled his shirt back on. It stuck to the salve on his skin. He leaned back against the wall for some rest while the town fell asleep.

Hours later the Imperial closed its doors. The last drunk staggered away from the saloon and down the road, singing a song about a horse. Roy figured it to be four a.m. He moved back through the empty town to the signboard. Underneath some ads there was a faded map made readable by the moon's light. Bracken was marked in the center with a black X. Charleston was forty miles due east and Colfax was ten miles to the northwest. The scope of the map didn't quite reach Chicago, but stitched train track markings went away from Colfax in the big city's direction.

Roy looked in a northwesterly direction to see the dark hills cut by logging trails. What had the shopkeeper called them? The Ledger boys. He touched the revolver on his waist. Best to start moving before the zealots got restless.

He set out of Bracken like a ghost, soundlessly passing Earl's Goods, the bank, and the Imperial. His hunger was sated. His skin felt good. His eyes were cool. His feet felt light as he walked the road out of town. After dawn he'd have to move into the safety of the trees, but for now the road was his. He walked down the center, breathing the night air evenly. His eyes caught a lightning flash in the distance. He began counting and got to six before he heard thunder.

14

"He can't go to school with you," Paul's mother said. It was midnight. She had awakened him to talk in hushed tones as Roy slept nearby. "I've been trying to tell you for weeks, but you boys are so inseparable." She smiled weakly.

Young Paul rubbed sleep from his eyes. He looked around the small room of their bayou home, trying to recall if he'd ever been awake so late. The fire was almost to embers and the silence of the hour was deeper than during the day.

"Do you understand?" his mother said.

Paul did. It saddened him. He knew Roy was different, had known it all along. He knew the kids at school would make humor of his friend. He knew it would be hard for Roy, but he hoped the others would grow to know him as he did. He hoped they could accept him as just another kid.

His mother's secrecy assured him he was wrong.

"We've been kind to him," she said, "and he's been so good for you, Paul. I don't know how that boy brought you out of your shell, but by God he did. I'll forever be grateful."

Paul looked at the sleeping Roy. The dying firelight danced across the boy's diamond scales, making him look like an animal in the night. Paul had never thought of Roy as dangerous, but he could see how others might.

"But it's been hard on me," his mother continued. She looked down at her clasped hands. "Word has spread about us taking care of Roy, and it's been difficult for me to go to town as normal. Mr. Smythe tried to charge me extra for milk the other day, saying I'd surely pay more if I would be serving it to a…"

"A monster," Paul said. He looked into his mother's eyes. She was ridding him of his best good friend and he needed to know her look. There was pain on her face. It wasn't losing Roy that pained her, Paul thought, but losing her husband to the war and her dignity to the strange boy left in her care. He put his hand on his mother's hands.

"You're a good son," she said, piling a hand over top of his.

"Where will he go?" Paul said.

Winny patted her son's hand. "Tomorrow night there's a show in town. It's the kind of show that, well, *specializes* in people like Roy. I'm going to take him to them."

"Will they want him?"

"I think so," Winny said. "I hope so, anyway. I think he belongs with them."

"What kind of show?"

"It's called a sideshow. They travel with the circus. You remember the circus?"

Paul nodded. The smell of animals and sweat and leather invaded his nose. Last year they'd gone to town to see the trapeze artists and the elephants. He remembered walking down the midway to the catcalls of outside talkers trying to lure him into dark tents. He recalled the battered banners with exotic images and statements like *Real!* and *Alive!* painted in their corners. He recalled the greasy snacks you could hold in one hand, the sugary treats that made you messy. He didn't want his friend to leave his home, but he wondered if Roy would be happier at the sideshow. He wondered if Roy would see it as great adventure. "It's dark in those tents," he said.

"It is," his mother said.

"He'll like the food," Paul said.

Winny stifled a laugh. She looked quizzically at her son. "Yes, I'm sure he'll like the food."

Now Paul walked the road south of Bracken. He figured to be about a mile out of town, having passed the five-mile sign just under an hour ago.

"Okay, then," he'd said to his mother that night, accepting Roy's dismissal so simply. And now, twenty-six years later, he was chasing his old friend across Hell's half-acre.

Lightning cracked in the distant sky. Paul counted to seven before he heard thunder.

15

The dawn brought rain. It continued through the late morning. Big drops pounded Roy's hat like falling acorns. The dark clouds kept the heat of the sun at bay, which was a blessing. Roy moved into the depth of the trees to remain unseen, keeping an eye on the road to guide him as he went. In the woods the downpour sounded like a round of applause, drowning out all other noise. Roy never heard the cart until it was passing him.

He stopped and crouched down. There was one driver and one horse pulling a flat, wooden cart carrying three other men. The cart's wheels sprayed mud in a looping arc. One man in the back carried a double-barrel scatter-gun while the others wore revolvers on their waists. All four were bearded. All wore dark dusters, square-toed boots, and black hats. All had sun-wizened eyes, scowls carved on their faces, and silver crosses around their necks.

The Ledger boys.

It was only by providence they hadn't seen him. Roy stayed low and still until the cart was well into the distance.

❉

Paul sat on the boardwalk in front of the bank. He watched rainwater bubble from an overflowing gutter. Raindrops hammered the tin roof above his head. It was the only roofed boardwalk in town, and he was happy to be dry beneath it. He'd stolen a nap near dawn and was now awaiting Bracken's awakening. He figured the best place to start searching for an ordinary man would be the saloon, but Roy wasn't ordinary. The general store across the street was Earl's Goods, a likely choice for a man in need of supply. The sign said the shop would be open by eight a.m., so the thing to do was wait.

As if on cue, a man appeared on the boardwalk across the street. Big and scruffy, he looked like an Earl. Ignoring the rain that pelted his clothing, the man walked to the door of Earl's Goods and produced an iron key ring. He eyed Paul suspiciously as he flipped through the keys.

Paul tipped his hat.

Earl nodded, and then he looked to Paul's left and nodded again.

Paul looked right to see two men approaching him. Both were dressed well, one in a banker's clothes, the other looked like he aimed to sell things. Their footsteps were barely audible against the downpour.

"Something I can help you with?" the banker said, speaking loudly over the rain. His face was round, his hands soft, his fingernails polished. His eyes were beady and sunken deep. He produced his own key ring and readied for the door.

Paul stood. He extended a hand. "Name's Paul Constantine," he said. "I'm from a county over-" the banker extended his hand to shake, "-in Hale."

The banker pulled back his hand. He and the salesman exchanged a glance.

"Redmine?" the banker said.

"As a matter of fact, yes," Paul said. He kept his hand extended.

The banker eyed him for a moment, head slightly tilted. The salesman came up reluctantly to shake Paul's hand. The banker, however, would not oblige.

"I'm looking for someone," Paul said.

"I'll bet you are," the banker said. "Got anything to convince me I should continue opening this door?"

Paul produced a strip of leather bearing the warden's seal. It was proof that he was a Redmine prison guard, not an escaped inmate, as he was certain the banker suspected.

The banker looked at the seal with one eyebrow raised. He tilted his head back and forth, as if changing his eye angle could squeeze lies from it.

"I didn't know they issued such nice pieces," the banker said, nodding to the Dragoon on Paul's waist.

"They don't."

The three men stood in awkward silence until, finally, the banker opened the door and escorted them in. "I've got a man here that needs to catch a train," he said, gesturing to the salesman. "I assume you won't mind me taking care of his business first?"

"That'd be just fine," Paul said.

"All right, then," the banker said. "Wait here." He pointed to a row of wooden chairs near the door.

The banker and the salesman walked to the office in the back. Paul took a seat and looked around. The bank was immaculate. It smelled like cedar and fresh paint. The chair was comfortable and plush, just like those next to it, and just like everything else Paul could see. One red velvet luxury after another, all collected together like they were common.

Paul looked out the window toward Earl's Goods. The man he assumed to be Earl stood behind the counter, staring back at him through the shop's front window. Paul averted his eyes. No point in giving Earl the nerves before going over to talk with him. He looked down at his hands. They were calloused and hard from digging so many graves. He turned them over, opened them, closed them. He liked the way his veins stood out on the backs. It meant he was no longer a soft kid, but a man, established in the world. He wouldn't get such hands from clerking.

He worked his jaw and felt the soreness. It wasn't as bad as before. He wondered if Roy had pulled the punch. He recalled Gloria's snicker when he told her how quickly the prisoner moved against him. Her eyes were bloodshot and her neck struggled to steady her drunken head, but her disdain was forever sober. He recalled feeling hatred for her in that moment. She was full of venom and so he must be poisonous, too. After all, he was in the right. His position was defensible, hers was not.

Defensible?

Paul shook his head. It was a word his father-in-law would use. He'd point out the drinking and the irresponsibility, he'd drill home facts and forget the feelings. He'd accuse, he'd make his case, and he'd win.

But Paul was no lawyer. He was a husband. He could accuse, he could make his case, and he could win, but what would he have won?

The office door came open. The salesman and banker came out. They shook hands. The salesman was now a paler color. His hands shook and he kept nodding and thanking and patting his chest pocket.

"You'll be fine," the banker said. "Just stick to the road."

The salesman kept nodding as he walked away, whispering words to himself and patting the pocket. Paul stood and tipped his hat as the salesman passed, but the man didn't respond.

"The name's Dillon," the banker said, approaching Paul. "What can I do for you?"

"He all right?" Paul said, thumbing toward the door.

Dillon took a seat behind a sturdy desk and leaned back in his chair. "I'm sure you're not here to discuss the well being of my customers."

"No sir," Paul said, sitting back down in the velvet chair. "I'm after a man who escaped prison, day before last."

"And you think he came through my town?"

"I'm hoping he hasn't come through yet."

Dillon nodded, pursed his lips. "Description?"

Paul pushed back his hat. "You'd know him if you saw him. He's got scales all over his skin, like a snake, and he'd be wearing-" he stopped when he saw the change in Dillon's face. "You've seen him."

"Scales on him, you say?"

"That's right," Paul said. "A disease since birth."

"I'll be damned," he said. "That girl. Sandra, I believe her name is. She's got more imagination than they know what to do with."

"They?"

"The orphanage. St. Luke's. The bank has a vested interest in-" he stopped, gestured dismissively, "-it doesn't matter. I was there yesterday afternoon and one of the girls was spouting off about a man she'd met. Said he had scales on his face and hands. We thought she created an imaginary friend."

"When was this?" Paul said.

"Yesterday."

"When did she meet him?"

"She said she found him in the woods while out playing." He blinked. "Goddammit. Are you saying that little girl had a run in with an escaped criminal?"

Paul put out a hand. "Now hold on," he said. "She ain't harmed, is she? I doubt Roy would be dangerous to a young girl."

121

Dillon's eyes sharpened. "First name basis seems awful familiar for a prison guard and his charge."

Paul closed his eyes to the mistake, wished he could suck it back in. He pressed on. "The girl, did she say anything more?"

"What did this prisoner do?"

"It's not important," Paul said. "I need to know where he might be headed."

"It's my town he's in. I need to know what kind of maniac we're dealing with. What was he imprisoned for?"

Paul sighed. "Murder."

"And you idiots managed to lose him?"

Anger bloomed in Paul's chest. Blood rose into his throat, into his head. His tongue tasted metal. His mind cleared and he found focus. The feeling was delightful. "That's a reckless insult for a man who doesn't pack iron."

Dillon smirked. "No need to pack iron in a town you own."

"Is that right?" Paul felt cool air on his widened eyes, the tickle of his hair coming to attention.

"You doubt me? Every loan in the county comes through this bank, meaning every goddamn one of those people out there are in my pocket." He tapped his breast pocket, which was stuffed with a silk handkerchief. "I'd say that puts me squarely in a position of ownership."

Paul looked down at his hands, shook his head.

"You disagree?" Dillon said.

"Funny thing about a man who thinks he owns things," Paul said, "he never understands that his things own him." He stood and leaned over the desk, knuckles against the wooden top, aware that his open jacket exposed the hilt of his Dragoon. He glanced at Dillon's breast pocket before finding the banker's eyes. "Next man you insult might put a hole in that pocket of yours, leak you right out of it."

"I think its best you leave now," Dillon said.
Paul tipped his hat and left.

16

Young Roy sensed the change when Winny Constantine gifted him a brand new hat. "Just like a gunfighter," she said, picking lint off the hat's wide brim. She placed it on Roy's bald head. "We're going on an adventure. Just you and me."

Roy had kept tabs on her unease. In the hour before they left, she kept rearranging things around the house, putting them just so. She moved the oil lamp on the table at least ten times, adjusted the salt and pepper shakers, and wiped her hands on her apron so often it couldn't be counted.

Paul sat still, staring into the fire that warmed their home.

When Winny came out of the bedroom dressed like an advertisement, Roy thought it best to pack his things. He loaded his knife, a couple books, and the extra clothes the Constantines had provided him into a crawdad net and tied it tight. His suspicions were confirmed when Paul didn't ask why he was packing.

"Come along now, Roy," Winny said, standing in the open doorway, the moon and stars peeking into the house from out of the black sky.

Roy slung his net over his shoulder and approached his friend. He stood at the side of the fireplace. "Thank you," Roy said.

Paul nodded, eyes still on the fire.

Roy placed a hand on Paul's shoulder. He was his best good friend and he didn't want him to live with pain. He wished to absorb Paul's misery and take it with him. Later, he could throw it up in some alley, down into the gutter, and let it wash out into a world where Paul could never find it again. He left Paul's side and caught up with Winny in the doorway.

As they crossed the threshold, Paul called out to stop them. "A three legged dog walks into a saloon…"

Roy turned an ear to his friend.

"… I'm looking for the man who shot my *paw*."

Roy smiled. "That's a humdinger."

The sounds of people and animals grew louder as Roy and Winny neared town. The din was occasionally cut through by a laugh, a squeal, or some variety of growl. The scents were exotic. His mouth watered. Closer still he could see points of light floating in the night air. Braziers pegged on high wooden posts, watching over the proceedings like guardians in the gloom. They shined down upon what Roy understood to be the circus and the sideshow. He'd read about them, seen drawings.

Roy halted when he saw the big top. The blue-and-white tent presided over everything like an enormous king, its sides swelling and collapsing like giant lungs. Roy's heart quickened. It was all he could do to stay by Winny's side.

She gripped his shoulder tightly.

At the striped king's feet roiled a sea of children, women, and men. Some were tall, some short, some wore big hats, some had their arms raised, others stood with hands in their pockets. Some were dressed in their Sunday bests, others looked as if they'd crawled from a ditch. Some stood in line to get into the tent. Others lined up for food. Still others circled something in the midway, something that spat fire. The audience cheered.

Roy longed to dash into the mix, but as his longing increased, so did the strength of Paul's mother's grip. The tips of her fingers cut painfully into his shoulder.

Thirty feet short of the crowd, Winny stopped and held Roy in place. She tugged his hat brim lower onto his head. She surveyed the grounds as best she could with her five-foot frame, standing on her tip-toes to get the best view.

Seeming satisfied with what she found, Winny drew Roy sideways, skirting the throngs of people. They moved behind the grandstands and food huts, cutting through the darkness like unwelcome spirits at the edge of a Pagan fire.

They came to a place where the crowds were less thick and the tents grew smaller. Here the din became distinct voices. Strange men stood outside small tents on wooden boxes, taunting passersby.

"You there, sir," a talker said, addressing a young boy. "You're not afraid, are you? Bring the young maiden with you." Next to the boy walked a giggling girl. They were together, but maybe not as close as the boy wished. He waved off the talker and laughed, keeping his eyes on the girl.

"You'll be back," the talker said. He turned his attention to two more boys coming down the midway, pointed at them. "I know two young men unafraid to enter the realm of the Fiji Mermaid!"

The boys shook their heads, unimpressed.

Roy and Winny moved farther down the midway, behind more tents. As they neared the midway's end Winny froze. She released Roy's shoulder and stared across the lane at a red-and-white striped tent. The low side of the tent was stained and ugly with mud. The entrance was littered with propped signs displaying what frights and fears may be inside—a bearded lady, a living corpse, a pinhead, something called an Aborigine, and dozens more. All the signs claimed that the beings were real, alive, and guaranteed. Above the tent hung a waxed banner of thick canvas and many colors. It read, *Jack McLean's Congress of Curiosities.* It was intricate and beautiful. Roy thought it must have taken a year to paint it.

On a soapbox in front of the tent stood an old man. He wore a black top hat and a red jacket with long tails. His pants were black and his boots shined unnaturally beneath the braziers. A riding crop was tucked under his arm. His gloves glowed a stark white. His face seemed wooden. The way he looked down upon those that passed told you he was born on that soapbox and had lived there all his days.

As the boy and girl approached, they fell under the talker's gaze and slowed their pace. He eyed them for a moment before speaking.

"The young lady is frightened," he said, eyes on the boy. His voice was a deep toll. The girl's body went rigid. If she wasn't frightened before, she was now. "You must draw her in closely," the talker continued, gesturing with his arm.

The boy took the command and wrapped his arm around the girl, seemingly grateful to the talker for giving him permission.

"That's right," the talker said, his voice shifted into a terrible whisper. "Protect her. Protect her from the *evils* of this world." He waved one arm across the expanse of night. He then leaned on the small podium and smirked. "But can you protect her from what lurks in my tent?"

The boy steeled up as if he'd been challenged to a fight. He clenched his available fist.

"I don't think you can," the talker said. He falsely checked his nails through his white glove. He shook his head and turned his gaze elsewhere. "Cowards don't do well in my hell."

The boy nearly tripped as he lunged forward, discarding the girl and digging into his pockets. "We'll take two," he said, slapping some coins down on the podium.

The talker accepted the boy's fee with a movement Roy almost missed. He smiled broadly and pulled back a fold in the tent, exposing a darkness like Roy had never seen. He imagined drooling demons inside.

"The show starts in five minutes," the talker said.

The two kids disappeared into the black. Roy looked down the midway to see the oncoming boys already digging into their pockets. Roy touched his own pockets, checking for coins that weren't there. He would have given his shirt to go into the tent.

The two other boys paid their fees and entered without a word.

Winny looked up and down the empty midway before drawing Roy forward. They crossed the lane quickly and came to the talker.

"Are you McLean?" Winny said.

"I am," McLean said.

She pulled Roy's hat off, exposing his bald head, his scabbed skin. McLean looked down at Roy. He blinked once, and then he smiled.

On the road to Colfax Roy crouched again. Another cart was passing. A lone driver and horse. This cart held no men, but a slatted box strapped down with thick rope. The well-dressed driver rode furiously against the rain. The cart jostled and banged against the rough road, but the box held tight. Roy waited for silence. He waited until the cart was lost to the horizon before he began again. He took one step before a distant gunshot stopped him cold.

17

Paul opened the door to Earl's Goods. Copper bells jingled above his head. He shrugged off the rain. The shop was clean, the smell medicinal and pure. The floor was worn with gaps between the boards. Paul moved past a rack of rock candy and thought of Jacob, wondered how the boy was faring.

The man Paul assumed to be Earl stood behind the counter wearing a brown apron. He smiled like a shopkeeper, but his arms were folded over his chest in a go-to-Hell kind of way. "What can I do for you?"

Paul approached the counter. "Well, I'm hoping you can help me out."

"Anything you need," Earl said.

"That's good," Paul said. He rapped his knuckles on the counter, still buzzing from his encounter with the banker, still savoring the anger, like a swallow of wine that coats the mouth and teeth. "I'm looking for someone."

"Imperial's just down the way," Earl said. He gestured down the boardwalk with his head. "If you're looking for someone in this town, you'll find them there. Don't think she's open yet, though."

"The man I'm looking for isn't just any kind of someone."

"Ain't no other kind of someone I know," Earl said. He moved down the counter and laid his attention on straightening some items.

Paul followed him down the counter. "He isn't a regular man." He waited until Earl looked up. "He's different."

Earl shrugged. He straightened a box of cigars, wiped the counter with a rag.

"Scales," Paul said.

Earl kept wiping.

"Diamond scales on his body. Like a reptile."

Earl looked up. "What is it you want, sir?"

"Have you seen him?" Paul said.

"You've heard your answer," Earl said.

"You've given no answer."

"As you say."

The bells above the door jingled. Quick footsteps banged the floorboards. A little girl appeared amongst the shelves and racks. "Hey, Earl!"

"Hey there, Sandy," Earl said.

Paul looked out the shop window to see a horse-drawn carriage in front of the bank. The door on this side was open and still swinging on its hinges. Two nuns sat inside, side-by-side, shaking their heads. Sandy reached up and slapped down three pieces of rock candy on the counter before Earl. "When you gonna get some strawberry?"

"Soon," Earl said.

Paul looked at the rock candy the girl had put down. Two were green, one was yellow. Lime and lemon.

"How about *June?*" the girl said. She placed three pennies on the counter next to her goods.

Earl looked up at the ceiling, thought for a moment, and then pointed at the girl and said, "Maybe in a blue *moon.*"

Sandy giggled. "Strawberry," she said, "would make me *swoon.*"

Earl laughed. "It would certainly be a *boon!*"

Sandy slid her rock candy off the counter and into the front pocket of her bib trousers. Earl slid her pennies his way. The girl regarded Paul. "Howdy mister."

Her eyes struck Paul like cattle prods. In that moment it came to him that he had never known the color of his own daughter's eyes. She had never opened them, of course, and it was a detail he'd never thought to check. It would have been a morbid thing to reach down and pull back her tiny eyelids. As he imagined doing it now, he found them black. Paul blinked away the vision and regarded the girl before him, Sandy. *She is what we might have had.* This bright person, this wonderful bundle of energy, might have been his own daughter, given the chance at life. He tipped his hat. "Howdy."

The girl squinted her eyes at him. "You okay mister? You look a little pale."

The nuns were out of the carriage outside and moving toward the store now. Paul squatted to match the girl's height. "If I'm pale, it's because I've lost track of someone."

The girl's eyes sparkled. "Well, that's no *fun.*"

"Maybe you've met him," Paul said, "this man on the *run?*"

The girl lifted a hand to her cheek, ready to tell a secret. With an exaggerated whisper she said, "Maybe he's the *scaly one?*"

"He is," Paul said. "No doubt he is… um…" he struggled to find a rhyme.

"Is he a bad man?" Sandy said.

"No," Paul said.

"I didn't think so."

"He's a good man in a bad situation."

Sandy put a hand on Paul's knee. "That's not why you're sad."

Paul blinked. He searched the little girl's face. The bells above the door jingled. He looked up. The nuns were in the doorway. "Here now, Sandra."

The girl leaned in close to Paul. "Tell Roy I said howdy." She ran off.

Paul stood from his squat as the nuns escorted the girl out of the store. He looked at Earl, whose jaw was clenched. He breathed through his nose. "Might be the last time I see that little scamp."

"How's that?" Paul said.

"Heard tell they found her a family."

"Well, good for her."

"What makes one man follow another?" Earl said.

Paul turned to Earl. "He's an escaped prisoner."

Earl placed two hands flat on the counter before him. "He ain't no danger to people. People are a danger to him. People like you."

"He killed a man. I'd lay dimes to nickels he didn't tell you that."

Earl took a moment to digest the new information, then he said, "I let him in here last night, after closing. Figured a fella with his… problem… could use some help. Didn't know I was aiding a criminal."

"Which way was he headed?" Paul said.

"I imagine he'd be looking to catch up with his old sideshow."

"You know where Redmine is?"

Earl nodded.

"Coming from there and ending up here, which way would you go?"

"I'd find the nearest train," Earl said, "and that's in Colfax."

Paul pulled off his hat and dropped his coin bag into his hand. He opened the bag and produced a penny, which he put down on the counter. "For one of those rock candies on the way out."

Roy watched the scene from a distance. The lone driver's horse was shot dead, the slat box busted, the cart overturned. One wheel spun slowly in the wind, dripping collected rain. Inside the slat box there had been a black chest. The chest was now on the ground next to the overturned cart. The driver knelt before the four men from the other cart, knees in the mud, his face turned down, his hands pressed together like prayer.

Through the drumming rain Roy could not make out the words, but two of the Ledger brothers were arguing. Frank was one of them. The artist that had captured his likeness on the wanted poster should be lauded, for the sketch was dot on. He wore a black sack suit and a bowler hat. A silver cross gleamed on his chest, suspended by a silver chain. If not for the scatter-gun casually laid over his left forearm, Roy would swear the man was an aristocrat. His brothers were woodsmen. Their clothing was similar to his, but unkempt, scruffy and wild. Each was adorned with a silver cross.

Roy chanced closer in the downpour, secure that the sound of rain masked his movements. He stepped through the leaves made soft and found cover once he was close enough to hear.

"Thou shalt not steal," one of the brother's said, pleading with Frank. The pleader was the most theatrical one, waving his arms about, pacing back and forth. The others kept their mouths closed and their guns trained on the kneeling man.

"It's a sin," the pleader continued, "a commandment. Ain't no way around it."

Frank Ledger lifted his right hand and inspected it. It trembled like palsy. He shook his head in distaste, closed the hand into a fist, and returned it to his side. Addressing his theatrical brother, he said, "Thievery is not the soul of this matter, Steven." He then lifted his scatter-gun to the kneeling man's chest and asked him, "Is it, sir?"

The kneeling man's face turned the colors of fire and ash. "I meant her no harm."

"A sad last bastion," Frank Ledger said.

"You bastard," the kneeling man said. "You were the one who set me free. Why now? What is this?"

"A proper judge requires the preponderance of evidence," Frank Ledger said. He clicked back both the hammers on his gun. "There wasn't enough on you."

"You're no judge," the man said.

"And I ain't proper," Frank Ledger said. He squeezed the triggers. The blasts were muffled by the kneeling man's chest. He spilled backwards into the mud and flopped over to his side.

In the echoing aftermath of the scatter gun's blast, Frank Ledger began whistling a slow, haunting rendition of *Clementine. Oh, my darling. Oh, my darling.* The notes of his melody were like drops of gloom paying out into the silence.

Two of the brothers went about the business of picking up the black chest while Frank and Steven headed toward their distant cart. No one noticed that the shot man was still alive. After a moment of writhing around, he pulled a small revolver from his waistcoat, aimed it unsteadily in the direction of the Ledger boys, and fired.

One of the brother's yelped. He dropped his end of the black chest and reached down to his thigh. "Aw, hell!"

They all spun toward the dying man and drew their guns, but no one shot. The man had fired once, fell back, and was now gone, his face as slack as a fish.

Steven Ledger stepped in to help with the heavy chest while his wounded brother limped about. They loaded the chest on to their cart and hopped aboard. All but the brother who'd taken the leg shot. He said a few words and waved the rest off. The cart pulled away as he limped into the woods and eventually out of sight.

Roy moved closer to the wreckage, inch by inch through the downpour, revolver at the ready. He came to the dead man's side.

He touched the man's neck to find a pulse. No dice. The skin wasn't yet cold, but it felt indifferent and waxy. The blood that had seeped through the man's waistcoat was spreading out as it mixed with raindrops. Damn fool, Roy thought. He looked at the man's hand to see his trigger finger still extended, the small revolver hanging from it.

Something metallic laid in the mud near the cart. Roy picked up the object and examined it. A spoon of polished silver. Its delicate carving was crafted with passion. Its maker was right; people in Chicago would have paid good money for his product. Probably they still will, Roy thought. He pocketed the spoon.

He moved into the western woods opposite the side into which the leg-shot Ledger had gone. He picked forward at a slow pace, reminding himself to move like a turtle. It helped to think of time's slow passing at Redmine. The interminable minutes, hours, and days, only cut through by the rising and falling bucket. He thought of the varied faces that looked down at him as the bucket moved. The guards. They were men of no consequence, no future, and meaningless pasts. He felt no hatred for them, only pity. He wondered which of them would be sent after him, if any at all.

And then he knew, somewhere deep and unexplained, that it would be Paul.

18

Paul smiled when the last drops of rain fell pitifully on his hat. The pines zipped by as he walked the road to Colfax at a brisk pace. The air was sweet and cool. Roy couldn't be far ahead, a day at the most. At the least, he could be around the upcoming bend.

Instead there was an overturned cart.

Paul slowed his pace and gripped the Dragoon on his side. His heart-rate increased its volume. This hadn't been a square dance. A man was face down next to the cart, shot up something bad. Dead. Paul recognized the salesman's clothes, and when he turned him over, his face. It was a strange thing to see a living man not but a few hours before, only now to see his eyes without light.

Whatever the salesman had been aiming to sell was missing from the busted slat box, and there was nothing to identify him. A shotgun blast at close range had opened up his chest; his waistcoat was singed with fire.

Roy?

It made sense. Roy was a desperate man, and desperate men don't resemble themselves. Hell, he was an escaped prisoner and convicted murderer, which was enough, but he was an outcast, too. Why not steal from a society that was repulsed by you? Why not kill those that meant to harm and control you? Why not take on the disposition of the monster they assumed you to be?

Paul tried to shake the notion that Roy could be so cold-blooded. It had unnerved him to know Roy killed one man, but now two?

It doesn't matter. Just find him.

The train out of Colfax went straight through to Chicago. Chicago was a big city with lots of places to hide, even if you were an outcast. If Roy could catch that train, he may be lost for good. Paul scanned the wreckage, studying the scattered footprints in the mud. Random patterns. This couldn't have been the work of one man. Most of the footprints disappeared next to some cart tracks heading north.

His heart tripped out of rhythm when he saw a line of his own initials trailing through the center of the mess. The prints went up the road and then disappeared into the woods on the western side.

Paul stepped alongside the prints, following them. A scream stopped his movement. It was a high-pitched, terrified sound from the eastern woods, behind him. Paul loosed his Dragoon and crossed to the eastern side in a crouch, moving quickly. The tall grass at the roadside was splattered red. He moved into the trees, following the blood trail.

He stopped when he saw the little girl, Sandy. She was standing rigid in front of a collapsed man. The man was up against a tree, crumpled forward over himself. His upper right leg showed a bullet hole. Bad spot. His pants were darkened with blood. He must have sat down and bled out. Paul stepped closer to the scene. "Sandy."

The girl turned to Paul.

The collapsed man sat up. He produced a revolver and pointed it at Sandy's face. Paul's guts shrunk like a closing fist. All function stopped. His mind's eye saw Gloria giving birth. He saw his daughter's black eyes. He saw his son pointing a pretend pistol. The boy's little thumb-hammer came down. *Pow.*

Sandy's lower lip trembled. Her eyes dilated.

"Over here," Paul said.

The man turned his aim to Paul. The gun began to shake in his weakening grip. The silver cross hanging from his neck jangled back and forth. Paul shifted his gaze to the man's face. He was pale as an albino. His eyes kept blinking and refocusing.

"Who the f-f-f...?" the man said.

"Who shot you?" Paul said.

The man cocked back the revolver's hammer. The gun shook wildly as he struggled to keep it centered. Paul holstered the Dragoon. He raised his hands and showed empty palms.

"B-Bastard," the man said, "lucky sh-sh-shot."

"What did he look like?"

The man blinked slowly. His head fell forward. His arm weakened and the gun fell and fired, ripping a hole in the man's boot. Blood bubbled out the sole. He didn't react.

Paul jumped forward. He propped up the man's head and slapped his cheek rapidly. "Did he have scales on him?"

The man seemed to think on the question for a moment, looking off and up. He then said, "Are you Jesus?"

Paul shook his head, no.

The man smiled before dying.

Paul turned to Sandy. She was catatonic. He went to her, knelt down, and hugged her. At first her arms remained at her sides, but slowly she unlocked, wrapped her arms around him, and wept.

Paul carried her out of the woods to the road. He walked north until the wrecked cart was out of sight and the girl had stopped crying. Paul set her down on her feet and held her by the shoulders. "What on earth are you doing out here?"

"I don't want to go with them."

"The sisters?"

"The Johnsons."

Paul coupled her story with what the shopkeeper had said about a family adopting her. "What's wrong with the Johnsons?"

Sandy looked down.

Paul picked up her chin with two fingers.

The girl sighed through her nose. She looked away and said, "The wife, Mrs. Johnson, she smiles like a clown."

Paul snorted. "That's the reason you don't want to go with them?"

"You don't understand," Sandy said. "She just… she just sits there smiling, like a stupid clown, with her hat and her gloved hands, while Mr. Johnson talks and decides everything. They're rich."

"Seems like a pretty good deal, you ask me."

"She's got no mind," Sandy said, stomping her foot.

Paul sat back on his haunches. "So what then? You don't want to end up like Mrs. Johnson?"

"Never."

Paul smirked. "You'd rather stay *clever*?"

Sandy rolled her eyes as she took a moment to think, and then she said, "That is my *endeavor*."

"Come on," Paul said. He stood.

"You're following Roy?"

"I am."

"I'm coming with you, then."

As far as Colfax, Paul thought.

They tread down the road for several minutes in silence. Eventually, Paul said, "How'd you know something was bothering me?"

"What do you mean?"

"Back there in Bracken, in that store, I said I'd lost track of Roy, and you said 'That's not why you're sad.'"

Sandy shrugged.

"Now hold on," Paul said. "You can't just shrug that off. Why'd you say it?"

"People don't follow what makes them sad," Sandy said. "They follow what makes them happy, and run away from what makes them sad."

They walked for another silent stretch before Paul said, "Some people prefer to be sad."

Sandy said, "Then some people are goddamn fools."

19

Roy reached Colfax in the late afternoon. The rain had stopped, but his clothes remained wet. He didn't mind; it kept his skin cool.

Colfax was larger than Bracken. A tourist trap. The main street was all shops, no blacksmith, no tannery, no whorehouse. The boardwalks teemed with people coming in and out of storefronts, wearing nice clothes and laughing with each other as they walked. Horses lined the boardwalk edges. They were tethered and seemingly oblivious to the comings and goings of their humans, their leathery lips moving for unknown purposes.

Roy wanted to go into town to check for a red placard, but there was no need; he was certain there'd be one. This kind of town was a sideshow's dream—ripe with loose money. Besides, entering the town would bring trouble. Too many people, and twice the eyes. A farmer or a blacksmith might not take a second glance, but a tourist was on the lookout for something different. Their jaws would fall, their fingers would point.

Roy stayed in the wilderness, circling the city until he came to the train tracks. He followed the tracks to the edge of the rail yard where he set up camp in a clump of trees. He would wait for nightfall, and if it were in the cards, he would hop an outgoing train.

Lunch was jerky, hardtack, and water. With time to kill, he indulged in another application of salve. His skin had taken the first like a desert takes rain, and now it was thirsty again. The second application would last longer.

The trains came and went, trailing steam and smoke, this way and that. People boarded and exited the cars. Boxes and luggage were loaded and unloaded. Workers in worn out overalls and sweat lined hats milled about in the mud, picking up this, pounding on that, directing heavy things on chains.

Roy envied the simplicity of their work. These men showed up each morning, beat their bodies to exhaustion, and then went home to good dinners and families. There was no thinking in it, and no worry. No time for trivialities, only time for the task at hand.

Working for the sideshow was never so simple. To look at it from a distance, most would think just sitting there was an easy job. *That's nothing*, they'd say, *try breaking your back on these tracks all day. Try looking at a hundred acres of grain, knowing you couldn't stop reaping until it was all down.* They would think he had it made.

But Roy would take their jobs in a beat. He'd break his back to come home to a good meal cooked by a loved one. He'd harvest grain until he collapsed, so long as when he opened his eyes someone was there for him.

Jesse.

His night with her had been finer than silk. He recalled the feel of her soft flesh under his hands, the way she moved and made small noises, the likes of which he'd never heard before. The climax of their love was like livewires tapped into his muscles and bones. Finer than silk, indeed. Afterward, she fell asleep quickly from the drink. He fell more slowly, watching the candlelight dance with her illustrations. Her ink seemed to darken and pulsate against the flickering light. He lay there wondering how she could give herself to a man like Samson, but then he bit back the thought. She was with him now. That was what mattered. He had some money. They could go somewhere. They could find a different life.

Sleep took him during visions of a farmhouse.

In the morning he awakened to find Jack McLean sitting in a chair across the room. The man had grown quite old in the years since Roy had joined the sideshow, and time's passing had been unkind. His once-wooden face was now soft, creased and folded like a well worn duster. His mouth showed colt's teeth. His skeletal hands gripped a cane. His top hat sat on his knees, exposing liver-spotted skin on a bald crown, ringed by a thin patch of white hair.

"How are you, Roy?" McLean said. His voice was no longer deep and imposing, but frail and desperate.

"I'm fine," Roy said. He looked for Jesse, but she was gone. McLean must've excused her. As much as he loved and respected his mentor, Roy didn't appreciate that he'd sent her away. He moved to the edge of the bed and plucked a tin of salve from the nightstand.

"She's my granddaughter," McLean said, tapping the empty side of the bed with this cane.

Ice formed on Roy's bones. He had smartly feared Samson's wrath, but this was unforeseen.

"That orphanage story was hooey," McLean said. "Her mother and father—my son—couldn't handle her, so they cut her loose. The girl's got fire. Never let it be said she's not her own woman."

"I didn't know she... I mean to say, I-," Roy said.

"Forget about it," McLean said. "We do what is-"

"-in our nature to do," Roy said, finishing the sentence he'd heard countless times before. The lesson had been beaten into his brain, not just by McLean's words, but by traveling the sideshow circuit for so long. Through all the years Roy had been shown the nature of humans. More importantly, he was shown that humans would always remain true to their nature.

"I'm here about something else," McLean said.

Roy exhaled relief. He opened the tin and started at his left elbow. His mind kept flicking through images of last night. He fought back a smile.

"How long have you been with the show?" McLean said.

Roy blinked. He did quick math. "Twenty-five years."

"Twenty-five years," McLean said, nodding his head. His movements were slow and calculated. "A long time."

"As you say."

"I reckon you've been with me the longest now," McLean said. He looked off in thought. "It was Delia, Gorgo, the original Samson, and then you. After Samson died, just you."

The original Samson had been McLean's first strong man. He was a specimen of size and strength in his youth, but through his adult years and into old age his strength had naturally declined. His last day as a strong man was the day after Winny Constantine had given Roy to the sideshow.

Roy spent his first night sleeping on a straw bed amongst the stagehands. McLean awakened him in the morning to show him around. Young Roy shook hands with dozens of characters, none of which recoiled at the sight of his deformity, nor he at theirs. That same night McLean let Roy watch the show from backstage. It was their final night in the Bayou Rouge.

"We're hot tonight," McLean said after introducing the original Samson and returning backstage.

His expression soon took a downturn. The original Samson had taken the stage with vigor, but his old body had clearly begun to fail him. He struggled to bend a nail. He winced when a stagehand dropped a considerable weight on his hardened stomach. He failed to heft an iron ball over his head.

"Get off the stage, old man!" came a lone voice from the booing crowd.

The raucous tent went silent.

Samson opened his mouth to respond, but he was breathless from attempting his feats. His hands went to his knees as he gasped for air.

"What humor," the voice said.

Backstage, McLean's eyes thinned. He stepped out in defense of his strong man. "Who speaks?"

At the back of the tent a hand went up. It was the size of a brick, the forearm a tree trunk.

"You feel you can do better?" McLean said.

"Better than that corpse? Yer goddamn right."

The original Samson came up from his bend. He looked out into the crowd, still breathing hard. When the loudmouth stood, Samson's head bowed. He was already beaten.

The loudmouth approached the stage. He was not a particularly tall man, but imposing, nonetheless. *Stout* seemed an inadequate word. Each muscle was like a separate live animal trapped beneath the skin. They flexed and jumped as he walked.

Jack McLean and Samson stepped aside. The man gripped the handle on the iron ball and it went up like a star-shot. The train track Samson had mustered six inches off the ground went up with little effort. The man pressed the weight from his shoulders above his head seven times before he dropped it on the stage with a thunderous crash.

The crowd erupted in ovation. The original Samson left the stage, and a new Samson was born. The switch was made with no hiccup. The new Samson fit into the old Samson's leopard-skin singlet as well as the old Samson now fit into a stagehand's overalls. The weights that old Samson once struggled to lift were made into bigger, heavier things. Audiences that once groaned to see the old Samson struggle now gasped at the new Samson's might.

After the switch there was simply Samson and a new stagehand named Walter.

Walter did his new job well until he fell dead off the back of a cart as the caravan crossed a bridge from Kentucky into Ohio. They'd just performed a free show for a Louisville consumption sanitorium. After taking down the tent, Walter dropped to all fours with the sanitorium's girls and boys. He let them climb all over him. He was the wild bear and all the kids laughed and reeled away from his growls and swiping paws. He played with them until it was time to go. His heart shut down on the bridge out of town. He was eating an apple when he fell. It bounced and seemed to float on air for a moment before disappearing over the side. Roy always thought he could have caught that apple, had he simply reached out for it.

"I need a favor from you," McLean said.

"Anything, Mr. McLean."

"Gene," McLean said. "My name is Gene."

Roy's blank expression must have given him away, because Gene laughed in a way Roy hadn't seen Jack McLean laugh in years. The way his body shook and creaked, Roy thought the old man might break into dust.

Gene finally settled. "That was priceless."

"Gene?" Roy said.

"Jack McLean is nothing more than a stage name, Roy," he said. "Or should I say, *Scales*." He offered a wink.

Roy nodded. He continued to apply salve, moving across his chest now. Her hands had been here, too, he thought. They'd been everywhere on him. He thought of her above him. He thought of the way she arched her back and pushed her hips forward. The way her breasts hung freely.

"No one would come to see Gene Rattenburg's Congress of Curiosities, would they?" McLean said.

Roy shrugged. He thought it had a nice ring to it.

"Bah. What do you know?"

"I know enough."

"In any case," McLean said, "I'm getting too old for it now. It's time to take a cue from old Samson and step out of the light."

Roy looked into Gene Rattenburg's failing eyes. He'd known for years the old man was looking for a successor. He figured Cecil Darton was being groomed for the role. Roy never thought it possible the riding crop would be passed his way. "You don't mean me?"

"No," McLean said. "You're a fine man, Roy, but we both know you're no outside talker."

Roy agreed. His skin alone disqualified him for the job. The idea was to entice people into parting with their money, not frighten them into keeping it. Darton was custom made for the job. His smile weakened the knees of girls and boys alike.

"What I need from you," McLean said, "is to help me make the switch. The others respect you. I need you to approve of my successor and make it okay with them."

"They like Darton well enough," Roy said.

The old man's eyes fell to the floor. He rubbed his hands. "It won't be Cecil."

"Then who?"

"Samson."

Roy shook his head. Jack McLean was a good man. He treated his performers with respect and dignity. They thrived under his care. The show did well under his supervision. Darton may not be a kind man, but he was harmless. An animal like Samson would destroy it all. McLean had to know this.

"Why?" Roy said.

"Jesse's the only family I have that gives a damn," McLean said, again tapping the empty side of the bed with his cane. "All I have—hell, Roy, all we've built over the years—it's hers."

"Fair enough. But I don't see what that has to do wi-"

"They're not just together, Roy. They're legal. They're married."

Roy heard the salve tin clang the floorboards. Images of last night flipped through his mind in quick stills, but the firelight faded and her body fell into shadow. All except the round scar of the cigar burn he'd seen on her ribs. Last night he'd noticed the scar for the first time, all the time hidden beneath clothing that never came off on stage. He told himself it could have been an accident, something she gained as a child. But a single thought gnawed at him then, and it gnawed at him now—Samson smoked cigars.

"I don't know what happened here last night," McLean said, sweeping his cane through the air to indicate the room, "but I believe she loves her husband."

"Don't do this," Roy said.

Gene leaned on his cane and stood—shaky, but not too shaky. He put on his hat. He sucked in a deep breath and released it slowly. "Well," he said, his frail voice returned to the outside talker's deep toll, "I may have a few more shows left in me."

Roy nodded. There would be time to change McLean's mind, time for him to claim Jesse as his own and leave the sideshow behind.

"After our swing down the east coast", McLean said, "we'll see how I feel. Meantime, you start spreading word to change their minds on Samson."

Outside of Colfax Roy watched the last rays of the sun get lost in the trees. A day's worth of action at the train station had slowed, but a vein of activity would pulse throughout the night. He rubbed the silver spoon like a charm, circling a thumb in the bowl, around and around, enjoying the smoothness, the perfection.

Dusk brought the forest alive. The wind pushed through the trees as the birds and squirrels made their last attempts for the day.

A robin crossed Roy's camp, pecking the ground at each hop and looking around with sudden head movements. It snapped down and tugged a worm from the earth. There was a short struggle, but the worm stood no chance. It writhed in the robin's beak as the bird flew off.

A freight train pulled in from the northwest. Each connected boxcar read *Chicago Mercantile* on the side in big, yellow letters. Some of the boxcars were numbered. When the train eased to a stop, men moved frantically, some unloaded boxes, others loaded boxes on. They opened boxcar doors and clanged them shut and locked them. There was one car with no door. Number seventeen.

This train was set to go back the way it came, Roy thought, and it appears it's running late.

He collected his things.

20

Colfax's town constable, Deputy Chief Randall, held tightly to Sandy's hand. The man was shaped like a barrel and seemed plenty powerful, but the girl at the end of his arm yanked and spun and kicked and howled like an animal.

"I'm sorry," Paul said to the lawman, raising his voice over Sandy's screams. The tourist-laden crowd inside the train station murmured around them. Paul heard someone whisper, "That girl's a menace."

"It's no trouble, sir," the constable said. "We'll have her back where she belongs straight away." With his available hand he was attempting to pocket the small notepad he'd used to take down Paul's report of the bushwhacking on the Colfax road. Sandy was making this simple task difficult. She kicked the constable's shin. The lawman grunted, gritted his teeth.

Paul came down to Sandy's level. "Hey now," he said, holding out his hands, palms up.

Sandy regained some composure. Her breathing was fierce, her cheeks Macintosh red. "You betrayed me."

"It's not safe where I'm going," Paul said.

"You said I could help you find Roy. You *lied.*"

"I couldn't leave you out there in those woods. It was best to get you here, get you safe."

The constable managed his notepad into his breast pocket. With both hands now free, he scooped up Sandy and held her to his large chest. She beat his shoulders with fists, but they were glancing blows; the fight had drained from her.

"Off we go, young one," the lawman said, turning away from Paul.

Sandy eyed Paul over the lawman's shoulder as he took her away. Paul smiled in apology, threw up his palms. Her face darkened.

Paul said, "You'll thank me later."

Sandy sneered. "*Traitor.*"

Paul sighed. He watched until Sandy and the constable left the train station, then he moved to a nearby wall and leaned against it. He scanned the crowd, looking for his own good hat and a scaly face beneath it. He didn't think Roy would be so brazen as to waltz in and buy a ticket, but he took no chances. Besides, he was waiting for return telegrams. The train station had a Western Union. He'd sent two telegrams when he and Sandy had arrived. One to the warden's office at Redmine prison:

IN COLFAX. WILL BRING HIM BACK.

One to Delmont Graves' office in Hale:

IN COLFAX. TELL THE BOY HIS FATHER LOVES HIM.

He'd wanted to add more to the second note. A voice in his head had pleaded with him to relay an apology to Gloria, but he didn't want to be sorry in print. Printed words carried a different weight than spoken ones. Printed words persisted. When needed they were there, waiting to remind you, lest ye forget. They were a record of evidence, a weapon in a drawer. If he was going to be sorry, he wanted it in person. He wanted her ears to hear his voice, her eyes to see his face, and then he wanted disarmament. What's more, he couldn't be sure his father-in-law would deliver the message, or, considering her typical state of drunkenness, that any message to his wife would be properly understood.

Now the day's last sunrays reached through the windows, catching dust swirls in the act. The train station crowd had thinned out. Paul went to the ticket office. The clerk wore a green hat with a snubbed brim. He was sweating through a collared white shirt and his fingers were long and lean. His nails needed clipping.

"Help you, sir?" the clerk said as he thumped a stamper down on some paperwork.

"Any freighters come through this station?" Paul said.

The clerk squinted at him. Freight-hopping was a nagging problem for the fledgling train industry. Any man at a ticket booth asking about freight trains was no doubt a suspect. A stupid suspect, maybe, but a suspect just the same.

The clerk lifted his chin and looked down his nose at Paul. "Back and forth to Chicago," he said. "Why?"

"When?" Paul said.

The clerk mulled on it for a moment, then he smiled. "There are plenty of *commuter* trains to Chicago, sir. A deal at ten dollars a ticket."

"The freighter," Paul said through gritted teeth. "When?"

The clerk tapped a finger on the wooden ledge before him.

"Might be better if I report a freight-hopper than-"

Paul slammed a fist on the ledge. The stamper hopped up and flipped over on its side. The clerk came to attention. "Every night," he said. "Got one coming in soon. Running a bit late."

Paul went back to the telegraph booth. There was no message from Graves, but the warden had responded:

YOUR JOB DEPENDS ON IT.

Paul watched the ticket clerk disappear into the back. Good. He'd alert security of a potential freight-hopper. If Roy was out there, they might find him. He could take him off their hands and that would be that.

He went outside and came to the rail yard. Dusk had turned the horizon a deep red. The yard was a flat expanse, gravel in all directions. Smelled like coal and fire. A forest began a quarter-mile down the tracks. A Chicago Mercantile train pulled in, trailing smoke. Workers moved quickly upon it, loading and unloading.

The freighter.

Paul moved along the side of the train toward the forest, away from the thickest hive of workers. The boxcars went on for what seemed like a half-mile before terminating at the caboose engine, now heating up to become the forward engine. Connected to the freighter was one boxcar without a door.

The rail yard workers moved in and out of the boxcars. Paul sliced through them and continued down the length of the train, passing car after car to find them increasingly loaded, closed, and locked. A few more boxes and this train would be moving out.

He came to the forest's edge. Hardwoods mixed with evergreens, spreading out in three directions, the train station at his back. The tracks continued into the distance, bisecting the green and gray. Paul scanned back and forth, looking for signs of human life between the trees, but it was pointless. Impossible to see through the thick undergrowth with so little daylight left. He looked back toward the station. A moment ago the yard had been overflowing with workers. Now it was silent and nearly deserted. One man in overalls slapped a hat against his thigh before disappearing around a corner.

"Whatcha doin' out here?"

Paul turned to the voice. A man with a revolver stood before him. The gun's barrel was pointed at the ground, but the man's demeanor was threat enough.

Paul had expected someone official, a man with a badge. This man was clearly of the woods. He wore no badge on his chest, but a silver cross. He was bearded and dirty. His hat was creased and ripped. His teeth were discolored and of varying agendas. His wide nose had a crook in the middle. Paul imagined a fist might have broken the nose, and that the man who'd had the stones to throw the punch was probably dead.

There were two other men, deeper into the woods, undoubtedly kin to the first. Brothers. Each one could be a ghost of the dead man on the Colfax road. The two at the cart were wearing crosses similar to the first, but otherwise they were a study in contrast. The one on the left was a twin to the woodsman before Paul, but the one on the right was a different breed altogether. His clothes were impeccable, his demeanor relaxed, his eyes as vacant as porcelain knobs. He looked an official of some kind. Someone who makes the rules, not someone who breaks them. He held a scatter-gun by the shortened stock, broken open and resting over his shoulder. A one-horse cart stood beyond the two, and between them, on the ground, there was a black chest.

"Back off," the nearest man said.

"I-"

The train whistle screamed, dousing all other sound.

The revolver man went back to his brothers. He and the other scruffy one picked up the black chest. The scatter-gun man trailed them, looking somewhat disinterested as they loaded the black chest into the boxcar. The revolver man hopped in. The second scruffy one stayed on the ground while the scatter-gun man hopped effortlessly aboard the boxcar as the train chugged and started moving.

The remaining brother gave Paul a long, hard look before heading back toward the one-horse cart.

21

The train whistle screamed.

Roy was a hundred yards up from the open boxcar, crouched in the woods, rubbing his spoon and watching the shadowy figures at the edge of the rail yard. The Ledger boys were threatening his old friend. Roy envisioned Frank Ledger blowing a hole through Paul's chest, just like the man he'd killed on the Colfax road. The thought made him touch the revolver on his waist, but he stayed put, reminding himself that Paul was surely here to escort him back to Redmine.

No chance at that. The only way Roy would go back to prison was as a bloodstain on his would-be captor's clothes.

Two of the Ledger boys loaded a black chest into the open car. A treasure of fine silverware, no doubt. They struggled with the weight as they hefted it aboard. A fortune in waiting, Roy thought. The big city would ingest their offering and spit money back at them like a riverboat payoff. All they needed to do was arrive on the Lake

Michigan shore and open the chest in front of fine people.

One brother stayed on the ground while the train jerked into motion. The mechanical arms pushed the wheels around. The engine blew off steam. The remaining brother faced down Paul before heading back into the woods.

As much as Roy wanted to ditch any pursuer, he felt good knowing it was Paul. It was comforting that a friend was near, even if that friend meant to imprison him. It would be the same as their childhood games. Back then Paul was always the hero and Roy the villain. Dozens of times a stolid Paul walked the wayward Roy back to some imaginary prison at the end of a hazy summer day.

Roy stepped into the open where Paul could see him. They stared at each other, a hundred yards apart, the train accelerating beside them. Dust and leaves lifted and twisted in the wind. Roy smiled. From such a distance he couldn't see well enough to know if Paul smiled back, but he could see that his old friend nodded in response.

He took the nod as Paul's guarantee—*I'm coming*. He tapped Paul's father's revolver with his index finger—*you better be*. He lifted his hand from the gun and formed a thumb-finger pistol. He aimed it at Paul and dropped the hammer. *Pow*.

Paul's shadowy figure reached up and clutched its heart.

The train had gained momentum. The number seventeen boxcar nearly passed Roy before he reached out to the open doorway. His hand clamped the steel frame like a vise. He pulled his light body aboard in a flash of motion and knelt in the doorway. The wind buffeted his hat and cooled his skin.

The Ledger boys stood against the far wall, bookending their treasure. The silver crosses on their chests winked in the darkness. Frank Ledger looked at Roy with his head cocked sideways like a curious dog. The other man reached for his revolver. Roy smiled when he heard a howl outside the train.

❋

The sound had jumped from Paul's lungs without warning. He held the howl as long as his breath lasted, watching the train get smaller as it pulled away. It clipped toward the big city with a fight in its belly, and already Paul was far behind. He wondered if he should keep on. He might retain his job, sure, but he could always find another. And why not let Roy live his remaining days in peace, should he survive his encounter with the Ledger boys? Was it regaining his father's gun that drew him? Could a simple object hold so much value that he'd trek across the country, re-imprison an old friend, and leave his wife and son behind just to retrieve it?

He walked back to the train station and checked with Western Union for word from home. There was none. He pulled the warden's message from his pocket and read it again.

YOUR JOB DEPENDS ON IT.

He squeezed the paper in his fist, felt it crinkle. The paper would never be perfect again. It would always have those ridges now, those scars. He sent another message to Delmont Grave's office:

ON TO CHICAGO. ILLINOIS CENTRAL.

Paul walked to the ticket office thinking of his son, Jacob, sitting on their front porch swing, waiting. Waiting to play games and laugh. Waiting to grow up. Waiting and watching for dad with those bright blue eyes. Pain emerged from his back and moved into his neck. The train he found was an overnight commuter to Chicago. His ticket offered no sleeper car, but Paul was certain it wouldn't matter; sleep would not likely come to him this night.

22

Frank Ledger stayed his brother's revolver with a gesture.

Roy crouched in the doorway with two hands flat on the rusted floor. The train clacked on the rails. The weight of the car shifted back and forth like a seagoing vessel. The front of the car was empty, the backside filled with wooden crates, each one numbered and marked with black paint, one to twelve.

Frank Ledger leaned forward, his head still cocked sideways. He blinked. There was no fear there, just simple fascination. "What are you?"

Roy said nothing. His hands throbbed for action. His legs ached to propel him forward. He wanted to bite and kick and punch. Outside a ringing station bell shot by the doorway.

"It's the devil," Steven Ledger said.

Frank ignored his brother. Addressing Roy, he said, "Do you speak?"

"It's the devil," Steven cried, "can you not see that, brother? It's here to steal back the salesman's silver." He cocked the hammer and raised his gun at Roy. "That silver was from our mountain." With his off hand he gripped the silver cross on his chest and thrust it at Roy. "The salesman had no claim, devil. Be gone."

Roy cocked his head to meet Frank Ledger's gaze at the same curious angle he was receiving.

Ledger smiled. "The devil," he said, "the proud spirit, cannot endure to be mocked."

Roy nodded. His hands closed into fists. His jaw ached from tightness, his tongue found the gap where the fat guard had knocked out his teeth. If there was any animal in him, any mystical gator blood, it was well in control.

Frank Ledger's eyes grew wide with revelation and, Roy thought, some ghastly level of glee. "You're from Redmine," Ledger said. "You're on the run."

Roy exploded forward with both fists against the man's chest. Ledger's back slammed the boxcar wall. Roy got a face full of beard. He smelled soap powder. He drove the crown of his head under the man's chin, heard clicking teeth and a groan. He seized the scatter-gun by the barrel and ripped it from Frank Ledger's hands. He spun and dropped the scatter-gun's short stock on Steven Ledger's shoulder like an axe. A bone busted with a satisfying crack. The revolver clattered against the floor. Steven staggered backward, gripping his shoulder. His lips curled with rage. Roy snatched up the revolver and pointed one weapon at each of his adversaries.

For a moment everyone stood still, just breathing. The train clacked on.

Roy nodded at the door, insisting them toward it.

"It can't kill us both," Steven said. "Let's rush it."

"Quiet," Frank Ledger said. "This convict won't hesitate to end you."

He was wrong about that, but Roy didn't mind Frank Ledger's way of thinking.

"It ain't no convict," Steven screamed, "and it ain't no man. It's the devil, brother, have you gone blind?"

Roy gestured toward the door again. The brothers moved into the windy opening while Roy kept their own guns leveled on them.

"You've lost your way," Steven said to his brother. "I knowed it's been coming a long time." He cringed at his shoulder pain. The break was bad. The shoulder sagged down and away from his neck and there was a cleft in the middle, the broken bone pressuring the skin. "I'd rather die in God's glory than let this beast steal directly from Jesus' ha-"

Frank Ledger shoved his brother off the train.

Steven bounced and rolled in the cinders along the train tracks. There'd be more broken bones, but likely he'd live.

"My brother often loses himself," Frank said.

Roy nodded toward the open door.

"The name's Frank Ledger," he said, removing his bowler hat and taking a small bow.

Roy moved forward with the scatter-gun, leveling the barrel just inches from Frank Ledger's nose, the barrel holes as close as spectacles. Up close Roy could see the man's eyes were bloodshot red and sickly looking. Roy touched the trigger, felt the mechanical pressure as it began to move.

Frank Ledger said, "Just wanted you to know the name of the man who's going to deliver you to justice."

"Get in line," Roy said, but only the wind heard him; Frank Ledger was already gone.

❧

Paul grasped a brass handle and pulled himself on to the diner car.

The aisle was carpeted and the ceiling was a landscape mural. Beneath the mural there were advertisement boards. All of them were filled, but with only one repeated ad: *Come See Edison's Electric Light! New Year's Eve in Menlo Park.* The hectographed image next to the words looked like a closed question mark. There was a spire on top and a looped filament in the middle. The contraption was called a light bulb, and it was said to run on electricity.

The train, however, was still lit by oil lamps. Each side of the car was lined with four-person booths—two benches squaring off around a wooden table—and they overflowed with people. Tourists. Only a few booths remained open. Paul squeezed into one and sat on the aisle side of the bench, hoping to fend off anyone who might want to sit with him.

He found himself surrounded by the rich. Colfax was a fanciful destination for those who had too much time and too much money. They called it quaint and considered it rough, having no idea what the latter word really meant. They came and went in droves, spent money on things they would soon forget they owned, and complained about poor service behind the closed doors of barely suitable hotel rooms. Gaudy hats riddled the car. Each one hovered in a fragile state upon their women's heads. Men in impeccable clothing checked pocket watches to see that the train was running a few minutes late. They shook their heads with a kind of disdain only the opulent could muster. Paul's ears caught phrases like *these people* and *ingratitude*. He closed his eyes and sagged low in his seat, hoping to gain some rest.

"Well, I just know he's here somewhere."

Paul's eyes snapped open; the voice was familiar. He sat up and searched the car slowly, scanning front to back.

The little girl's voice sounded out again, "I don't know how on earth we got separated, but he told me if we do, just meet him in the diner car."

She was behind him. Paul turned, gritting teeth as he did so. "Daddy!"

Sandy released a rich woman's hand. She bolted down the aisle to where Paul sat, hopped into his lap, and hugged him. Begrudgingly, Paul returned her embrace. She smelled faintly of the woman's perfume.

"She's yours then?"

Paul looked up to see a man standing over him. His face showed the same contrived displeasure as Paul's father-in-law, plus the same style of clothing, the same stance. If the man wasn't a lawyer, Paul wasn't Cajun. He stood next to the woman that'd been holding Sandy's hand. She was beautiful, young, and kept.

Sandy wriggled over Paul's lap to find the inside half of the bench. She sat down pretty and pleased.

"Please don't be upset with my daddy, sir," Sandy said, "I tend to run off and get lost. It's my own fault." She batted her eyes. "I'm like a dog that just won't heel."

"And a mouth that just won't close," the lawyer said. "Stay quiet while I'm talking with your father."

"Now just hold on," Paul said.

"Keep an eye on your brood," the lawyer said. He pointed at Sandy. "And keep her quiet." He gripped his woman's arm and they turned away. Over his shoulder he said, "No need to repay me for her ticket."

Paul plucked off his hat and grabbed his coin bag. He stood and began untying the leather string, but stopped. His own ticket had cost him the lion's share of his coin. The cost of Sandy's ticket was more than he had to give. He slumped back into his seat as the rich man and woman took seats of their own, just down the aisle, the man with his back to them, the woman facing them. She was striking. Crimson hair and emerald eyes. The kind of woman you could watch dance or scrub a floor with equal fascination, though Paul doubted she had ever scrubbed a floor. She smiled at Paul, by way of apology.

"You see that smile?" Sandy said, elbowing Paul's ribs. "That's what I mean."

Paul sighed. He put a hand over his forehead, two fingers on one temple, a thumb on the other. "That's what you mean about what?"

"That's the clown's smile."

Paul snorted. "Is that right?"

"That's right."

Again Paul sunk low in his seat. Sandy mimicked him.

"How'd you know where to find me?" Paul said.

"I watched you buy your ticket," she said, "followed you here."

"How'd you escape the constable?"

Sandy winked. Otherwise, she offered no reply.

Again, Paul snorted. "You sure are something."

"She is beautiful, though," Sandy said, "isn't she?"

Paul looked again at the woman. She was rummaging through a bag, pursing her lips in concentration. A lock of her hair, somewhat lighter in color than the rest, played in the mysterious hollow between her neck and shoulder.

She looked up and caught him.

Paul looked down, suddenly interested in his thumb.

"Well, Jesus," Sandy said, "no need to stare."

"I wasn't staring," Paul said. But he looked at the woman again. She was smiling. Not at him, but at something she held in her hand. Indeed, she was beautiful. Paul found himself wishing he was the reason a woman smiled like that. He recalled his wedding day, when Gloria had smiled at him as she came down the aisle, arm-in-arm with her father. He had been a hell of a reason for a woman to smile on that day. The woman turned the object in her hand. Paul saw it was a polished stone—flat, dark, and about the size of her palm. It was the kind of thing you'd find piled amongst hundreds of others in a bin in any shop in Colfax. Parents bought them for their squawking kids. Shopkeepers kept them out front and didn't mind if they were stolen. Why would a grown woman find a cheap gift so fascinating?

The woman caught him staring again, and again he averted his eyes. Dammit, he was acting like a fool. He had a wife and son at home, and here he was blushing over a strange woman on a train.

The train whistle sounded. A conductor yelled, "All aboard."

Paul stretched out his legs. "When we get to Chicago I'll have to find you a smarter constable."

Sandy stretched out her short legs to match Paul's sitting position. She seemed to think for a moment, and then said, "Nothing rhymes with constable."

"Well, good," Paul said. He pulled down his hat to cover his eyes, peered sideways into the window glass. At this angle he could again see the woman. She was a translucent vision in the window's reflection. She held the stone between two delicate hands like she was praying on it. Her lawyer said something and she looked up at him. She blinked and recoiled as she put down her stone. For a moment she looked scared, and then her smile returned.

Good lord, it was *a clown's smile.*

The train's brakes released and the car inched forward. Paul caught a glimpse of movement on the boardwalk outside. His eyes shifted focus. Through the woman's reflection and through the glass he saw Jeb Crittendon and Cyrus Lee. They were boarding the diner car.

23

The music box struggled on.

for... I... come.

Cecil Darton jolted into a sitting position, coughing and hacking. He gripped his chest and winced. Alive.

Roy pulled the pillow away.

Cecil looked at Jukey's dead face, looked at the pillow in Roy's hand. He shrunk against the bed. His face contorted. "Don't hurt me."

"I'm not going to-"

"Help!" Cecil said. He scrambled on to the bed. "Somebody help me!"

Roy dropped the pillow and stood. Shut this idiot up or run?

Run.

He turned to the door to find it already opening. Samson stepped into the wagon. His bulky frame filled out the doorway. His shoulders looked like medicine balls. He chomped a stubby cigar.

"What seems to be the problem here, Cecil?" Samson said. His eyes never left Roy. The cigar shifted from one side of this mouth to the other.

"He killed him," Cecil said. "Look. He k-ki-"

"Shut up," Samson said.

Cecil curled into a corner. He sniveled and quivered. A greasy lock of hair fell away from its slicked position and spilled over his eyes. Samson flexed his fingers and cracked his knuckles. He flexed his arms and cracked God knows what. The sounds were like shifting ice. "Time to stove your head in."

Roy knew what this was. Jukey didn't matter to Samson. None of them did. This was about Jesse. He'd learned of her infidelity. Roy thought of Samson's big hands pressing a burning cigar into Jesse's ribs. He flicked out his father's blade.

Samson smiled. "That supposed to scare me?"

Roy had no answer. It *was* supposed to scare him. He fired the only other ammunition he had. "You don't deserve her."

Samson's face turned to rage. He growled and swung a paw at Roy. Roy side-stepped. He plunged his knife into the big man's shoulder and drew it back.

But his hand came back empty.

Samson's shoulder muscles clenched the knife like Excalibur's stone. The big man thrust a forearm across Roy's throat, drove him against the back wall, rattling the wagon. The jewelry case fell and burst apart, spilling golden cufflinks. Roy felt like his head would pop off. He reached for the knife but found himself pinned. He squirmed against the big man's might. He clawed at the blade, trying to loosen it. If he could just-

Samson punched his ribs and ended the confrontation. Roy fell forward, seeing black and purple dots. He was sure he'd never breathe again. His guts must be crushed. He crawled toward the wagon door. A big hand grabbed his shirt and the seat of his pants. He flew through the doorway and landed in the dirt like a rag doll.

The caravan's din fell silent. The pinheads, who had started playing War in the absence of other poker players, looked up from their cards. Girda shifted her weight and a wagon hinge creaked. Camilla looked up from her makeup mirror.

Samson came out of Cecil's wagon. He carried Jukey's body like a child in his arms. A trickle of blood dripped down his shoulder, away from Roy's knife.

Roy came up to his knees, but Samson kicked him back down.

"Look at your brother," Samson said. He lifted Jukey over his head. "An innocent man, killed by one of your own."

Roy heard gasps. The performers exited their wagons and circled around. Samson lovingly laid Jukey on the ground, a showman in his own right. He pulled Roy's knife from his shoulder. It looked as small as a thorn in his hand. "And for what?" he said. "A few dollars?" He threw Jukey's wallet down next to Roy. It was brown leather with a few bills peeking out from a corner. There was a wild horse stitched into the leather. Roy recalled Jukey, on stage, removing bills from the wallet with only his feet. The audience had clapped to the fact that he could pull out just one bill at a time.

Samson went back to the shadowy space between the carts. He came back with a handful of pipes and chains. He dropped them on the ground with a clank. Roy scanned his fellow performer's faces. Girda held a meaty palm over her mouth. Camilla shook her head. Randy and Miriam looked confused and anxious. Cecil Darton followed Samson out of his wagon. No longer cowering, he threw back his hair and drew up a shirtsleeve, suddenly a thug.

"No," Roy croaked, but with broken ribs it was all he could manage.

Samson pointed at Girda and motioned to Roy. She shrugged her shoulders and turned up her palms, uncomprehending.

"Hold him down," Samson said.

"Now just wait a second," Camilla said. "We don't know the whole story here."

Samson took a stride toward her. Camilla jumped back as if he'd slapped her. Samson turned back to Girda. "Now," he said, still wielding Roy's knife, "hold him down or I'll gut you like the hog you are."

Girda stepped heavily off her wagon. It rose behind her. She moved toward Roy like a living wall.

"No," a voice said.

Girda stopped. Everyone turned to the source of the sound. Miriam. She stood with her fingers in her ears, shaking her head violently side to side.

"Yeaaah!" Randy said, agreeing with his sister. "No!"

Samson went to Miriam. He gripped her polka-dotted costume by the front and lifted her off her feet. She continued shaking her head, eyes closed, feet struggling to find the ground.

"Yeaaah," Randy said, "No!"

Samson threw Miriam against the ox cart. The slat walls shuddered with her impact. She yelped and went silent. Playing cards fell from the table and flitted down upon her limp body. Randy ran to his sister's side. "Yeaaah," he said. He knelt beside her. More silently he said, "No, no, no, no, no."

Girda moved toward Roy with no more hesitation. Roy lost focus. He blinked dust from his eyes. The performers gathered closer. "Please," he wheezed, still reeling from Samson's gut punch. He struggled to one knee, but was kicked down again, this time by Camilla, driving a foot into him like a donkey. She and Cecil grabbed Roy's arms. They pinned him down while Girda straddled his legs. She came down with tremendous pressure. His bones would surely be reduced to sand.

"Everyone takes a turn," Samson said.

The performers exchanged fearful glances. Iron and steel clanged as Samson picked up the items he'd brought out. He handed out pipes and chains. With each weapon came a threatening look.

There was a silent moment while the performers examined the objects in their hands. Some looked at Jukey's lifeless form, his overturned wallet like a dead bird on the ground. Their doubtful expressions gave way to wrathful sneers.

The punches and kicks came from all sides. Their faces hovered above him like disembodied heads. A chain came down across Roy's stomach. An iron pipe bounced off his head. They screamed with rage and laughter. They pushed each other out of the way so they could measure their blows carefully, and, Roy thought, so they could ensure that Samson knew they were giving it their all.

As the blows rained down Roy thought of home. The day that gator took his mother. For an hour he laid on that dock, watching his reflection in the water. The boy he saw was no boy at all, but a beast. He wasn't part of the human race, and never would be. He knew it then and he knew it now. Why hadn't he had the courage to end himself?

It mattered not. It was okay now. Like Jukey, he wanted no more from this world. What was it that Jukey said?

Existing is not living.

Roy leaned into their blows for maximum impact. He wanted their punches and kicks to do real damage. He wanted the pipe to come down harder, to crack his skull and destroy his thoughts. He wanted a chain around his neck, stringing him up. He wanted Girda to fall forward and smother out his life. These freaks were his angels, come to take him back to his mother and father, to take him back to the bayou where all cities and towns and sideshows and guns were imaginary.

But they simply couldn't oblige. At length they grew tired. Their fire dimmed. They stopped swinging and kicking. Roy heard only the rush of his own blood. They stood above him like blurry ghosts, their shoulders heaving with each breath. They'd given him all they had, spilled their pain into him. He wanted more, but they had no more to give.

Samson appeared, Roy's knife in hand. He held it with the blade pointed downward for a killing stroke. Roy silently thanked him. He nodded his bloody head in approval.

As Samson took aim at Roy's chest, one of the freaks stepped forward to stay the strong man's hand. It was Randy, coherent and calculating well beyond his standard character. He whispered something in Samson's ear. Samson smiled. He turned the knife over and began carving into Roy's chest. Roy felt the pressure of the blade. He felt his scaled skin coming apart like pages of a book. He turned his eyes away. Through a forest of legs he saw Jesse in the distance. She stood between the wagons, glowing like firelight. Her hair was tied up behind her head. Some locks had come loose to lie across her cheeks and frame her face just so. She was Aphrodite. Her body was not tense. She did not rush to save him. She looked upon him with no expression, as a queen might look upon the peasantry.

❧

The train barreled into the night, its iron skin highlighted by a half-full moon. Roy sat on the boxcar edge, letting his feet dangle. The occasional tall weed whipped his soles. He liked the sensation. He unloaded the Ledgers' weapons and threw them into the darkness where they landed without sound. Silhouetted silos and barns passed slowly in the distance. Roy rubbed the silver spoon.

He had been ready to die that day. He had wanted it. He was done with a world that wanted him tucked away until they were ready to pay for repulsion. Despite a lifetime of effort to see it otherwise, he now saw the sideshow as a traveling prison. Its warden was a nice old man that conjured the illusion of freedom. All a lie. They were not performers, but freaks. No one would look upon them unless they'd paid for the pleasure. But give it to them for free, on the streets? The real sideshow was a performance just for him and his kind. The real performers were the audience, those that kept him believing he had purpose. Those that made him think he was not a caged animal but a free man. Tear down the tent and open the cages to watch the audience stop acting and start imprisoning, start killing.

He was willing to die believing he had Jesse's love. He could leave this world knowing he could go to their farmhouse and wait for her there. He would tend to the crops and keep things clean for her. He would wait out the years while she grew old, mourning him and forsaking all others. She would live a quiet life before one day rejoining him. There would be days and nights between them. There would be pain behind them and forever before them. But did he have her love? Had he ever? He tried to think of their special night. He tried to flip through the beautiful pictures in his mind. No dice. He could only see her standing between the wagons, impassive and alone, while the freaks poured their pain into his body.

24

"Warden said it was our fault, too," Jeb Crittendon said. He was squeezed into the bench seat across from Sandy and Paul. The table between them cut into his huge belly, bisecting it top and bottom. His lips were moist with sweat and his breathing sounded difficult. Paul felt queasy looking at him, listening to him. Cyrus Lee sat on the outer half of the bench, skinny as a branch and fidgeting. Together these two looked like a nightmare version of the number ten.

"He said we shoulda known that freak was still alive," Crittendon said. "But that's not what I say." He leaned in on his elbows, eyeing Paul. The table creaked under the pressure. "Want to know what I say?"

"Yeah," Cyrus Lee said.

"I say I beat that freak with no mercy," Crittendon said. Cyrus Lee nodded and nodded like his neck was hinged on a spring. "I say I beat him bad," Crittendon continued, "and he was dead as shit when we loaded him in that bag. I say he was still dead as shit when we left him in the dead house to rot."

"There's no need to cuss," Sandy said.

Crittendon turned his eyes to Sandy. "And just who the hell are you?"

"My name is Sandra MacGillicutty Rae," Sandy said, thumbing her chest. "My friends call me S-"

"Well keep your fuckin' mouth shut, *Sandra MacGillicutty Rae*."

Sandy's brow furrowed. She said, "You, sir, are a nincompoop."

Crittendon snatched out and gripped Sandy by the shirt-front. He lifted her half out of her seat, brought her suddenly terrified face near his own. "Use that keen tongue again, and I'll cut it clean out of your-"

The click-clack of a revolver's hammer stopped Crittendon's words. Paul had the weapon's barrel against Crittendon's belly beneath the table. "That'll be enough from you."

Crittendon looked incredulously at Paul. He kept Sandy in his grip. Pulled her farther out of her seat.

"Something wrong with your ears?" Paul said.

"You ain't got the stones," Crittendon said.

Cyrus Lee quietly set a knife down on the table before Paul. "That's my friend you're threatenin'."

"And he's threatening mine," Paul said, eyes still on Crittendon.

Crittendon released Sandy. She fell back into her seat with a thump. He showed his open palms.

Paul uncocked his revolver, holstered it.

Lee sheathed his knife.

"Well now," Jeb Crittendon said, "ain't this a fancy little party?"

"And you're the host," Paul said.

"Right you are," Crittendon said. "I believe we was discussing an acquaintance of ours?"

Cyrus Lee said, "Tell 'em, Jeb."

"I believe there's some voodoo mumbo jumbo going on with this fella," Crittendon said. "We ain't dealing with no man, but some kind of black magic devil that needs putting down like a dog."

Paul looked away. The train was at full speed now. It rocked back and forth like a cradle. Most of the rich folk had already headed to their sleeper cars, but the rich man and woman who had delivered Sandy were still there. She had put away her souvenir and they were now engaged in a hushed conversation. Next to his fellow prison guards the woman's radiance was that much more brilliant. Paul imagined she was suggesting bedroom things to her man. Underneath their table her foot came to his leg. She'd kicked off a steel-buckled shoe and was toeing the pale skin beneath his pants. His curly black leg hair made Paul want to vomit. The oil lamp above her head swung in rhythm with the train, changing the shadows on her face from dark to light to dark again.

"Warden says we gotta bring him back," Crittendon said. "I asked if he preferred dead or alive." He smiled broadly. Cyrus Lee followed suit. "Want to know what he said?"

"Yeah," Cyrus Lee said.

"He said he's already dead, ain't he?" Crittendon slapped the table. "Ain't that something? That's about as close as you get to a killing license, you ask me."

"Sure is," Cyrus Lee said.

Sandy elbowed Paul's ribs. "Does he mean Roy?"

Paul sucked through his teeth.

"Well, well," Crittendon said. "Seems like someone's become awful familiar with the devil he's chasing."

Unwilling to meet Crittendon's eyes, Paul continued to watch the woman. Her foot still played with her gentleman's leg. She took his hand into her own, giggled.

"You listening to me?" Crittendon said.

"I am," Paul said.

"All right," Crittendon said, "then why don't you tell me how it is our little freak got away from you?"

Sandy elbowed Paul again. "Are they talking about Roy?"

"I mean, I could understand if it was just *you* out there," Crittendon said. "But with those Boyle twins it just don't make no sense. Them boys are as big as the hills, and yet they came back looking like they got trampled by a horse team. What in the hell was you all doing out there, you managed to fuck this up so bad?"

The woman slipped her shoe back on and stood. She collected her bag and hat and led her man by the hand. They headed toward a sleeper car. Paul felt a sickness in his guts. That man would take her in his arms. He would untie parts of her clothing and see parts of her body only a rich man could see. He would do things she would only allow a rich man to do. The woman looked back and Paul saw a young version of Gloria. He wanted to blackjack that lawyer and replace his hand with his own. He wanted to follow his wife back to a different time, a time before their daughter's death had corroded their lives.

Jeb Crittendon's hand appeared before Paul's eyes. He snapped his fingers. Paul blinked, sank deeper into his seat.

"You want to know what happened?" Paul said.

"That I do," Crittendon said.

"Yea-" Cyrus Lee started, but Crittendon silenced him with a hand gesture.

Paul looked back and forth between the two members of his audience. Their eyes were alive with anticipation. He thought of the month he'd spent at Roy's bedside while his new friend's broken ankles healed. In the same way Paul's mother nursed the boy with fresh splints and salve, Paul nursed him with fresh stories. It was his way. It was what he had to offer. He started each tale with a bang and drew out the tension long and slow, building toward a hair-raising finish. He watched Roy's reactions and listened to his breathing, knowing just when to ratchet things up or slow them down. And every story, whether comedy or tragedy, was met with reverence and respect. Every story ended not with Paul's words, but Roy's bemused response, "That's a humdinger."

Roy Pellerin had been Paul's best audience.

But these two?

Paul sneered. Such effort would be wasted on Crittendon and Lee. They were ignorant creatures, existing only to destroy or be destroyed. They were no different than dogs, in that they lived life with limited tools. "Get used to disappointment," Paul said.

"Look here, you son of a bitch," Crittendon said. "If we're gonna track this thing down and kill it, we need to know what it's capable of."

Cyrus Lee went back to nodding. The train was slowing down, coming to its first stop. Throughout the night they'd be coasting in and out of small stations along the way to the big city, stopping when necessary to drop off travelers or pick them up. This first stop couldn't have been but ten miles from Colfax. All the rich had gone to their sleepers. Paul imagined no one would be getting off so soon, so someone must be getting on.

"We need to know what kind of black magic the devil can throw at us," Crittendon said. He drew out a revolver and clapped it down on the table. It was a battered, rusty thing that looked plucked from a swamp, but surely it would perform its single, powerful trick. Crittendon smiled, showing yellow and brown teeth. "I need to know if this little fella will tear holes through lizard flesh the same as any other."

"Please tell me they're not talking about Roy," Sandy said.

The train's brakes squealed. The car slowed. Paul looked at the bench seat where the woman had sat. He imagined her skin smelled of scented soap. He thought of her face, not with a smile, but alive with the pleasures of sex. Again she became Gloria, the way she used to be. Her face once expressed the same pleasures. Her body once moved both above and beneath him all in the same night. He tried to recall how long it'd been since he'd seen her like that, since she smelled like scented soap instead of whiskey, but couldn't find the memory.

The train stopped, the doors opened, and a lone passenger boarded the diner car. Paul closed his eyes at the sight of the scattergun man.

25

Correction—the man no longer possessed a scatter-gun, nor was he wearing his cross. His face was scratched and his nice clothes were torn. His neck was scraped where the cross seemed to have been ripped away. His bowler hat was in his hand, only now it was beaten and dirty. An elbow bled. A knee was red raw and exposed through a fresh hole in his pants. His eyes, however, were clear and direct. They were filled with unappeasable anger. He was whistling a slow, painful tune. Sounded like *Clementine*.

The train kicked into motion. The scatter-gun man walked to a bench at the far end of the car. He slumped into the seat as if the string had been pulled from his spine. He was tired and hurting, but there was serenity about him, a peacefulness that seemed out of place. It was as if pain and violence were as common as breakfast and lunch to this man. And if so, Paul thought, supper would certainly be vengeance. He slid closer to the Sandy, hiding his face behind Crittendon and Lee. The less association with the scatter-gun man, the better.

"You know that fella?" Crittendon said.

Paul shook his head.

"I do," Sandy said. "That's Judge Frank Ledger."

Cyrus Lee pulled an intake of breath. His eyes widened, his skin reddened in some parts, paled in others.

"Don't look like no judge to me," Crittendon said. "Looks more like he's off his chump."

"He isn't a judge anymore," Sandy said, "he's an outlaw now. Haven't you seen the posters?" She pointed at Cyrus Lee. "He's seen them."

Crittendon looked at Lee, who was nodding gravely.

"What's he wanted for?" Paul said.

"Killed a man in Bracken," Sandy said, "shot him dead right in front of The Imperial. Opened his belly and knocked his guts clean out."

Crittendon snorted. "Fella probably deserved it."

"Waylon Fremont was the fella's name," Sandy said, "and apparently he did deserve it. He was a known cattle thief and bushwhacker. He'd been on trial in Judge Ledger's court for killing that old married couple that lived out on the Bariat road. Took their life savings and left them to die and get eaten by the blow flies."

"Sounds like Mr. Fremont pissed off the wrong judge," Crittendon said.

"He got off is what," Sandy said. "Not enough evidence to support the county's case. Way I heard it, Judge Ledger told Fremont he was certain of his guilt, but without the evidence, he could do no sentencing. To that Fremont said-"

"Jesus will be my only judge."

It was Cyrus Lee who had spoken. All eyes turned to him.

"Fremont told the honorable Frank Ledger that a judge could do nothing to him," Cyrus said, "even if he had evidence. He said the only one fit to judge him was Jesus, and he'd be meeting up with him on the day he died. To that the judge said, and I do quote, 'Son, that day may come sooner than you think.'"

Jeb Crittendon looked at Cyrus Lee like he'd just dropped down from the stars.

"What?" Lee said. "Don't you read?"

"Fremont was just the straw that took down the mule," Sandy said. "I hear it was one after another getting off with no evidence in Ledger's court until the judge went loony. They say he never sleeps."

Paul watched Frank Ledger lean against the window and close his eyes. He seemed to fall asleep in an instant. "Guess you can't believe everything you read."

Crittendon holstered his revolver and pulled down his hat. Cyrus Lee mimicked him. They settled into their seats for some sleep of their own. Paul took off his hat and placed it over Sandy's head, pulling it down to shade her eyes. Beneath the brim he could see her smiling. "Get some rest," he said. She didn't fight him on it. Paul, too, slouched down in his seat.

Though his eyes burned with fatigue, Paul couldn't rest. He'd already assumed he'd get no sleep, but with Frank Ledger in the same train car there was zero chance. From a distance he could see Ledger's dreaming eyes moving wildly beneath the lids. His lips were whispering threats and his teeth were snapping like a dog chasing rabbits. He was chasing Roy, now, too.

They all were.

Paul stifled a chuckle. It was so absurd. The shopkeeper in Bracken had asked him, *what makes one man follow another?* Paul had given him what he thought was an acceptable answer. He was sure all these men would give acceptable answers, too. Answers they could give their wives and sons and still be held in proper standing, answers that society would regard as good and true. Keeping a job. Protecting society. Even vengeance could be respected, and in some cases heralded. But none of these answers were at the heart of the matter. These men cared little for right and wrong. They followed because secretly they wanted to bleed. They wanted scars. They wanted to taste bitter confrontation. They wanted to inflict pain and suffer wounds. They wanted to survive tests that make everything else seem small. They followed because they sought the kinds of answers good homes and comfortable beds can't provide. They followed because sleeping awkwardly on a train a man can dream of agony and death, and when he awakens he can have them.

❊

Roy opened the black chest. It was filled with dozens of forks, knives, and spoons just like the spoon he carried. All the same, all in sets, and yet all different. Each piece was brilliant. Each with its own personality, an individual work of art with little nuances that made it just different enough from its partners to be special. Roy wondered if one set was missing a spoon, or if the spoon he carried was unique—a display model molded with the most amount of care. The best of them all.

Yes, this had to be the case.

He considered collecting one knife and one fork so he could have a complete set to carry with him, but there was something wrong about ruining the unity of the sets in the box. The box was pure. Whomever should find it should find it whole. That would be the glory of it.

He moved the chest to the edge of the boxcar and sat next to it, his feet once again dangling out the doorway. He rested an elbow on the chest and continued rubbing the spoon. The ground sped by. Roy thought of the creatures living out there in the ditches and fields, sleeping in trees or holes, maybe hunting at night. They lived by their own terms. They moved through their own small worlds like kings. He imagined they were aware of humanity, but only in as much as it meant to their survival. Humans were to be avoided, their machines to be tolerated, their guns to be heeded. Cross them and death would follow. This was the capacity of animals. It was all they needed know.

The train began to slow. As the train was a freighter Roy didn't figure there'd be any stops between Colfax and the big city.

No dice.

The train stopped and whistled its arrival. Outside the car a sign read *Knoxville*. The station was a small wooden shack with two black eyes for windows. Every second or so a bell rang. It seemed like a ghost station until a worker lit the gas lamps on the stunted boardwalk.

The freighters must be routed on a separate track, Roy thought, away from the commuters.

More workers poured out of the station. They moved toward the boxcars wearing gloves and tired faces. Some carried boxes, some limbered up in anticipation of the same task. There would be more loading and unloading, just like at Colfax.

Roy hopped back into the boxcar. He slid along the near wall and crouched down in a corner behind the wooden crates. He pulled his hat low and his collar high. He pocketed the spoon and produced his revolver.

Shadows floated past and mingled on the walls. Voices carried into the boxcar and echoed. Some near, some far. Commands from a foreman to the laborers to hurry up and get to it, to load this, unload that. One command increased Roy's pulse. *Make sure you get everything off seventeen.*

A man appeared in the boxcar door. Above the man's head, held in his left hand, was a lantern. The man wore brown overalls and a bowler hat. He had a young face with a patchy beard. He set down his lamp and placed his hands on the boxcar floor, ready to hop aboard, but the black chest gave him pause.

"Now what in the hell is this?"

From all his years of traveling, Roy knew accents like bankers knew coins. This man was Kentucky, straight through. He pushed the chest deeper into the car. He looked left and right and then hopped aboard. He crouched down to the chest and ran a gloved hand over it. He whistled, not like you would for a dog or for a woman's attention, but like you would when you saw something impressive. He unlatched the chest and opened it, took off a glove and reached inside. An outside voice stopped his movement.

"Get moving, Wade! We ain't got all day."

"Yes, sir," Wade said. He closed the chest and slid it along the floor until it was covered in shadow. He put the glove back on and began unloading crates, handing them off to a man on the ground outside the car.

Roy breathed through his nose. His ears rushed with each heartbeat. He released his breaths evenly and soundlessly. Still crouched, he held the revolver down by his ankle. It came to him that he'd pointed the gun at everyone and everything he'd met since taking possession of it, and yet he still hadn't squeezed the trigger. His hand yearned for the kickback. His ears wanted the explosion and the uneasy silence that only follows gunshots. A silence where the world comes to attention and petty things are forgotten. All the same, he wanted to throw the gun away. If he used it society would look upon him. Be they butchers or bankers, whores or thieves, they would stop what they were doing and look. They would point. They would talk. And they would eventually chase.

Wade worked with purpose. He was wiry, but his forearms were furry and strong. One by one the crates disappeared. His pace was methodical. In thirty seconds he'd be removing the final crate and looking upon an armed freight-hopper.

26

The three other men and one girl in the diner car slept like babies rocked by the train's rhythm. Jeb Crittendon snored. Paul, still awake, wondered how well his son was sleeping at his grandfather's house. No doubt Jacob would be in a lush bed with countless pillows and servants at his call. Too much time there and the boy would come back soft. Jacob loved his grandfather for the reasons a boy should love anyone—toys and gifts. The old man rained them down like a god. A rocking horse, tops, marbles, a drum, and a cup and ball that the boy had yet to master. The old man confused gifts for affection.

No, that wasn't right. There was no confusion about it. Delmont Graves *substituted* gifts for affection, saving himself from the burden of the time and energy.

To the point, Delmont Graves was spoiling Paul's child. Paul had always bitten his tongue on the subject. Gloria would blast with both barrels if he said anything, and he hadn't the will to fight her on it. His silence was pain avoidance, he knew that. He had come to terms with it, but the row was no less hard to hoe. He couldn't offer gifts like Delmont. And even if he could, he wouldn't. In Paul's way of thinking, a boy needed only his imagination and a world to explore. A down tree could be a rocking horse, stones replaced marbles, and who needed a cup and ball, anyway? Gifts would take away the boy's imagination and drive. They would give him expectations when it was best to have none. They would make him think a man needed only to exist and the world would open its doors.

But how do you tell a five-year-old the world is a cold and terrible place, and to move through it thinking you had a right to peace or happiness was a mug's game?

Jeb Crittendon snorted in his sleep. Paul looked at Cyrus Lee for a matching snort, but none came. He peeked at Frank Ledger to find the man's eyes open. Ledger looked like a demon possessed him. He still slept, of that Paul was certain, but his open eyes watched a nightmare. The man's mouth came open, slowly and steadily, to the point where the jawbone would either lock or crack. A silent, horrified scream. His body convulsed. A knee banged the table from beneath. His eyes widened and widened. His jaw worked up and down like he was mouthing, "Ah, ah, ah."

Paul grabbed the hilt of his Dragoon.

Ledger's legs extended and his boot heels banged the floor. Froth formed at the corners of his mouth. Some kind of seizure. Paul slid to the edge of his bench and pulled his legs underneath him, ready to pounce at God knows what. The seizure went on for several minutes. Paul wasn't well-versed on such things, but the length of the affair seemed extraordinary.

And then, as suddenly as it started, it stopped. Ledger's body went flaccid. He blinked. Awake. He wiped froth from his mouth as his eyes searched the diner car. They paused for a moment at the revolver on Paul's waist, and then moved up to match Paul's gaze. "I've seen you."

"The Colfax rail yard," Paul said. "You and your brothers."

Ledger nodded. "You know something about the lizard."

"I do," Paul said.

"Where's he headed?"

"Don't know."

Ledger looked at Crittendon and Lee, and at Sandy, all still sleeping. He lifted a chin to them. "Who're they?"

"What happened in the boxcar?" Paul said.

Ledger sneered. He looked out the window.

Paul waited, but after a moment it was clear no answer was coming. "They're prison guards," he said. "Save for the girl, we all are. Redmine."

Ledger laughed. The sound was not of joy, but of sarcasm. The kind of laugh a madman might let out before spitting in the faces of the men dragging him away. "Prison guards?" he said. "You boys couldn't guard your own acorns."

"Mind your tongue."

It was Jeb Crittendon that spoke. He was awake now.

Frank Ledger regarded Crittendon calmly. There it was again—that out of place serenity. It seemed the man was at home with conflict and at odds with peace. When he slept there were nightmares and seizures, when threatened he was tranquil as a monk. "There's an eternity box in your future, fat man," he said. "Don't hasten yourself to it."

Crittendon slapped Cyrus Lee's shoulder, jolting him awake. Lee looked around, confused. Crittendon produced his revolver and kept it hidden behind the seatback. Lee saw the revolver and registered the situation. He turned his gaze to Frank Ledger as he reached into his jacket for his knife.

"What I see is one man against three," Crittendon said, lifting his battered revolver so Frank Ledger could see it, "and two guns against, well, whatever you got. If a man in this here car should be in the market for a coffin, *your honor*, I'm thinking it's you."

Frank Ledger began to reach inside his jacket.

"Enough," Paul said.

Ledger's hand stopped moving, save for its tremoring.

For a moment the men remained silent, all eyes unblinking.

The train clacked steadily on.

Sandy slept.

"It's a few hours to Chicago," Paul said. "Just keep your peckers in your pants 'til we can separate ways."

Frank Ledger nodded. He wiped his hand on his chest, as though he'd been intending that move all along.

Crittendon and Lee relaxed. They put away their weapons.

To Paul, Ledger said, "Meantime, you'll tell me about the lizard."

27

Wade reached the last line of crates. There were three of them stacked on top of one another. He put his hands on the topmost crate and stopped. He focused on the wall in front of him as if he were speaking to it, "I can see you there," he said, then he hefted the crate and carried it to the open door.

Roy stayed motionless, pistol at his side. His stomach was a prune. The knot at the base of his skull began to ache, a dull pain slowly grew and spread out across his neck and head.

Wade came back for the second-to-last crate. Again, looking at nothing and talking to no one, he said, "They make me check for freight-hoppers." He put his hands on the crate. "I'm supposed to roust you fellas out and kick you in the ass for good measure. Supposed to alert authority so you can learn a little something about being *civilized*." He picked up the crate and carried it away.

A voice from outside the car said, "Who you talking to in there?"

Wade handed off the crate and said, "Just one more." He then crouched down in the open doorway, forearms resting on thighs, gloved hands dangling in the space between his legs.

"Well, hurry up then," the outside voice said. "Standing around ain't getting me any closer to bed."

"Hold on, Bob," Wade said. "I got an issue here."

Roy raised his revolver. He aimed it at Wade's temple from ten feet away. His mind's eye saw flashes of the day they took him to prison. He recalled looking up at the sky from a roadside ditch where the sideshow had discarded him with their horrible word carved into his chest, plus a note explaining his crime stuffed into his pocket so the law would know what to do. He recalled the constable's deputies picking him up. After that it was a short ride in a caged cart to Redmine. The cart never actually stopped. It only slowed enough to make the turn and sling him out. The guards at the prison wrapped him in burlap before picking him up, one at each arm. His toes dragged across the hardpan as they walked him beneath the portcullis for registration. He signed his name, as asked to do, and then they dropped him in the hole.

The pain in his head now reverberated through his jaw. His chest tightened. The gun remained surprisingly still. His aim would be true. Wade's final thoughts would be spelled out in blood and brain matter on the boxcar wall.

Bob said, "What is it?"

"I checked the manifest," Wade said, "and it showed we have twelve boxes here on seventeen, right?"

"Yeah," Bob said. "What of it?"

"There's thirteen."

There was a beat between them, and then Wade nodded with his eyebrows raised.

"Well c'mon then," Bob said. "Let's get this done and get on."

Wade's voice fell to a whisper, though loud enough for Roy to hear. "Well, like I said, I got an issue. My guess is the freight-hopper on this here car might not take too kindly to us taking his treasure."

Another beat passed.

"Is that right?" Bob finally said, menace in his tone.

Roy figured they were used to pounding the tar out of freight-hoppers, and that Bob was likely pounding a fist into his open palm at the moment.

"That's right," Wade said. "In fact, he's got a gun pointed at me right now."

Roy cocked back the revolver's hammer. The sound was plenty loud enough for both Wade and Bob to hear.

Bob whistled that same kind of whistle.

"Here's the thing, though," Wade said. "Something tells me—I don't know, call it a hunch—that it might be more important for this here fella to stay on this train than to keep this old chest he don't need, anyway."

"You think that's right?" Bob said.

"I surely do," Wade said. "And ain't it funny that we know how this here train won't be stopping again until just outside of Chicago? A little place called Hyde Park where they need to drop off all them grapes and fine things on twenty-one for some rich boys to have a party with their day-bue-tants."

"That *is* funny," Bob said.

"It is," Wade said. "And I'm betting this fella might like to know that getting off this here train at Hyde Park would be a cinch, while getting off in Chicago… well, with all their law enforcement and high ideas about what it means to be *civilized*."

"It sure wouldn't be no cinch," Bob said.

"No cinch," Wade said.

For the first time Wade looked directly at Roy. Roy could see his courage was only halfway real. If the eyes truly were the windows to the soul, Wade's soul was flat terrified. Who wouldn't be with a revolver aimed at their face?

Wade stood. He rubbed his gloved hands together. "I'm gonna take this here last crate," he said, keeping his eyes on Roy but still talking to Bob. "And then I'm gonna have you come aboard and help me with this chest. That all right?" The question had a dual purpose, one part aimed at Bob, the other at Roy.

"Sounds all right to me," Bob said.

Roy clicked down the hammer and brought the gun back to his waist. He kicked the final crate and it slid across the boxcar floor until it bumped against Wade's feet.

Wade smiled.

28

"What do you want to know?" Paul said, now sitting across the aisle from Frank Ledger. He'd heard Ledger's account of what happened in boxcar seventeen. The man had been surprisingly honest in recounting the event, admitting to being too slow to react to Roy's movements, admitting to being easily beaten. He explained how he pushed his own brother from the train and then jumped off himself. He was also honest in his intent to bring Roy to justice.

Execution, Paul thought.

Ledger spoke of his intent matter-of-factly, like a man might speak of what he did for a living. Hell, judge or no judge, murder *was* what Frank Ledger did for a living. Or maybe it was just something to do because men like Frank Ledger needed something to do. He'd been for the law, and he'd worn a cross, but what did that say? How many lives had been forfeit, and how much blood had been shed in the name of religion? If anything, the cross was a dead giveaway.

"What is he," Ledger said, "part animal?"

"I don't think so," Paul said. "It's some kind of skin disease put on him at birth. It doesn't do anything for him but make him look different."

"That isn't right," Frank Ledger said, shaking his head. "He moves like nothing I ever seen. That's something more than just bad skin."

Paul shrugged. He had to admit that Roy seemed different than the boy he once knew. Despite his thin body, he seemed stronger and more agile. Like a machine. But there was something else, too. His eyes, even at a distance, showed a different kind of fire than before. Not a fire for adventure, like when he was young, but the smoldering embers of a jaded and unpredictable man.

"Some kind of reptile blood," Ledger said. He was looking out the window. "Makes him naturally hard where most men are soft."

"Is that right?" Paul said.

Frank Ledger allowed the hint of a smile across his face. Paul stifled a laugh. He imagined this was about as tickled as Frank Ledger may ever get.

Paul looked at Crittendon and Lee. Both were once again sleeping on benches near the front of the car. Crittendon spilled out over the sides like a sack of guts. Lee was curled up in the corner like a house pet. Sandy was awake now. Still in Paul's hat, and still with it low on her head, she watched Paul and Ledger from across the train.

Paul smiled at her, nodded.

Sandy glanced fearfully at Ledger.

The man had gone into another seizure. It was milder than the first, but unmistakable. His eyes were like melting glass. His fists trembled. His teeth showed. He emitted a string of small grunts. This went on for thirty seconds, and then, very quietly, it was over. Ledger blinked and composed himself. He went on as if the seizure never happened. "What I mean to say is when his fists touched my chest it was like two cannon balls had hit me. I never saw him coming. He moved like a ghost. And when his head touched my chin, I thought my teeth would explode. There's armor on him." He ran his hand over his forearm as if to show where armor plates might go.

Paul nodded. He recalled the events around Roy's intended burial. How quickly Roy had moved. How his lights were out before he could spit. Maybe Frank Ledger was on to something. Maybe there was animal blood in Roy after all, a mystical gator's curse.

"I feel sorry for him," Ledger said.

Paul cocked his head. This wasn't on Paul's list of things a scourge like Frank Ledger might say. If there was animal blood in anyone, it was in Ledger—cold, merciless blood that only knew survival. If Roy could be compared to a gator, Frank Ledger was a scorpion.

"I guess he escaped your prison?" Ledger said.

"He did," Paul said.

"And what was he in for?"

"Killed a man," Paul said.

Ledger contemplated a moment, and then said, "I never put him there."

"He was awaiting trial when he escaped."

Ledger snorted, shook his head. "Wasn't any trial coming."

Paul studied Ledger's face. Up close he could see there was a long scar along the side of this face, nearly hidden by his beard. His eyes were bagged and bloodshot. He had the look of an insomniac. Paul knew the look well; Redmine turned healthy men into insomniacs, prisoners and guards alike. They walked the prison's cells and halls like marionettes, strung up and teetering on the edge of sanity.

"Nevertheless, justice will be served," Ledger said.

"Is there such a thing?" Paul said.

Frank Ledger regarded Paul coolly, then his eyes shifted toward Sandy. He watched her, and for a moment Paul thought the man might smile, but he didn't. "That girl," he said, "she's yours?"

"Not by blood," Paul said.

"But she's in your care?"

Paul nodded.

"And what would you do, sir, if she were harmed? Call it molestation, rape, or murder. That beautiful child?"

Paul's heart rose and thumped inside his throat. He considered Sandy, innocent and helpless beneath her tough little facade, now under some man's brutality. She stared back at him, smiling uneasily, seeming to know they were speaking of her. Frank Ledger was right; Paul would see justice for her under any circumstances. Even at the cost of his life.

Frank Ledger put his hands on the table before him. He spread his fingers wide and drummed them in a rhythmic fashion. His knuckles were bulbous and calloused. Scars crisscrossed everywhere. He'd been a judge, but there was no doubt he'd come up the hard way. Still watching Sandy, he said, "Oh, she may not be your blood, but she's certainly yours."

"That salesman on the Colfax road," Paul said, "did he receive justice?"

Ledger's eyes sharpened. "Hell you know about that?"

"I found him," Paul said. "Found your brother, too, bleeding out on the roadside."

"Still breathing?" Ledger said.

"Just barely."

"Dead now?"

"Died while I was with him," Paul said. "Thought maybe I was Jesus, come to save him."

Frank Ledger looked down at his trembling hands. That unnerving peace was once again in his insomniac eyes, it was all around him. He touched the empty place on his chest, where the silver cross had recently been torn away. He said, "Jesus only saved himself."

29

Roy walked along the train tracks between Hyde Park and Chicago. There was a distant patchwork of farms to his left, dense forest to his right. The midday sun shone straight down, as if magnifying only on his head and shoulders, trying to melt him away. The sky was spotless and unending. Insects chirred. The nearby trees contracted and moaned like old men in the heat. His eyes were swollen and his vision blurry. His cheeks were wet with thrown water and gritty with salt. There may have been a drop or two in his waterskin, but he refused to check in case the news was deflating.

Getting off the train at Hyde Park had been a cinch, just as Wade said it would be. As the train had slowed, Roy hopped off and slid down a steep bank. At the bottom was a valley of tall weeds. Roy crouched down and lit out from the station unseen while the train was unloaded. By the time the train was again on its way, Roy was already a half mile down the tracks in front of it. When it passed him the wind felt good, but then the heat clamped down.

He was now six or seven miles from the big city. Already he could see the buildings and smoke. In a strange way he felt he was returning home. His mind's eye saw the streetlights and alleys, the fire escapes and tall brick walls, the faces that looked up from the gutter, and those that looked down from on high. Chicago was a place for both the well-to-do and transients. It was mother to those that sought something more from life than a farm or a trail. And yet the city embodied detachment. Roy once heard someone say Chicago could chew you up and spit you out. He disagreed. The big city breathed you in and absorbed you. It swallowed you and forgot you were ever there.

He recalled his first pass through Chicago. He was eleven years old and had been with the sideshow for just over a month. His only job, so far, had been shoveling horseshit.

"Everyone pitches in," McLean had said, handing Roy a shovel. "I'll take it back when you're ready."

As much as his own parents did their best by him, they didn't revel in his difference like McLean did. Out of love they kept him hidden, but hidden just the same. McLean taught Roy to display himself and profit from his difference as though it were a skill, just as the skill of an actor or a blacksmith. He taught him to come by it honestly and feed off society's repulsion with no reservation, for there would always be a bounty.

Young Roy bellied up to the feast for the first time in Chicago. His banner had been created but kept under wraps until he was willing. Roy peeked in on it from time to time, stealing away from his wagon at night and unwrapping and unrolling it carefully. Across the top, in red letters, it read *Scales, the Crying Lizard*. In one lower corner it read *Born Alive!*, and in the other corner, *Why?* In the middle was a painted picture of a giant, green lizard with a boy's head. It looked nothing like Roy, and in fact the image scared him. It only served to make him more hesitant to go on stage.

McLean was patient, but only for so long. They were on the south side of Chicago when he set out the banner for the first time. Standing in the empty midway in the early afternoon, he unwrapped the banner lovingly, like he was removing the swaddle from a newborn child. He unrolled the canvas and tapped nails into the corners, applying it to a wooden stand not unlike an artist's easel. He propped up the stand dead center amongst the others, making it seem important. When he was done he stood back, put a hand on Roy's shoulder. "You ain't here to shovel horseshit, son."

At the time Jack McLean doubled as both outside and inside talker. The show was not yet profitable enough to afford one of each, so McLean corralled audiences into the tent before quickly moving backstage to introduce the acts. Over time McLean would grow to introduce Roy in varying ways—mostly speaking of a marriage between man and beast, the swamp or bayou, and a reference to Africa or the Amazon when the crowd needed some extra flair—but his last line was always the same. Roy heard the line now as he heard it the first time, and as loud and as clear as if McLean were walking right next to him.

Witness, ladies and gentlemen, the awful price of a woman's sin.

After *sin*, Roy had been instructed to come across the stage, turn a full circle, and then sit down. That first time, on Chicago's south side, he stepped timidly out, a leopard skin loin cloth around his waist. Dozens of eyes were once again upon him, just like at the schoolhouse when he was a boy. However, there was no Paul this time. There was no one looking at him with something different than repulsion. He walked toward a chair in the middle of the stage trying to catch just one set of eyes with which he could connect.

No dice.

Fear welled up inside him, but he recalled McLean's advice to view his skin as a skill. It helped him quiet the fear and continue to move. He focused his eyes on the tent wall just beyond the crowd. There was a brown stain there. It was in the shape of a kidney bean. The stain was faint in the middle and dark rimmed at the edges. He tried to imagine how it got there and what had caused it. Mud? A rotten tomato? Blood?

At that final thought a coldness came to Roy, and he understood that detachment was the real skill. The actor detached and became someone else when he walked across the stage. Afterward he was again himself. He could be sad, happy, or crazy. He could be a woman or a man. He could be dressed as an animal. Roy once read a play where a man acted as Faust making his pact with the devil. Roy felt he should do the same. He should walk across the stage and become the cold-blooded reptile they paid to see, making a deal with his own devil.

At present Roy neared a scarecrow. It wore a Union army jacket over a stuffing of straw and leaves. Years of neglect had worn the scarecrow down and robbed it of its former glory. The right arm was broken off and the sleeve hung limply, twisting in the wind. The left arm pointed toward Chicago and held up a murder of crows. The crows were defiant to the scarecrow's original intent, perching in mockery. They squawked as Roy approached. Roy vaguely recalled his father once saying something about keeping friends close and enemies closer. The crows seemed to heed the advice.

Roy moved with suddenness and the crows scattered, laughing as they went. Roy came to the scarecrow and faced it. The scarecrow's stitched eyes were level with his own. It had a ripped, all-knowing smile, and its hat was eaten through with dark holes.

"That way to Chicago, eh?" Roy said, nodding to the scarecrow's pointed arm.

The scarecrow held its silence.

It occurred to Roy that someone viewing from a distance might not know, between he and the scarecrow, which man was living and which was nothing more than straw and stick.

Roy heard a distant train whistle. He looked over the scarecrow's broken shoulder. A mile off he saw the black, smoking line of a commuter train chugging toward Chicago.

30

Paul exited the diner car holding Sandy's hand. Crittendon and Lee followed close behind. People milled before them like a roiling sea. Chicago. There were hats and shoulders, smoking pipes and newspapers, suitcases and boxes, dogs on leashes. Frank Ledger had gotten off before them. Despite his roughed up clothing, the man merged into the mix of humanity at the Illinois Central Station and was gone. Losing sight of him both troubled and relieved Paul.

"Good riddance to that bastard," Crittendon said.

"Yeah," Lee said.

Paul could hardly hear them over the din. He weaved through bodies like an eel through a weed bed, sliding into gaps and turning and twisting his body as he moved toward the Western Union with Sandy in tow. For her part, she didn't complain about being dragged through the crowd.

Paul hoped he could lose Crittendon and Lee like Ledger had

lost them, but it wasn't to be; Crittendon was a cattle catcher. He barged through the crowd in a straight line, discharging bodies left and right, invoking ill commentary.

At the Western Union there was a message from Delmont Graves:

SHE MADE AN ATTEMPT ON HER LIFE. MIGHT NOT SURVIVE.

Paul read the message once.
Twice.
A third time.
The din faded away and was replaced by a high-pitched keening. He looked up. Jeb Crittendon was saying something and Cyrus Lee was nodding in agreement. They were mimes. Paul thought they should join variety theatre. He looked around to see all the bodies and mouths and eyes moving. All these people, living their lives and doing their things. Talking, eating, working, smoking. They were sleepwalking, unaware that his wife had attempted suicide.

Sandy tugged at his duster. He looked down at her. Sound returned in parts. First a bell, somewhere outside the station, pierced through the high-pitched tone in his ears. Then a man selling boiled peanuts called, "Get 'em while they're hot!" A boy dropped a marble and it clacked against the bricks.

"Constantine," Crittendon said. Paul watched as the heavy man put a hand on his shoulder, but he didn't feel its weight. He didn't feel himself being shaken. "Still here with us?"

Paul looked up at the big board. A man on a ladder was posting train arrivals and departures. A train left for Colfax that afternoon. If he hurried he could be home by mid-morning, tomorrow.

Gloria was a drunk, yes, but so desperate as to take her own life?

How could he have been so ignorant? She needed him and he'd been cold. A bad husband. An unacceptable father. He conjured an image of Gloria's face, drunk and incapable. He saw his hands go to her throat. Her eyes turned to surprise when she felt his touch. At first she seemed to hope for a caress, but her surprise turned to a darker realization. As he squeezed, blood rushed to her ears. Her teeth showed and her tongue fell out. It turned blue. Paul blinked and her face changed, the moment changed. She was young and full of laughter on the day they met. Delmont Graves had come to Redmine to see a client, and his daughter had insisted on tagging along. Barred from the room where her father and client sat down, she was left under the watch of a young prison guard. Paul told her a story.

"This is one about little Tommy," he started, "and Tommy was a naughty young boy."

"Are you sure his name wasn't little *Pauly*," Gloria said, winking.

Paul blushed. He stood silently for a moment, doubtful on how to proceed.

"Well, go on then!" Gloria said.

"Are you sure?"

She threw her hands on her hips and tapped her toe.

Paul nodded. "Now," he said, "everyone knew little Tommy was a foul-mouthed boy—his classmates, his parents, and even his schoolteacher, Ms. Jones. After years of trying, they'd all given up on correcting him, but they certainly weren't going to encourage him. His parents did what they could at home, and Ms. Jones did what she could in class, but as you can imagine, keeping Tommy from cursing a blue streak was a tough job."

"I'll bet it was," Gloria said.

"One day Ms. Jones started a lesson, saying, 'Okay, class, I'm going to give you a letter of the alphabet, and I want you to raise your hands when you have a word that starts with that letter. We'll begin with the letter *A*'"

Now it was Gloria that blushed, seeming to realize which word a foul-mouthed boy like Tommy would associate with the letter *A*.

"I'm sorry," Paul said, "this story is out of line."

"Hush now," Gloria said. "Get on with it."

"Very well," Paul said. "'We'll begin with the letter A,' Ms. Jones said, and of course Tommy raised his hand. Ms. Jones knew better than to call on him, as he might say *ass*, so she called on bright-eyed Susie in the second row.

"'Apple!' Susie said.

"'Very good, Susie,' Ms. Jones said. 'Now everyone, how about the letter *B*?'"

Gloria snickered.

"Some of the kids raise their hands," Paul said, "but Tommy's hand was up the highest. Still, Ms. Jones couldn't call on him, for if she did he might say *bastard*. Instead the teacher called on quiet little Gloria in the very first row."

Gloria batted her eyes and smiled.

"A beautiful young girl, that Gloria," Paul said, "her voice was as sweet as a summer breeze when she said, 'Banana.'

"'Very good!' Ms. Jones said, 'and now class, how about *C*?'

"At this letter Tommy's hand shot up like an arrow. He waved it back and forth. Ms. Jones gave it a split second before opting to call on another student. Heaven forbid she allow little Tommy to say…"

Gloria's pink blush went crimson. She slapped him playfully on the shoulder.

Paul soared at her touch. "So she called on another student, and they said, 'Carrot.'"

Gloria raised an eyebrow.

Paul knew then that he had her. "Now," he said, "when Ms. Jones got down to the letter *R* she found that not a one of her students had raised their hand. Not a single one, that is, except for little

Tommy. Ms. Jones thought long, and Ms. Jones thought hard, but she couldn't come up with a curse word that Tommy might use. So, with an increasing sense of trepidation, she called on the foul-mouthed boy.

"'Rat!' Tommy said, beaming triumphantly."

Paul watched Gloria's face switch from curious to stunned. "'Very good, Tommy,' Ms. Jones said.

"'Yeah,' Tommy said, 'A big bastard rat with a fat ass and a huge cock!'"

Gloria's laughter crushed him. He remembered wanting only to hear that sound for the rest of his life. He remembered the way she stuttered nervously when she said goodbye and thanked him for such a good time, as if they'd been on a date.

And now she'd tried to kill herself?

"Go on without me," Paul said.

Crittendon's face twisted up in confusion.

Paul ignored him. He turned to the Western Union counter. The clerk smiled. "I need to send a return on this," Paul said. He handed the clerk the message.

"Certainly, sir," the clerk said. He produced a pad of paper and a pencil.

"I'm coming back, stop. I'll-" he felt something hard against his ribs. A single point of pressure, undoubtedly a rusty revolver barrel. After a beat, the clerked looked up from his writing pad.

"He won't need to finish that," Crittendon said.

The clerk glanced at Crittendon, and then back at Paul.

"Isn't that right, Mr. Constantine?" Crittendon said.

Paul nodded.

"Let's take a walk," Crittendon said.

"Yeah," Lee said, "a walk." He now gripped Sandy's wrist. The girl was wide-eyed and staring at the spot beneath Paul's duster where Crittendon had placed his gun.

Crittendon led Paul with one arm over his shoulder like they were brothers. The man smelled like he hadn't bathed this year. He kept the revolver tucked tight against Paul's ribs. They maneuvered through the crowd and out of the station, into the blinding sunlight.

Outside, the crowd was thinner. The group moved along the station wall until they came to an alley just on the other side of a produce stand, not yet open for the day. The alley was dark and the ground was covered with trash and stacked crates. It stank of rotting fruit.

"Keep an eye out," Crittendon said. He shoved Paul into the alley and followed, gun raised. Cyrus Lee stood at the alley mouth with a tight grip on Sandy's wrist.

"My wife is in trouble," Paul said.

"I don't care," Crittendon said.

"You don't need me," Paul said. "You can find him on your own."

"Now ya see," Crittendon said, "I just don't think that's true." He smiled like the childhood bully he still was. Paul's neck throbbed. His hands went cold. He considered the revolver on his waist. Could he snatch it up and rip off a shot before the fat man burned him down?

"I think you ain't letting on as much as you really know about our little freak," Crittendon said. "See, me and Cyrus, we been thinking. Ain't that right, Cyrus?"

"That's right," Lee said.

"We been thinking you're the only guard that never went near that freak when he was at Redmine. At first we thought you was just scared, you being a yellow belly and all. But we knew someone had been giving that freak all them Beadle books. Couldn't quite figure it, but then something hit me. Something as big and bright as the day." He pantomimed a bright, sunny day. "What was it that hit me, Cyrus?"

"Cajun," Cyrus said.

"That's right," Crittendon said. "In all that time at Redmine our little freak didn't say more than a few words, to be sure, but the words he said, they sure sounded like Cajun."

"That they did," Lee said.

"Get to your point," Paul said. Suddenly his accent sounded thicker to him than before.

Crittendon smiled. His eyes grew wild.

Paul's hand moved slowly toward his revolver.

Crittendon spat. The glob splattered against the ground near Paul's feet.

"Here's the point," Crittendon said. "We're wondering if you ol' boys don't stick together. We're thinking maybe it wasn't one against three out there with you and the Boyle twins. Understand? We're thinking it was really two against two. Ain't that right, Cyrus?"

"That's ri-"

He was going to say *right*, Paul thought, but little Sandy's bootheel came down on his toes. He cried out and released her hand. Sandy ran down the alley toward Paul. He reached out to her as she came, but Jeb Crittendon intercepted her. He gripped the girl by her hair and used her momentum to pitch her against the alley wall. He pinned her down with a large hand on her tiny chest. He flipped the revolver in his other hand, reared it back, and started the butt end down toward the girl's face.

Paul stepped forward and caught Crittendon's arm at the wrist. His gravedigger's grip squeezed until the man's two forearm bones clicked together. Crittendon yelped and dropped the revolver. Paul caught it with his off hand, flipped it, and brought the butt down on the back of Crittendon's head.

The fat man tipped over backwards, clutching the back of his head. He curled up and covered his face. Paul corralled Sandy behind him. He stood over Crittendon enraged with the memory of what this man had done to his friend in the prison yard. He hammered Crittendon with blows to the ribs, to the back, and to the arms until he uncovered his face. Paul then worked over the man's facial features with blind fury. The eyes, the nose, and finally the mouth, the teeth.

"Stop!"

Paul looked up to see Cyrus Lee on one knee at the alley mouth. He'd pulled a single-shot Derringer from his boot. A small gun, but not so small it couldn't open a man's skull from its current range.

31

Roy unbuckled his gun belt, threw it on to his shoulder, and stepped off the road. He marched into the water until he was ankle deep in Lake Michigan. His boots flooded and his feet cooled down—a well-deserved treat after miles of walking in the sun. His skin was on fire. His eyes were bursting dams, his throat a corroded pipe. He began to fill his waterskin but then stopped. Instead he flipped off his hat, opened his shirt, and flung himself down to his knees where he gulped water like a dog.

At length he stopped drinking. He came back on his haunches and belched. He scooped up a half-gallon of water with his hat and placed it on his head, letting the water splash over his shoulders. His coin bag rested on the sand beneath the surface, dropped from his head when he'd removed his hat.

Before him was an expanse of green, white-capped water to rival the oceans.

This was not the water of home. The bayou was a brown, boggy mess. It was ugly and dripping like an infected wound, a series of clogged veins with dangers and traps at every turn. It purveyed death and pain. It didn't want humans, and it killed them for trespassing.

But this water was life itself. A cleansing pool. There were no gators or snakes to speak of, only freshwater fish seemingly designed to be food, to gladly give their lives to the prosperity of man. It was no wonder the big city sprouted and thrived on these banks. No wonder civilization set up its permanent camps so close to a loving bounty. If God's image was reflected anywhere in this world, Roy thought, it was in the water of Lake Michigan.

He grabbed a handful of sand, squeezed it, and let the dirt fall through his fingers in clumps. He enjoyed the plopping sounds as the sand returned home.

He filled his waterskin and ate what remained of his food, savoring it to the last. He patted his belly. It was distended and uncomfortable from overdrinking, but it was a good pain and he savored it, too. He absently traced the letters carved into his chest.

A half-mile to the north was Chicago. The skyline looked like the spiked backbone of a great beast dozing in the heat. The thought gave him pause. As much as the city felt like home, as he'd drawn closer he felt more and more unwelcome. A prodigal son, gone wayward and meant never to return. His journey, up until this point, had been fueled by glorious visions of love and revenge. The visions had pushed at his back like hot wind, propelling him toward a dime novel destiny, but the wind had cooled and died. Such toothsome visions were now more difficult to conjure. They were blotted out by a thought he could no longer put away.

Jesse left.

McLean hadn't dismissed her that morning at the Corktown Inn. He hadn't awakened her happy slumber and asked her to leave so he and Roy could talk. She had left on her own, and was gone before McLean arrived. She had tiptoed quietly away in the dark of dawn. Roy had heard her go. He could admit that now. He heard the creaking floorboards and the tiny strike of wood against wood as the door was secretly pulled shut. He had pushed the sounds out of his mind, pretending he'd never heard them, telling himself there was no need to reach across the bed and find her because she was certainly there, and there was no reason to doubt it. He kept his eyes closed and forced himself back into slumber, knowing when he awakened he'd find her breathing evenly in sleep, her ribs rising and falling, her devils and dragons at home in the warm bed they shared.

No dice.

They had shared nothing, or at least not enough. He saw the truth of that now.

The waves of Lake Michigan rolled in. They whispered. They asked him to keep coming out, to swim into the deep and forget. To swim and swim until nothing but water could be seen. There he could discard the hat, the rope, the bag, the clothes, the boots, the gun. It would all sink away. He could float naked on his back and stare up at the endless blue, up at the foundation of Heaven until God reached down and collected him.

He stood and began moving forward. In the distance he heard galloping hooves. The pale horse of the apocalypse, he thought. He took more steps. The gallop grew louder. He imagined the reaper upon the pale horse, scythe at the length of its cloaked arm. He saw its hollow eyes and perfect teeth. He welcomed its coming. He closed his eyes and walked blindly into the depths. The gallop grew louder still. The hooves pounded and echoed, drowning out all other sound. He slid off the burlap bag and discarded it. The water gathered around his waist. The hoof-beats pounded in his ears. He slid off the rope and tossed it aside. The water came to his chest. His eyes still closed, he saw visions of the farmhouse burning. And then it was gone. Left behind was an empty field with a black crater in the middle. She wasn't there. She never was, never would be.

Roy lifted the gun belt from his shoulder. The sound of the galloping hooves stopped growing, started fading. He moved his arm to toss the gun and belt away, but stopped. He turned an ear to the fading sound. The horse was no longer riding toward him, but away. Death was passing him by. He looked back over his shoulder. The horse was not pale, but brown, and its rider was not the reaper, but Sully. The advance man was crouched low against the horse's back, riding hard away from the city. Strapped behind him were two familiar satchels, presumably filled with red placards.

Away from the city.

Roy loosed the revolver and fired a shot into the air.

32

Cyrus Lee squinted behind the tiny sights of his Derringer. The man held the pistol straight and unwavering. If he fired, that would truly be that. Paul dropped Jeb Crittendon's revolver on to the prone man's belly. He raised his hands and whispered to Sandy behind him, "Stay calm."

"Back away from him," Lee said.

"You have only one shot," Paul said.

Lee smirked and pointed the Derringer at Sandy. "Back away."

"He's here," Sandy said.

Her ears were young. She'd heard Frank Ledger's funerary rendition of *Clementine* long before Paul and Cyrus Lee. The low melody echoed down the alley as Ledger's shadow appeared. It blotted out the sun and stretched over and past Cyrus Lee, engulfing the man in darkness.

Lee's eyes widened. His fidgety lips went thin. He swallowed when the judge's blade came to his throat from behind.

"That'll be enough from you two," Frank Ledger said.

Cyrus Lee dropped his Derringer. It clattered against the ground. He slowly raised his hands. Ledger safely removed the blade and kicked Lee's back, sprawling him across the alley floor.

"Cyrus?" Crittendon said. His eyes were swollen closed, his mouth bleeding from the beating he'd taken. "You all right?"

Cyrus Lee crawled across the alley toward his partner.

"I can't see," Crittendon said. "Where are you?"

Paul was put into mind of his old grandpap and grandma. All their lives the old man berated his wife and beat her down, kept her behind him. She just took it silently and held the marriage together, kept the home in order. Once Paul was old enough to feel like he knew a thing or two, he determined that his grandma had no backbone. But when grandma died, grandpap came apart and followed her to the grave like a parakeet. Up until this moment Paul thought grandpap had been the strong one all along. Now he understood the opposite was true.

"Answer me, Cyrus," Crittendon said, rocking on his back like a turtle. His searching hands were turned up like beggar's palms.

"I'm all right," Cyrus Lee said, arriving at his partner's side. "I'm here."

Jeb Crittendon found Lee's jacket. He gripped it and pulled the man close.

Frank Ledger kicked Cyrus Lee's boot. "Get him up."

Lee helped Crittendon to his feet. The man's revolver fell off his belly when he stood. Ledger picked up the revolver and put it in the holster on Crittendon's waist. "You're too fat," he said. Then he cut through the leather of Crittendon's gun belt. The belt lost several inches where Ledger hacked it, but it fit its new owner perfectly well as Ledger tightened it around his own waist. "Now," he said, "you two go on. Go back to your prison and tell no stories."

"This ain't right," Jeb Crittendon said. He spit out the blood that'd been welling in his mouth. His head turned back and forth as he spoke; his swollen eyes blind to whom he was addressing. "We can't go back with nothin'. We'll lose our jobs."

Frank Ledger sighed. He said, "You keep standing there, talking. I don't like you."

"Fuck you, outlaw," Crittendon said, leaning toward the sound of Ledger's voice.

He leaned back when his own pistol barrel arrived on his forehead. Ledger pushed him back against the alley wall, using the gun like a bully's finger. "I'm allowing you to leave with your pitiful life," he said. "You'll go back to your prison and tell no stories. Do that, and I won't come to your bedside one night, as silent as the air you breathe, and take back the gift I've just given you. Do it not, and you will never sleep well again."

Jeb Crittendon opened his mouth to reply, but the words never came. Frank Ledger removed the revolver from Crittendon's forehead, leaving behind an indented red ring.

"You have our word, sir," Cyrus Lee said, "I mean, your honor." He helped his partner down the alley and out.

Frank Ledger holstered his new revolver. He turned to Paul and said, "That true?"

"Is what true?"

"You in league with the lizard?" Ledger said.

"No."

"Know where he's going?" Ledger said.

"I need to go home," Paul said. "My wife."

Frank Ledger shook his head, no.

Paul considered drawing his gun. At the thought his skin seemed to tighten on him. His hand must've twitched because Ledger looked down at it, but his expression didn't change. He just stood there, waiting. His inaction spoke a volume. Paul wondered how it was possible

Roy had out-quicked this man. He may have been able to take Jeb Crittendon, but going against Frank Ledger was a death sentence. He relaxed his hand and let it fall to his side. "The sideshow," he said. "I reckon he's trying to find it."

Ledger looked down at Sandy. "And what about you, little one?" he said. "Do you think the bad man is going to the sideshow?"

"He's not a bad man," Sandy said.

Frank Ledger squatted to her level. He regarded Sandy with interest, smirked, and said, "We are all bad men."

Sandy moved closer to Paul. She gripped his duster. Paul put a hand on her shoulder.

Frank Ledger stood up. "A signboard," he said. "If there's a show there'll be an advertisement. He'll aim to find it." He walked to the end of the alley and waited, seeming to give Paul a chance to consider his next move.

Right now, Paul thought, shoot him in the back, *right now*.

But he could not make his hand move. Frank Ledger would find Roy. Paul was certain of it. He would find Roy and kill him without passion or anger, for Ledger's task was not vengeance, but a simple rebalancing of the scales. Rage was always in this man, so much so that it no longer qualified as rage. He was as indifferent to vengeance as a farmer was to shucking an ear of corn, but it was his task all the same, and it would possess him until its end. Paul could abide Roy's death, even at the hands of Jeb Crittendon or Cyrus Lee. Even, God forgive him, at his own hands. There would be a final glory in dying with passion, be it hatred or love, intolerance or mercy. What Paul couldn't abide was the indifference. He couldn't let Roy's life fall away without sound or resistance, like a dream forgotten upon waking.

Paul gripped Sandy's hand. They walked down the alley until they caught up to Frank Ledger at the mouth. They stood behind him. Two men and a little girl faced the whole of Chicago.

They walked into the street.

❧

Sully's horse reared and kicked its front legs. "Whoa!" Sully said. He looked back over his shoulder at Roy. He squinted in concentration, and then his eyes widened. "Scales?"

Roy walked out of the water and came to the road.

Sully turned the horse and trotted back to meet him. "Took you for dead." He hopped down from his horse.

Sully stood a full foot shorter than Roy. He wore a wide brimmed hat with a domed top. His skin was leathery from the constant wind and sun that came with his job. One of his eyes was always a little more squinted than the other, and it seemed to everyone who knew Sully that the suspect eye always flipped back and forth between the two. It was something he and the other performers had once laughed about. At the moment the suspect eye was Sully's left.

"I heard what they did to you," Sully said. "That wasn't right."

Roy shrugged.

Sully patted the horse. "You trying to catch up with them?"

"Thought I'd look in on Mr. McLean."

Sully shook his head.

Roy understood his meaning. "Heart?"

Sully nodded.

"Who's outside now?"

Sully patted the horse again. He looked out over the water. Finally, he said, "I stay in front. It's only in the cities they catch up to me. You know that."

"I do."

"And you know how they are with me," Sully said.

Roy nodded. Sully was referring to how the performers confided in him. He was their oracle. He was a safe place to unload the thoughts and feelings they collected along the road, knowing their words would not be repeated to anyone that mattered. A family of freaks was as maladjusted as any other, and they needed the same release other families needed—to talk behind each other's backs so they could face each other again. Roy himself had confided in Sully many times in his day. Always in the cities at their back-alley saloons, always just a day or two before Sully was off again with a new set of placards, staying ahead. Meeting and talking with Sully had become a rite of passage in their family, an honor and a privilege.

"Then you know how strange I would find it," Sully said, "that no one said a word when I asked about the new outside talker."

"You don't know?"

"Oh, " Sully said, "I know." He threw a foot into the stirrup and hopped back into the saddle in one slick move. He picked up the reins and directed his horse back in the direction he'd been heading. "I guess you'll want to know where they are?"

Roy nodded.

Sully regarded Roy with a perplexed expression. "You should know by now, Scales, the danger of expectations."

Roy raised his bald eyebrows.

Sully sat up straight in his saddle and cleared his throat. He threw out an upturned hand. Affecting a foreign accent and a commanding tone, he said, "No one is born into this wretched life with expectations. We learn them while we are young, while we are but ore yet to be forged in the crucible of being. We learn them and they make us brittle. But just as the strongest steel emerges when the slag is burned away, the strongest man emerges when he's burned of expectations."

"That's mighty fine," Roy said.

"I thank you."

"I'm plenty burned," Roy said.

Sully smirked. "North side," he said, falling out of character.

"Lincoln Park. They've been there almost a week. Tomorrow morning they'll head out to Gary."

Roy pointed to one of the satchels. "May I have one?"

Sully produced a red placard from the satchel and handed it over. "It's nice to see you again, Scales."

"Roy," he said. "My name's Roy Pellerin." He tipped his hat.

Sully tipped his hat in return. "Of course it is."

He rode off.

Roy read the placard.

> *Jack McLean's Congress of Curiosities*
> *Together with the Top Tent Circus*
> *is Coming to Gary, Indiana, June 3rd at 6 p.m.!*
> *Come see the spectacle! The ten-in-one tent featuring*
> *Camilla, the Camel Girl*
> *Girda, the Heaviest Woman Alive*
> *Scales, the Amazing Lizard*
> *and many more!*

Amazing?

Roy's stomach soured. They'd replaced him without missing a beat. They found some other afflicted soul and the show went on, as always. Even Jack McLean's death seemed to cause no ripple. But what had Sully said? No one said a word about the new outside talker.

Samson.

Roy looked at Chicago. The city was a dozing dragon with a spiked backbone, its nostrils blowing smoke. People and horses and trains buzzed it like flies. Roy crumpled the placard in a fist and threw it aside. He tipped down his hat, pulled up his collar, and walked toward the slumbering beast.

33

Frank Ledger carved a straight line through the crowd. Unlike Jeb Crittendon, who had barged through, Ledger walked with no resistance as civilized people parted before him. Their irises touched the corners of their eyes to inspect him as he passed.

Paul followed in his wake, Sandy at his side. His heart ached more for his family with every step in the wrong direction. He envisioned Jacob, motherless and lost in a big city like this, scared and searching for dad.

MIGHT NOT MAKE IT, Delmont's telegram had read. That meant she was still alive. There was hope.

But first the task at hand. How could he ditch Frank Ledger and get to Roy first? What was the plan? He could just stop walking, right now, and let Ledger continue on. The crowd would swallow him up. He and Sandy could duck into an alley and disappear.

No. He thought of how Ledger had appeared at the alley mouth after they lost him once before. The man was a shadow when need be. And besides, Jeb Crittendon had had a plan, too.

Paul would have to plan better. He needed more than just a head start. He needed to put sizeable distance between himself and Ledger.

How?

With no answer to the question, he followed.

They had agreed that Roy would likely make his way through the city. He would look for signs of the sideshow and go to them, so they should do the same.

They moved away from the train station and up Pine Street toward the city center. Beneath their feet were cobblestones, and to the left and right were buildings in varying states of construction—some residential, some industrial, and some still burned out by the fire of 1871. Desperate faces peered out from underneath the fire escapes that zigzagged the alley walls. The rich passed the poor without a glance. The streets were littered with trash and discarded food. A raggedy pigeon with pink feet watched two gulls bicker over a moldy crust. The combatants pecked each other's chests and came away with fine down feathers. As they squabbled, the pigeon snuck in and snatched the bread away from them.

"I'm hungry," Sandy said.

Paul felt the weight of the coin bag on his head. He couldn't remember his last meal. His stomach gurgled. He was surprised to feel hunger in this situation. In the stories he'd heard and read—hell, even in the stories he told—the good guys never ate. They were impervious to hunger and thirst, while villains ate and drank with fervor. It was a character thing. Food represents gluttony. The good side should appear strong and willful, while the bad should appear gluttonous and weak. Paul wasn't sure what it said about him that he was starving.

Frank Ledger stopped and rubbed his elbow. He looked up. "It will rain again."

They came to a city square. In the center was a base for a statue not yet built. The base was a concrete block, larger at the bottom than at the top, and there was a readymade place for an iron plaque. Paul wondered what kind of figure might grace the statue's base some day. Likely a Federal war hero.

"There," Ledger said. He pointed across the square.

At first Paul couldn't see, due to the number of people milling about. He moved up to his tiptoes and peered around heads until he saw the signboard. It was a squatty thing. Two stout wooden legs stuck out from underneath a mountain of paper and nails. They moved through the crowd to find the signboard plastered with ads. One for a Nodark Camera, six dollars. Another claimed that baldness is curable with a simple tonic. Brain Salt. Laudanum. Upright Pianos. Paul eyed a whiskey ad. Sour Mash. Bourbon. Straight. A sweet pain came to his jaw, his salivary glands excreted and begged him to make real the words he read. His stomach began a revolt. He peeled the ad off the face of the board. Ledger followed his lead and peeled back some others. They tore sheets away until a red placard emerged. It told of the circus and sideshow going on this week in north Chicago at Lincoln Park.

Paul felt a sensation like snakes crawling up the backs of his legs. Roy was close. He knew that. He would go to his sideshow, to his kin.

"Will he join them?" Ledger said.

Paul pretended to think on the question. He needed to temper Ledger's haste and buy some time to clear himself of this man. It would do no good to march him straight to Roy. He shrugged. "They cut him up and left him for dead."

Frank Ledger nodded. "We'll move upon them tonight. Let him go to them before we take him down. If we're there first, he'll know, and he'll run." He lifted his right hand and looked down at it. It trembled. Ledger shook his head. "Meantime, we'll eat."

Sandy gripped Paul's hand more tightly. He looked down at her. She smiled.

Paul looked around the square's outer rim. Most of the buildings were tenements, but along the near side was the Fisherman's Inn. The building was constructed of red and brown brick, the sign was a carved wooden plaque hanging from dark chains. He pointed at the inn, but Ledger was already walking toward it.

The sky blinked white with lightning. A brooding storm, just as Ledger had predicted. Plump, dark clouds moved toward them over the tall buildings.

Paul began counting. The thunderclap stopped his counting at three. The first drops of rain touched the cobblestones, touched his hat. He saw their dark circles collecting on Frank Ledger's shoulders as they walked. He watched the man shake off the rain in a move not unlike one of his seizures. When they pulled open the door to the Fisherman's Inn, Paul realized he had a plan.

❊

Roy blinked at the lightning flash, struggling to believe he was watching Paul Constantine follow Frank Ledger toward the Fisherman's Inn. He stood in an alley bordering the square, absently counting as the rain began to fall. Had they formed an alliance? Did Ledger have something on Paul?

The thunderclap stopped his counting at three.

Ledger, Paul, and oddly, the little girl he'd met in the woods outside of Bracken, entered the Fisherman's Inn and disappeared. There had been no gun at Paul's back. It was as if Ledger had Paul leashed like a dog.

Roy swallowed back bile. His old friend was apparently no friend at all, but a man concerned solely with returning him to prison, or worse.

The rain came quickly. The remaining people in the square scattered with hunched backs and newspapers over their heads, protecting themselves as though the water were acid. The square was cleared in the space of a minute.

At first Roy found it hard to make his feet move. He stared at the Fisherman's Inn in a daze. He imagined Paul in there, laughing and drinking with an outlaw as though they were old friends. The vision hit him in an unmarked place, a hollow in his chest that had, until now, gone undiscovered in his life. His breathing hitched. He forced a few deep breaths to bring back order.

If this was Paul's play, he thought, then so be it. He'd burn them both down when the time came.

He left the alley and edged along the building fronts, avoiding the Fisherman's. He didn't bother with the signboard as he passed it; the bright red placard shone like a beacon, and he already knew the way to Lincoln Park.

The rain grew heavier as he moved up Pine Street. The sky hovered lowly. He had the road to himself. He was sure the windows above held ghostly faces looking out at the rain, possibly looking down at a gator man walking their street. Let them look, he thought. He took off his hat to reveal the diamond scales on his bald head. He turned up his face and opened his mouth to take in some of the cold drops. Let them whisper and point and gawk. Let them tell stories of the thing they saw walking in the rain.

34

Frank Ledger moved into a booth against the inn's front window. Sandy slid in opposite him. The glass was streaked with rain. It made the outside world look broken. Ledger took off his bowler hat and placed it on the table before him. There were a few patrons scattered about in booths and on stools, all proper types—quiet and non-threatening.

Upon inspecting Frank Ledger, two men downed their drinks, tipped their hats to the bartender, and left.

Paul checked the barroom for a wanted poster, but found none. He guessed the men didn't know Ledger personally, but he counted them as particularly observant for getting out.

Paul went to the bar. The bartender had more hair on his face than on his head, and even there it was only whiskers. His shirt was white and his apron straps sunk into his shoulders as though, over time, they'd grown into his skin. A cocktail stick moved around in his mouth. He toweled a shot glass and eyed Frank Ledger with distaste as Paul approached.

"How's the food here?" Paul said.

The bartender nodded toward Frank Ledger. In a low voice, he said, "Friend of yours?"

"Yes," Paul said. His own voice sounded harder than he might have intended. Frank Ledger was no friend of his, yet the bartender's demeanor irked him.

"Eyes here," Paul said. He snapped his fingers before the bartender's face.

The bartender looked Paul up and down. "What'll you have?"

"Two whiskeys", Paul said. And then, "Milk?"

"Surely," the bartender said.

"And what's on the menu?"

"Beef stew."

"Three."

The bartender nodded. He threw the towel over his shoulder and set the glass on the bar top. He produced a whiskey bottle and a second glass. "You're Cajun," he said, pouring the shots.

"I am," Paul said.

"I know some of your people," the bartender said, his voice once again low, "and I trust them. I'd usually let you start a tab, but…" His eyes shot to Ledger and back.

"He's no threat to you," Paul said, unsure if what he was saying was true.

"Just the same, there'll be no tab."

Paul leaned forward and let his hat fall into his hands. He pulled out the coin bag and paid the bartender more than the whiskey, milk, and stew could possibly have cost. He picked up the two glasses. "Send two more whiskeys out with the stew."

Frank Ledger stared through the rain-spattered glass. His fingers drummed the table before him. Paul set one glass between Ledger's splayed hands and slid into the booth next to Sandy.

Ledger looked down at the whiskey. His shoulder and head twitched like the muscles themselves held a bad memory of drinking. He shook his head and returned to staring out the window.

Sandy reached for the shot glass.

Paul slapped her hand lightly, looked down at her like she'd lost her mind.

The little girl shrugged.

Paul downed his shot and silently cursed his luck. He hoped the whiskey would loosen Ledger up, possibly tire him, but it appeared he'd have to work through his plan without such help. At the thought, he took Ledger's shot and downed it, as well. The whiskey burned beautifully. It tasted of smoke and wood and earth. It quelled his wild stomach.

A woman emerged from the back room. She had blonde hair and was as big as a Viking. Her chest was like a shelf above a green apron. Her long hair was braided behind her head, and the braid swung back and forth as she walked. Her tray balanced a glass of milk and three brown bowls with handles on the sides, their contents steaming. As she moved toward the booth the bartender poured two more shots and set them on the bar top. The woman snatched them up with one hand and placed them on her tray without slowing down. "Three stews and two whiskeys?"

Paul nodded.

The woman plopped down a stew in front of each of them. She clacked down the shots dead center on the table, and then lightly set the milk in front of Sandy before she headed back toward the kitchen.

Paul looked down at the stew. Brown liquid held up a glistening layer of rendered fat. Small potatoes and carrots broke the surface, along with some beef and what looked like sausage. There were no spoons. Paul gripped the bowl's handle and drank quickly, gulping chunks as they came to his lips. He barely bothered to chew. The broth was salty with a hint of peppers.

When Paul put the bowl back down it was half empty. He wiped his lips with the back of hand. Young Sandy had apparently matched his fervor; her bowl was half empty, as well.

Frank Ledger hadn't yet touched his food. He looked at the stew like it was a bowl of vomit. He lifted his right hand and watched it for a moment. It continued to tremble, maybe more than out in the street. He picked up the bowl and took two medium-sized sips. He then slid the bowl down to the far end of the table.

The man refused anything that might cause contentment or the satisfaction of an urge, Paul thought. It seemed his trembling hand told him how much food was required to keep him going, and he went to the task of eating as though it were an annoyance.

Paul slurped down the rest of his stew in another long session. Sandy did the same. When she was done she slid her bowl aside and pulled her milk closer. Paul picked up Ledger's nearly full bowl and slid his and Sandy's empty bowls beneath. He drank a third shot and set aside the empty glass. His stomach felt stretched and full. His throat was hot and his head was clear. He steepled his hands before his mouth and breathed in and out through his nose. His right leg bounced involuntarily, like a dog's tail.

Frank Ledger turned his sleepless eyes away from the window. Paul saw torture in them. This man had never been allowed peace. Any moment of contentment or rest, possibly since birth, had taken him to a dark place. A place where his body betrayed him and left him frothing like an animal in a humiliating state of weakness. It was no wonder he avoided pleasure like it was disease, and that he sought out the bitter and painful things in life. Pain was the only state of being where this man was in control.

Paul said, "I want to tell you a story."

35

Roy stood at the fairground's edge. The circus tents looked dreary and lopsided in the dusk. The place was all mud and sadness, and it was nearly deserted under the pissing sky. Some boys braved the downpour, trudging up the midway toward the sideshow tents. Likely they'd had their hearts set on this event for weeks. No rainstorm could stop them from going home with honey-coated stomachs and empty pockets.

Roy drew sideways behind the grandstands and food huts. He stepped around the circles of light shed by the hanging oil lamps. Steam rose from their metal lids and glass sides. There were a few outside talkers still making a go of it. One made a half-hearted attempt at the passing boys.

"Want to see a show?" the talker said.

The kids shrugged.

"Aw, to Hell with ya," the talker said. He picked up his podium and disappeared into his tent. The remaining talkers followed his lead, and soon, save for the boys, the midway was empty.

Roy moved unseen until he came to the midway's end. Across the path he found the red and white stripes of Jack McLean's tent. Mud spattered the lower sides, but the top was still clean and bright, shiny from the downpour. The tent stood out in contrast to the dark forest beyond. Out front were all the banners, their easel boards slick and darkened by the weather.

As Roy read each banner, he felt more at ease. The scents he found in the evening air unlocked memories. Familiarity flooded his system. He saw visions of each performer's face, both when they were themselves and when they were angered freaks above him, brutalizing him. Both visions resonated. Both reassured him he was home.

Scales, the Amazing *Lizard*.

The cover-up was well done. To the inexperienced eye it would seem *Amazing* had always been there, but Roy could see the slight discoloration of paint beneath the word, the thinness of the letters crammed into the space where it once read *Crying*.

Jack McLean's podium was empty. Roy frowned. McLean would have been out there. He would stand out front until the very last rube staggered by, come Hell or this selfsame high water.

Roy watched the boys approach. They seemed interested in the banners, but it would take some doing to bring them in. As in all the big cities, the kids here were either of great privilege or of the penniless masses. These boys were clearly of the former. Their clothes were wet, but being well made they kept their shape and color. Their hats discarded the rain as though they were made from duck backs. There was no doubt these boys had coins to spend, but they'd part with them only if the temptation was unbearable.

A voice was heard. Roy recognized it as Jack McLean's, as if the man was speaking to the kids from within Roy's own imagination. "Boys, boys, boys," the voice said. Each word was drawn out slowly with space between. The talker's tone was deep, but maybe not so deep as Roy thought it should be. Strange, he thought, how could his own memory betray him?

A figure emerged from the darkness of Jack McLean's tent, showing Roy that the voice had not been imagined, but it was the voice of the show's new outside talker. The talker's head was turned down so that the top hat's brim masked his face. His jacket was red and his pants and boots were black. As he moved toward the podium he spun the riding crop deftly around a white-gloved finger. He was lean, and he walked with a cat's grace.

This man could not be Samson. He was half Samson's size, if that. Roy imagined Cecil Darton's face below the hat's brim, but the voice didn't quite match. It was deep, yes, but a forced deep. There was effort in it.

"How brave you truly are," the talker said. His head was still down and his face still in shadow, and yet the kids were aware they were being addressed. "How brave to be out here in such *harsh* elements." He waved an upturned hand through the rain.

Roy smiled at the professionalism. The talker's approach was simple and effective. One could spend a lifetime honing such a skill. A young talker would start out poorly, cramming too many words into his speech. thinking, much like with his own manhood, size and length would prove impressive. Over time a talker would learn that less could be more. He'd learn that correctly chosen words aimed at just the right trigger would draw crowds to the tent like sin draws souls to Hell. This talker's skill was honed to a blade's edge. He must have mentored beneath Jack McLean himself.

But if it wasn't Samson, and if it wasn't Cecil Darton, then who?

The talker's head tilted back to answer Roy's question. Beneath the top hat's brim was Jesse's beautiful face.

"But are you brave enough?" Jesse said to the boys. She stopped twirling the riding crop and in one smooth turn used it to pull back the tent's opening, just a sliver. She raised an eyebrow to the boys, knowing she had them, and that no more words were required. Her beauty was the reveal, hidden from view until it was time to strike. It was the neatest trick Roy had ever seen. McLean may have spoken to morbid fascination, but Jesse spoke directly to lust. The boys practically ripped off their pants as they went for their coins, and Roy found himself touching his hat, searching for a coin bag that he'd left lying in the sand beneath the surface of lake Michigan.

The boys were whisked into the tent, and Jesse was left alone at the podium. She tucked away her riding crop and looked up the midway. No one else was coming. The night air was cold and she was wet. Thinking she was unwatched, she rubbed her arms and allowed a shiver. She moved back the podium and made her way around back.

Roy followed.

36

Paul waited for Ledger's reaction. He expected to be told to keep his mouth shut. At the least he expected a stern look, but Frank Ledger turned his eyes back to the window, blinking his insomniac blink. Paul checked with Sandy. She looked up at him with milk on her upper lip. He tousled her hair before starting his story.

"My grandpap always said you can turn your back on your family, your job, and all of your responsibilities, but you can't turn your back on your heart, for it turns with you."

Frank Ledger's head moved. A tiny nod. The movement was so slight Paul wondered if he imagined it. He pressed on, both legs now bouncing.

"And there was no doubt my grandpap's heart was set on a whitetail deer by the name of Stygian.

"Now, most people don't think of deer when they think of the bayou. Instead they think of gators. Always the gators. But make no mistake, the deer are out there, and I should know, for every fall my grandpap and I spent a week hunting them. And every fall, while sitting around the first night's campfire, my grandpap told me the story of his beloved Stygian.

"As legend had it, Stygian was a massive black stag with antlers so wide you'd swear they were the outstretched limbs of a live oak. A devil, some thought, due to his fabled black fur. Grandpap spoke of red eyes and fire-breath from Hell. Others said he was the king of all deer, an ancient and immortal beast, set on earth to haunt hunters' dreams. Still others claimed he was a collection of old hunters' spirits, back for some unexplained vengeance.

"No one was sure what he was, or how he came to be, but they all reckoned he was out there, for each year at least one or two new Stygian stories emerged. Tales told over the orange light of campfires or in the back booths of inns. Tales of a perfect shot missed because the black stag seemed to disappear into the brush," Paul snapped his fingers, "just before the bullet found its mark.

"Stygian was always one step ahead of them, they said. And always he'd twitch that goddamn white tail at them just before he was gone."

Frank Ledger nodded again. This time Paul was sure he'd seen it.

"Of all the storytellers," Paul said, "my grandpap was the worst. He had more Stygian stories than you could count, and with every new season he tempted fate by shaking a fist in the air, saying, 'This year he'll be mine.'

"Now, even as a boy, I believed Stygian was a myth. For Heaven's sake, a black stag with antlers the size of tree branches? Red eyes and fire-breath? Ridiculous. The whole of it was nothing but drunken lore shared between frustrated hunters and old men. It was a story concocted to keep them in the woods and away from their wives. At least that's how I felt until the day I saw Stygian, myself."

Ledger's eyes turned to find Paul. They stared at each other for a moment before Ledger glanced at Sandy, and then returned his gaze to the window.

"It was a cold, fall morning," Paul said. "Unseasonably cold for the time of year, and just plain cold for Louisiana, at all. I remember it well because it was the first time I'd ever seen frost. The trees were bare and gray, and the ground was thick with their fallen leaves. Each leaf was frosted in its own unique pattern, and they crackled underfoot like bird bones. Back then we camped in the woods and lived on grandpap's gruel and coffee for the week, so in the mornings, and with a fire no bigger than the base of a coffee pot, the only way to get warm was to get moving. This day was no exception. We set out in the pitch black before dawn, crunching through the frosted leaves like frozen maroons. It wasn't long before grandpap called it off. He cursed the frost, saying there was no way we could track anything while making such a racket. He wanted to turn back and wait for the afternoon hunt.

"I told him to go back, but that I would press on. There was something about the cold that drew me forward, something about the sharpness in my throat and the shivering of my hands that appealed to me. It meant there was more at stake, a bigger risk, and this brought a new kind of clarity."

Ledger was now nodding now, almost continuously. Sandy sipped at her milk, unblinking.

"Now rid of the old man," Paul said, "I moved slowly through the darkness, carefully picking my steps to make as little noise as possible. It went like this for some time, and after awhile the sun peeked over a ridge. Red and yellow shafts of light split the trees and defrosted the leaves.

"About a mile from camp I came to a downed tree at the base of a ridge. Its trunk was so wide you could hide a house behind it. I leaned my back against the trunk to catch my breath. The forest was coming alive all around me. Birds began to chirp, trees groaned in a fresh wind… and then my ears piqued to an unmistakable sound—something was moving through the undergrowth."

Again, Frank Ledger looked away from the window. This time his eyes stayed with Paul.

"If I thought I was cold before," Paul said, "I was freezing now. In a moment like that your heart pounds so hard it loosens your nerves. Shivering like mad, I looked around the side of the trunk. Up on the ridge I saw a flash of black fur moving between the trees, a white tail twitching back and forth. I'll put my hand to God when I say that the legendary beast was mocking me.

"I stayed still for a moment, just breathing and letting the truth sink in. Stygian was not a myth. The black stag was real. All the stories were true. All the horseshit was porridge.

"And all those hunters, for all those years, were simpletons. Stygian was mine. I would be the greatest hunter Louisiana had ever known!"

Ledger allowed a small, upward curl at one edge of his mouth. Sandy's smile had grown full and wide.

"My rifle held just one shot," Paul said, "but something inside me knew one was all that would be necessary. My aim would be true and the stag would fall. It was my destiny.

"With all the energy I could muster, I launched from behind the trunk, slashing through the undergrowth. I ran up the ridge like a soldier to the gods, bouncing through the forest on winged feet. Moving up and up, I passed from our mortal world into the divine.

"Once I reached the top I splashed down into prone position, rifle aimed. Through the iron sights I scanned the ravine before me. At the bottom there was a small brook. Steam rose from the water, boulders riddled the ground, skeletal trees reached up. Birds flitted in and out of vision.

"But there was no Stygian.

"I brought my eyes away from the rifle sights and scanned the ravine a second time. Again the brook, the steam, the boulders, the trees, and nothing.

"How could this be?

"And then I knew. It was like all the tales I'd been told. The fleeting glimpses of the black stag, the perfect shots that impossibly missed their mark. I would be no different than the rest. My story would be just one more disappointing tale tossed on top of the pile."

Ledger's head tilted with curiosity.

Sandy said, "Come on."

"But then," Paul said, "from the corner of my eye I saw a flicker of bold white. Stygian's tail. It winked from behind a boulder not ten feet from my position. The tail sprouted from a mound of black fur and it was close to the ground, so I knew Stygian had bedded down. At this I cursed my luck, for the mass of his body was hidden from view by that damn boulder, leaving me no shot to take. The only thing was to attack, straight on. Of course, I could have tried to wait him out, but it's known that a smart stag might stay in one place all day. And this was not just a smart stag, but the king of all stags, and a fire-breathing demon to boot. Waiting him out would mean waiting out the devil.

"I came to my knees slowly and quietly, surprising even myself with the deftness of my skill. Up from my knees and to my feet I moved with the control and patience of a monk, eyes always locked on Stygian's tail, never leaving it. The tail continued to flicker and wink at me, to mock me. I drew a deep breath to steady my nerves. My hands did not shiver, my pounding heart was tame; my destiny awaited me, just on the other side of that rock.

"It was in that moment I saw my grandpap's face, bright with fire glow and filled with astonishment at the story I would tell. I saw scores of hunters and old men in inns, all riveted by my gripping tale. Mine. The tale of the man who took down the legendary Stygian."

A second small curl came to the other side of Frank Ledger's mouth. Paul could almost say he was smiling.

"In two giant strides," Paul said, mimicking the steps though stuck in the booth, "I crossed the ten feet of space between myself and destiny. I spun around that rock, rifle drawn. My eyes saw through the rifle's sights while my mind saw the glory of the gods. It was just a matter of squeezing the trigger and I would be at one with them."

Paul paused. He let a beat pass. He smiled. "But leveled in my sights," he said, "was no legendary black stag. There was no king. No fire-breathing devil. No Stygian. In fact, there was no stag at all… but a skunk."

Sandy pulled an intake of breath.

Frank Ledger's eyes widened. His would-be smile reached up toward his ears and made red knobs on his cheeks. His teeth were exposed to the world.

"And his tail wasn't mocking me," Paul said. "It was *aiming* at me." He lifted the final whiskey glass and toasted it first toward Ledger, then toward Sandy. He shot the drink and slammed the glass down on the table. He swallowed down the harsh liquid and said, "And I got sprayed in full."

Frank Ledger's hands came down so hard the empty shot glasses bounced around and Sandy's milk spilled. Ledger laughed, and he laughed well. Sandy laughed. Paul laughed, too. He couldn't help it. The delight in Frank Ledger's eyes was the unbridled delight of a child. Paul wondered if the man had ever laughed before.

And then, just like that, Ledger stopped laughing. A seizure took hold. His eyes focused on nothing and his hands curled into fists. White scars stood out against the redness of his skin. His mouth began to ratchet open, stretching to the locking point. He fell sideways in the booth and began to shake. His arms and legs trembled like he was being electrocuted. He spilled out of the seat and on to the inn floor.

Paul gripped Sandy's hand and got out of the booth. He lifted her into his arms and backed away.

"What's wrong with him?" the bartender said.

"He needs help," Paul said, moving backwards toward the door.

The serving woman came out of the kitchen holding a wet, wooden spoon. She lumbered over to Frank Ledger's side and knelt down. Ledger's mouth was opening and closing like a fish. She put the spoon between his teeth and he bit down on it. The wood crunched, but it held. The woman scooped Ledger up into her arms. Even though he shook wildly, she was big enough to control him. "There's a military hospital on Rush Street," she said. "Follow me."

Still carrying Sandy, Paul backed out of the door and held it open while the woman carried Ledger through. She ran down the street through the pounding rain, presumably toward the hospital.

Paul ran the other way.

37

Roy came to the back of the tent in time to see Jesse go in. She would watch the show from backstage, just as McLean had. Roy stopped and listened. From inside he heard murmurs from the audience.

"This better be good," a voice said.

"Damn right," said another.

Boot heels clacked the stage's floorboards in a slow procession. Cecil making his way across, Roy thought. The audience fell to a hush.

"Ladies and Gentleman," Cecil said. Roy envisioned the movements to accompany the voice—the removal of a hat, a bend at the waist, a broad smile. "All of you have braved the elements to be here with us tonight. You're wet, you're tired, and it sure is *dark* outside."

The murmurs rose and fell. There was a pause. Cecil holding a beat. Roy imagined the inside talker thrusting up a finger as he said, "You shall not regret your persistence."

A voice called out, "We better not!"

Others shouted their agreement.

Roy looked past the tent, out into the forest. A hundred yards away was their camp. It was set up in a small clearing amongst the hardwoods. He could only see pieces of wagons and faded paint through the trees, but there was enough for him to recognize his old home.

He went to it.

The camp was set up in a circle. It wasn't just convenience to set it this way, but an act of defense. Small towns inevitably contained easily instigated mobs. If one or two rubes felt the show wasn't worth their coin, or that one performer or another was in mock of their religious beliefs, the sideshow could find itself set upon. In such a case it was best to centralize and pack together. McLean had become an expert at diffusing such situations—particularly with Samson at his side—but on occasion it was necessary to appear as a unified force, to literally circle the wagons.

Roy moved past the still oxen and fidgety horses into the camp's center. He spun to look at all the wagons he recognized—Cecil's, Girda's, Camilla's, Jukey's, Samson's, Randy and Miriam's, and his own. All were empty, and almost all were the same as when he'd last seen them.

His wagon was the lone exception. It was molded and dirty. The falling rain gave it a filthy sheen. If the outside was so poorly looked after, he could only imagine the inside. He moved closer. A foul odor came from the wagon. It was as if they'd let it to a pig or a donkey. He twisted the latch and found it unlocked. He opened the door. The stench hit him like a thumper. Inside he found the wagon more spartan than when he'd been the owner. His bed and small dresser were gone. There was almost nothing inside. The floor was covered in straw and shit. On a ledge there was an unlit candle and an old cigar box. Tucked against the near wall was a water bucket. That was the whole of it.

Roy blinked and the wagon became his cell at Redmine. The floor turned from straw to clay, the shit turned into moldy bread crusts. The bucket grew a rope that headed toward the ceiling. Roy reeled away from the wagon with one arm covering his eyes. He backed into the camp's center, breathing hard and stumbling. He uncovered his eyes to find himself again in the prison yard. The encircling wagons had become the great wooden wall. The ground was riddled with solitary confinement cells.

He fell to his knees. His body shuddered. He pounded the earth with a fist, making dents in the forest floor.

The forest floor. It wasn't hardpan, but leaves and pine needles. He looked up. The camp was back as it should be. He smiled like a fool, threw back his head and laughed. The mirage had been uncomfortably real. He didn't believe himself mad, but to a degree he wished he was. There would be peace in such a thing, to be constantly lost and unaware, to be constantly confused. The pinheads were happy creatures, were they not?

He stood and went to Jack McLean's wagon. It was bigger and more well decorated than the others. McLean had once told Roy that he actually preferred a smaller, humbler space, but his position of leadership required things to be a certain way. "You can't have an outside talker living in similar quarters to pinheads."

Roy tried the latch but found it locked. He reached under the steps to see if the old man's hidden key was still in place. Sure enough. He slid the key into the lock and opened the door.

The scent here was different than he remembered. McLean's wagon had always smelled of wood and wool. Now there were the scents of spices and talc, and the room had a woman's touch. There were drapes where there had once been shutters. The bed coverings were a lighter color. The dresser, which once stood bare, was covered in trinkets. Porcelain and glass. Birds and turtles. Jesse had made this place her own, just as she'd made the sideshow her own. But what of Samson? In here there was no sign of a husband, no shaving kits, no men's clothing. If Jesse stayed here, she stayed here alone.

Roy shut the door behind him. Rain pounded the roof and made it sound like he was inside a drum. He sat down in a leather chair against the far wall. At least the chair was the same. It'd been McLean's favorite spot. A place to think and smoke a pipe. A place to read. Roy gripped his silver spoon, rubbed a thumb in the bowl. He closed his eyes and thought of his childhood home in the Bayou Rouge. He saw his mother's smile when he read to her, the dimples that came out on her cheeks. He saw his father's final wave as he left for the war. He saw his mother's face turn to horror when the gator took her. He saw the gator's smug expression just before he ended its life. He recalled floating on the river and being scooped up by Paul's father, opening his eyes to a young Paul Constantine. The boy that had watched while his parent's splinted Roy's ankles and salved his skin. The boy that had accepted him without hesitation. The boy that told him stories and kept him laughing while he healed.

His best good friend.

Roy's eyes threw water. For the first time in his life he knew weeping. His mother had wept, but until now he'd never understood why. Her tears weren't born of function, she had told him when he asked, but of feeling. A feeling, Roy imagined, not unlike what he felt now. Love. Love and loss. This was not what he had felt for Jesse. The candle he'd burned for her had been too easily snuffed. This candle's light had survived decades. No fierce wind had touched it. No downpour had doused it. No calloused hand had pinched out the light. This flame had burned on as Roy traveled the country exposing himself. He'd taken it from Paul's boyhood home and kept it in that unmarked place, that hollow in his chest where it had remained hidden. Now the feeling was all over him. It wracked his body and bent him forward. His eyes burned and boiled over with tears. He wept into his hands with no restraint. He hadn't come home, after all. The sideshow had become what he knew as family, but it was dysfunctional at best. His father displayed him on a stage and his brother's cheered the act. He'd lusted for his sister and committed incest with her. They were freaks reveling in freakish things. Not a family, but a gang of outsiders banded together against the mob of society. They'd leaned on each other because they had to, but would any of them stay if they were suddenly made normal? If Camilla's legs were put right, would she continue life with her adopted geek family or go find a husband and give birth to a mess of children? If Randy and Miriam could think straight, would they lose money playing cards on the back of an ox cart amongst foul animals and deformed beings, or would they go become bankers?

Roy wiped his eyes. He leaned back into the chair. If he had a family at all, if he had love, right now it was at the Fisherman's Inn. Paul was trapped there with a madman, and Roy had done nothing to help. He'd made assumptions based on what he saw, just as the schoolteacher had done, just as the prison guards had done, just as each and every man, woman, and child that had ever laid eyes upon him had done.

Roy gripped the chair's arms to stand, but he stopped when the wagon door opened.

38

Paul ran up Pine Street with Sandy in his arms. She clutched herself to his neck, her legs around his back. Cold raindrops stabbed at his cheeks and eyes. He could hardly see the road before him. His lungs burned hotter with each new breath. His legs flared and his feet ached. But there was something good in the running. The abandon of it. It was a purging, a molting. Behind him was old skin, in front of him something raw and unknown. He ran harder. He ran like a boy.

He came to the edge of the fairgrounds and stopped. He let Sandy down. He bent forward, hands on knees, and sucked air. His muscles were jelly.

"Oh my," the girl said.

Paul looked up. Colorful tents crowded the landscape, but the circus was deserted. A few workers milled about, checking tent ropes and kicking at things, seeming in a hurry to be under a roof, dry and warm.

Paul couldn't blame them. There was once a time when he'd wish to be dry and warm, as well, but right now he was one with the dampness and cold. He was making a pact with pain, and secretly he wished he were bleeding.

Sandy gripped her own arms against the weather. Paul removed his duster and put it over her small shoulders. Though it was miles too big, she threw up the hood, pulled up the sleeves, and managed. She grabbed his hand and drew him forward.

Paul regained his breath as they walked the deserted midway toward the sideshow tents. They passed a tent advertising a snake charmer and one advertising a six-legged cow. Another advertised a Cyclops, and still another offered conjoined twins. Near the end of the line there was a small tent proposing an *Anatomical Wonder*, but there was no picture to give any idea of the act, only a question marked cloaked in darkness. Paul wondered what it could be, and then he smirked, realizing the vagueness was a trick to lure him in.

No outside talkers were at their podiums. No one tried to convince them to come in, out of the rain, and bare witness to something awful and amazing.

They heard a crowd's muffled applause. It came from the last tent on the midway. They walked toward the tent slowly. It was striped red and white, which made Paul think of blood and bones. Above it hung a painted banner, *Jack McLean's Congress of Curiosities*. Numerous smaller banners stood out front on wooden stands. The falling rain made them hard to read. They moved closer. Paul eyed one banner amongst many. It depicted a being with a reptile's body and a human head. *Scales, the Amazing Lizard*. The image looked nothing like Roy, and no right-minded person would believe they'd see something like this beast once inside the tent. But Paul supposed, again, that this was the trick—you had to come in and find out.

Inside the tent, a crowd gasped and clapped. It seemed one of the shows was ending. A voice towered above the din. "Another round of applause, please, for Henry, the Ossified Man!"

The crowd renewed their applause. Someone whistled.

The inside talker continued. "And now, ladies and gentleman, I'll ask you to hold on to your seats, grab a neighbor's arm, or at least plant your feet to the earth. In a moment our beloved *Girda* will cross this stage, and her massive steps will shake the very ground!"

Paul and Sandy moved around the side of the tent. As they neared the corner he heard the squelch of wet footsteps above the sound of rain. He backed Sandy up against the tent until they were both in shadow. A woman walked past them, didn't see them. She wore a black top hat and a red jacket. A riding crop was tucked under one arm. She was exquisite. Her stride, even in the mud, was elegant. In her presence, Paul felt curiously less evolved, like she was from some future world and he was the equivalent of a caveman. She entered the nearby woods and walked toward an encampment.

If Roy had come to this place, Paul thought, this was the person he'd seek. There could be no mistaking it. This woman could drive any man to his brink and well beyond. One look was a vise on your heart. One touch and you'd swear to God.

Paul began to follow the woman, but Sandy stayed put. She held Paul's hand, not allowing him forward. He came back to her. "What is it?"

"That woman," she said.

"What of her?"

Sandy hung her head. She spoke into her chest when she said, "She scares me."

Paul set a lock of the little girl's hair back behind her ear. "Why?"

Sandy looked up. Her eyes searched back and forth across Paul's face. Raindrops tapped her cheeks, making her blink.

"What is it?" Paul said.

"You'll leave me."

A bird spread its wings in Paul's chest. He pulled the girl close and hugged her to him. She dug her face into his collar, clamped her hands around his neck.

"I won't leave you," Paul said.

Sandy gripped tighter at his words. Her body shook. He lifted her off her feet and hugged her tightly. She nuzzled into his neck. "Does he love her?"

Paul set her down. She backed up and wiped her cheeks.

"He might," Paul said.

"He must," Sandy said.

Paul nodded in the direction of the camp. "Coming?"

They moved quickly and quietly through the rain, picking up ground on the woman. The encampment was a circle of wagons, each one displaying a different circus scene. One showed the white clown's face of the legendary Joseph Grimaldi, another the three rings of a circus complete with lion tamer and lions, a third depicted a strongman hefting an iron weight. In all cases the paint was faded and peeling, the wood was cracked, and in some places, mended.

Paul and Sandy watched as the woman stopped at the doorway of the largest wagon, seeming perplexed by the latch. She reached beneath her jacket, into the small of her back, and produced a snub-nosed pistol. She drew one deep breath, and then another, before pushing aggressively through the door, pistol at her side.

❊

Roy hung halfway between sitting and standing up from the leather chair. In the doorway was Jesse's dark silhouette. One hand was tucked behind her waist, no doubt concealing a weapon. A lock of hair hung loose from beneath her top hat. Her body was tense.

Roy eased back down into the chair. He turned up his hands to her, showing only the spoon he carried, no gun.

Jesse relaxed. She entered the wagon and closed the door behind her. "You're alive," she said, sounding bored. It was as if a threatening intruder would have been the favorable thing.

"I am," Roy said.

"Good for you," she said. "What do you want?" She moved to the dresser and put down the small, silver gun she'd been holding. She pulled off her gloves, tugging one finger at a time.

Roy watched her delicate hands as she unsheathed them. They were as perfectly illustrated as he remembered them. He followed the contour of her arm up past her shoulder to her face. She pulled off the top hat and a few more locks of hair fell across her eyes.

She wasn't ordinary. Roy could not deny it. She was the embodiment of sex and lust. She was everything a man desired, and yet it was difficult to muster the feelings he once held. It was like understanding that a painting was beautiful and deeply moving to other people, maybe even once to himself, but he could no longer see its beauty, no matter how desperately he wanted to.

"Oh," she said. "I see." Her tongue rubbed across her teeth, underneath her lips. She put a hand to her chest. "Did you think it would be so easy?"

Roy felt a twinge of anger. She believed his sole purpose had been to seek her out, to be with her again. And of course she was right. "No."

She raised an eyebrow.

"You have a husband."

She looked away. Her eyes became unfocused. She placed the top hat on the same hook Jack McLean once used. The hat wobbled for a second before falling still. She began rearranging items on her dresser. She turned a glass turtle first left, and then right. She slid a swan from the back to the front. She swallowed. "It's my fault. Had I not spent that night with you, none of this would have happened."

Roy's heart and head played tug-of-war. His heart was a poet. It pulled for their special night, the most vivid and memorable thing in his life. It pulled to have that night grow in strength and purpose, to become a more important thing. His head was a tax collector. It pulled for protection against childish dreams.

"I was mad at him that night," she said. She took off the red overcoat, peeling it back from her shoulders, first the left and then the right. As she removed the jacket Roy watched her full chest and the flatness of her stomach stretch against her white, custom cut dress shirt. There were glimpses of the tattooed lines beneath, and the dimpled outline of a cigar burn. She was flawlessly shaped, designed by God to weaken men's knees and stiffen their loins.

"He burned you," Roy said.

She looked at him curiously.

"That cigar burn." He pointed at her ribs.

Jesse put a hand over the area of the scar and smiled. "This was our wedding vow."

Roy blinked. His heart let go of the rope. The tax collector reeled it in.

"I was mad at him," she said, "because he met with my grandfather alone. They talked family business without me."

Roy tried to stand, but his legs merely shook. He was no hero, no star-crossed lover. His motivations had been cheap. His mission hadn't just been a waste of time, but a hoax from the start.

"And then the old man died," she said, "before I had a chance to reason with him, to let him know the others didn't know George like I did. They wouldn't accept him as their leader."

She sat down on the bed, slid off one boot.

"Where is he?" Roy said.

She regarded Roy coolly. "He's different now, after what they did."

Roy waited.

She slid off the other boot and aligned both on the floor. She cracked her toe knuckles and then leaned back with both palms on the bed behind her. There was a time when seeing her like that might have dropped him in a faint.

"You saw the banners out front?" she said.

Roy nodded.

"Did you wonder why yours still stood?"

Roy said nothing.

"I'm sure you did. Well, we can't have a show without a lizard man, now can we, Scales?"

"My name's not Scales. It's Roy Pellerin."

"And my name's Jesse Fickas. So what?"

Paul stood on the steps outside the wagon, his hand hovering an inch from the latch. He stood there stupidly while Sandy looked up at him from where she was hidden beneath the wagon floor, behind a wheel. His movement had stopped dead when he heard the woman say *Fickas*.

The husband she and Roy were speaking of, could it be?

Voices and laughter cut through the rain to reach Paul's ears. He looked back to see a silhouetted cluster of sideshow performers moving through the woods toward the camp. Out front were two pinheads, dashing and laughing, playing tag. Behind them a woman walked on all fours like a dog. Next to her two men in overalls carried a board between them. No, not a board, a man. As they moved closer Paul could see the prone man's face was frozen in a horrified stare.

Paul came down the steps. He joined Sandy beneath the wagon, out of sight. He peeked from the darkness to watch the performers parade into the camp. They found their way to their individual wagons and went inside.

From a distance two more figures approached. One was a short, round mass of humanity. It hobbled in such a way to make Paul think the body was actually two side-by-side sections, with each side taking a turn to move out front and propel it along and pull the other side up. This had to be the fat lady. The second figure towered over the first. It lumbered next to her like a bear walking on hind legs.

Paul held his breath; he would recognize that gait anywhere. Even with the man's features concealed by darkness, Paul knew he was looking at George Fickas.

39

"The day before he died," Jesse said, "my grandfather announced to everyone that George would be taking over as outside talker. As you can imagine, they didn't take the news well."

Roy thought of the way they raged when provoked. Always the performers teetered on the edge of violence. Living life under constant scrutiny and threat made them volatile. On stage they performed and smiled, they did what was necessary to survive, but away from the tent they were jaded and intolerant. They'd grown up wanting acceptance, needing it. They'd grown into young adults holding on to the hope that one day their circumstances might change; either they'd somehow transform from ugly duckling into swan, or that society would evolve its way of thinking to accept them. As fully-grown adults they discovered the lie in Aesop's fable, and the cold truth that the world was as unchanging as their face, their skin, their size, their knees, their missing limbs. With this truth in hand, they no longer sought out acceptance from the outside world, but a healthy disdain for it, and fury for anything, or anyone, that smacked of it.

"They were angry," she said, "but trust me, Scales, their anger wasn't about you. They got over you quickly. Even my grandfather did. They say it's about family, but don't fool yourself, it's about money. You killed Jukey, and he was our biggest draw. You cost us all." She turned an ear to the wagon doors opening and closing outside. "They're back."

"What did they do with the news?" Roy said.

"They performed," she said, "what else? They smiled and pretended they couldn't be happier. They were convincing, too. Camilla even went as far as sewing George a new outside talker's jacket. Even I thought, for a moment, that it might work out. But secretly they were packing their bags. Can you believe that? A family of freaks ready to take to the streets just so they wouldn't have to be led by my husband."

"But they're still here," Roy said.

She leaned forward and placed her elbows on her knees. "It was one of them, I know that, but really it was all of them. They must have thought twice about leaving. Instead, they concocted a plan to make sure George wouldn't stand long behind the podium."

Randy.

"I found my husband lying behind our trailer, alone and bleeding on the ground, that horrible rock next to his head."

Roy envisioned Randy atop McLean's trailer, large rock in two hands, waiting for Samson to pass beneath. He shuddered to imagine the impact on the big man's head. In his mind he heard Randy whisper, "Yeaaah."

Tears welled in Jesse's eyes. She lifted her hand to wipe them away, but then stopped. Her face became tranquil. She straightened her spine and let the tears fall as they may. "But everybody pitches in," she said. "Isn't that right?"

"I don't imagine he's shoveling horseshit," Roy said.

"He's still a part of the show," Jesse said, "but his act is different now. *He's* different now." She looked at Roy's hand and shook her head. "That figures."

Roy looked down to see the spoon gripped tightly in his hand, his thumb involuntarily circling the bowl.

"He'll be escorting Girda," she said, "as usual. She's fallen a couple times in the last year and he's the only one with the strength to help her up. They'll be behind the rest." She went to the window and peeked through the drapes. "They're here now."

Roy came to the window just in time to see his old wagon door close. The camp's center was empty now. All the performers were tucked away and drying out.

"He's in my wagon?" Roy said.

"You've seen it?"

He nodded.

"Then you know what sort of state he's in." She moved away from the window and Roy once again found her scent. It cast a shiver over him. He stepped to the wagon door, put his hand on the latch, and looked back. She looked cold and frail. All her guile had fallen away.

"The show needs him," she said, forcing a smile that didn't have the strength to remain. "*I* need him. Don't take him away."

Her husband was a brutal sadist, and yet it was clear she loved him.

Roy left Jesse's wagon thinking how he'd spent his life catering to the nature of others—what they thought, what they felt, what they needed. But what had they given back? He tried to conjure an image of something he'd learned from them, something that made sense, something he could describe and cherish.

No dice.

The sour stench again assaulted Roy's nose as he approached his former wagon. The windows were covered with horizontal shades, but faint light sliced through the slots. The wagon was noticeably tilted to one end, suggesting the massive figure inside was at the back. Roy pocketed the spoon. He put one hand on his revolver and opened the door. Cigar smoke was the new scent. Cigar smoke and burning meat.

The creature that was once Samson looked up as Roy entered. It was sitting cross-legged at the back of the wagon. On its face Roy could see a manmade pattern in the flesh. Circles. And stretching away from its forehead was a long, red scar with white stitch-mark dots on either side. The creature's eyes were sallow and drooping, the irises gleamed in the light from the candle on the floor just in front of it. It grunted something like, "Hello."

Roy managed a small wave. He felt both silly and scared. In one hand the creature held a cigar butt. The orange, cherry end was glistening and crackling. The opposite forearm bled from a new wound. As Roy's eyes adjusted, he could see the pattern in the creature's flesh was not confined to the face. It spread out over parts of the creature's body like... Jesus, like scales. It came up from his hands and wrists and it marked his chest and lower legs. The work was intricate and no doubt time-consuming. Each individual scale overlapped two others below it and was overlapped by two above it. Each was a perfectly round cigar burn, raised from the skin in a bumpy cluster. There fresher wounds were at the edges.

Roy opened the nearby cigar box and looked inside. It was loosely filled with cigar butts and two full-length, unlit cigars. The butts weren't chewed and mangled like they'd be if someone had smoked them. Instead they were still round and uncut at the lip end. Roy picked up one butt and examined it. The burnt end was waxy and crusted over with the skin and blood that had been melted to it. He looked down to see all the butts had the same waxy look. There must have been a dozen of them.

The thing reached out its current cigar butt to the candle before it. It rolled the end in the flame. Absently, it said hello again. Its voice was rough, but still recognizable as Samson's. The butt grew bright with embers, and the creature found the appropriate spot on its arm. It drove the burning cigar into its flesh with a sizzle. Smiling at the pain, the creature began rocking forward and backward. The wagon moved under its shifting weight.

The thing extinguished the cigar butt on the floor and dropped it. It fished out something from a pile of straw and held it up. Roy's knife.

"Pretty," the creature said. It rubbed the knife's handle with its thumb, making sense of what Jesse had said about Roy's spoon.

"Yes," Roy said. "Pretty." He held out an upturned palm. "Can I see pretty?"

The creature clutched the knife close to its chest. It shook its head back and forth with a petted lip.

"Okay," Roy said.

The creature loosed one hand from the knife and pointed at Roy's waist. "Pretty!" it said.

Roy looked down to see that the creature was pointing at his gun. The candlelight gave the iron ring a yellow glimmer.

"This?" Roy said, indicating the gun.

The creature nodded.

Instead of reaching for the gun, Roy reached into his pocket. He produced the spoon and held it out. "What about this?" he said.

Candlelight splayed against the silver, making the spoon glow brilliantly. The creature's eyes widened. Its jaw unhinged. It stopped nodding. It stopped rocking. The wagon fell still.

"Mine," the creature finally whispered. One giant hand reached out for the spoon.

Roy pulled the spoon back.

The creature's eyes met Roy's. Its brow came down and a scowl came to its face. "Mine!" it said. It flexed a series of muscles in threat. Veins appeared everywhere.

"Trade," Roy said.

The creature blinked, seeming unable to comprehend the word.

"Trade," Roy repeated. This time he pointed to the knife.

The creature looked down at the knife in its hand. It looked at the spoon. It looked back at the knife, and then again at the spoon. "Trade?"

Roy nodded.

In a flash the creature's hand moved, snatching the spoon from Roy's grip.

Roy looked at his empty palm in disbelief.

The creature grinned. "Mine!" It pounded two fists on the floor, knuckles down. The wagon shook. The candle wobbled. The creature hopped to a crouched position with two feet on the floor, Roy's knife in one fist, his spoon in the other. "Mine, mine, mine, mine, mine!" It pounded the floor with each repeated word. The candle fell. Roy snatched it from the ground before it lit the straw. He drew his revolver and backed away.

The creature's body fell into shadow as the candlelight now hardly reached it. Roy saw only a black, hulking mass and two yellow eyes fixed on him. He cocked back the revolver's hammer and trained the sights on the dark space between the thing's eyes. He didn't dare move the gun off target when he heard the wagon door open behind him.

40

The wagon walls shook. The windows rattled. Inside George Fickas was screaming, "Mine, mine, mine." Paul gripped the door latch with an icy hand. He needed to turn it. He knew that. It was just that his hand refused to move. His neck throbbed. His mind was overrun with childhood memories. In one moment he was watching a scabby skinned boy run through the schoolyard. In the next he was lying on the ground, unable to breathe, with George Fickas standing above him. In another moment he and Roy were running through the bayou, laughing.

And then he was holding a stray dog underwater.

The dog's claw scratched his hand and made it move.

The wagon door fell open.

Paul stepped inside with Sandy just behind him. He saw Roy holding a candle in one hand, his father's old revolver in the other. The revolver's hammer was cocked back, the gun aimed. At the far end of the wagon Paul saw the target—two eyes reflecting candle-light in the darkness. He could make out George Fickas' weighty silhouette. The man was crouched like an animal and seemed ready to pounce.

Paul had expected to feel rage. He'd expected his mind to go blank and his hands to act on their own accord, loosing his Dragoon and filling George Fickas' body with bullets. But all he felt was pity. This creature was not the bully he once knew. George Fickas was nothing more than a bad memory.

"Hello, Paul," Roy said.

"Hello, Roy."

They stood in silence for a moment. A drop of wax fell from the candle and hardened, trapping a length of straw against the floorboards. Rain lashed the roof and walls of the wagon, but the dominant sound was the creature's labored breathing.

"Come to take me back?" Roy said.

"No."

"Come to kill me, then?"

"No chance at that."

Roy glanced at Paul. A smile came to his face.

Paul put a hand on his friend's shoulder. "Let's go."

"He's got my knife," Roy said.

Paul looked in the creature's direction. Its body was inflating and deflating with each breath.

"Let him keep it," Sandy said.

Both men looked down at the little girl between them. She was transfixed by the creature at the back of the wagon.

"Let him keep it."

Roy set the candle on the nearby ledge. He holstered his revolver and they turned to leave.

"Faggot," the creature said. The sound of the voice hit Paul like a punch to the kidney. His core went cold. Blood rushed to the extremities. His ears and eyes burned. He released Sandy's hand.

"Killer," the creature said.

"Keep going," Roy said. He put a hand on Paul's back, pressuring him toward the door.

But Paul slapped Roy's hand away. He came back and faced the creature straight on, ten feet between them. His right hand hovered near the Dragoon on his waist. A bit closer now, and with his eyes adjusted to the low light, he could make out the creature's horrible features, the scales and the closed scar on its head, the bleeding wounds.

The creature pounded the floor with two fists. "Why you here?"

Paul opened his mouth to reply, but he found no words. Throughout his youth he envisioned what he'd do differently if ever facing George Fickas again. Growing up he'd lie awake at night, seeing things in new ways. He would have run off with that dog, taken it home, and given it a name. He would have grabbed a stick and cracked Fickas over the head. He would have pleaded with those cowardly thugs to help him overtake their leader and do the right thing. But now here he was, given his chance to fulfill a myriad of vengeful dreams, and he had no words, no action. The creature had asked him why he was here, but he couldn't say.

Paul heard a metal *ting* against the floorboards. The beast had dropped something. A spoon. The horrible thing coiled back on its haunches into a bull's stance. It said, "*Dog* killer."

Paul stepped toward the creature, but Roy's hand came to his shoulder.

"Enough," Roy said.

Again Paul slapped his friend's hand away. He took another step toward George Fickas, but suddenly found himself against the wagon wall, his lips thumping in pain.

Roy had punched him.

Paul reached a hand up to his mouth, found his upper lip split and bleeding.

"Enough," Roy said. One of his hands was flat against Paul's chest, the other was a fist up near Roy's ear, ready to fire again. Paul looked down at his own hand. It trembled. He clasped it together with the other but the trembling wouldn't stop. He looked at Sandy. Her hands covered her mouth and nose in fear.

Roy drew back the hand on Paul's chest. He gestured for Paul to come forward. Paul did. He gathered Sandy to his front and they started again toward the door with the creature at their back. Roy reached for the door latch. As he gripped the handle there was the sound of a thrown knife splitting the air.

The blade appeared on Sandy's back, just inside the shoulder. *T. Pellerin* was etched into the metal.

The girl fell.

Four rapid-fire gunshots echoed in Paul's ears. A sulfuric scent filled the wagon. The creature that was once George Fickas teetered for a moment, and then crashed to the ground, face down in the straw. Paul found his arm was extended straight out. Clutched in his hand was his father's old revolver, ripped from Roy's holster in the moment when Sandy fell. His finger repeatedly worked the trigger, clicking the impotent hammer in the silent aftermath.

41

A pool of blood spread from beneath the creature's chest. Roy could see his reflection in the dark liquid, could smell the iron scent mixing with scorched black powder. Outside, wagon doors opened and closed. Voices punched through the drumming rain. Roy heard Camilla. "What was that noise?"

"They're coming," Roy said. He looked down at the girl, who was lying on the wagon floor, eyes closed. Paul had removed the knife and was packing her wound with material torn away from his shirt.

Outside, Cecil Darton said, "Sounded like gunfire."

"I'll explain it to them," Paul said, he gestured toward the wadded cloth over the girl's wound. "Just hold this in place to stop the bleeding."

"You have a family?" Roy said.

Paul nodded.

"Go to them. I'll take care of this." He gripped the door latch.

"No," Paul said.

"I'm not giving you a choice," Roy said. He turned to leave.

"Wait," Paul said.

Roy stopped, turned back.

"I followed you that night," Paul said. "That night my mother took you away."

Roy let go of the latch.

"I saw her give you to that man, Jack McLean. I went to him after my mother left, asked him if what she had done was right."

Roy saw a vision of a brave young Paul standing beneath Jack McLean's podium, looking up at the terrifying man, just as he himself had done.

"He told me you were with your real family now," Paul said, "and that you'd be happy with them all the days of your life. I knew then that I could let you go, Roy, but, God help me, I need to know now... have you been happy?"

A series of memories flooded Roy's mind. They spanned from his days in the Bayou Rouge with his parents to his days with the sideshow, with Jesse, with Jukey, with Miriam and Randy, and with Jack McLean. He saw all of their laughing faces, and he saw their sadness. He understood their tears. He saw visions of all the places he'd been—the lakes, the oceans, the mountains, the cities, and all the roads in between. He saw the wide-eyed stares of the audiences and he heard their applause. He saw the river in which he and Paul swam that fabled summer, the summer he'd spent with his best good friend. The hollow in his chest, that unknown and empty place he'd discovered in the heart of Chicago only hours before, now felt full and overflowing. It had been a good life. By God, it had been an adventure.

"It's been a humdinger."

42

Roy came out of the wagon, pulling the door closed behind him. He took off his jacket and shirt, exposing his carved chest. The freaks stood before him in a half circle. Beyond them was Jesse. She stood on the steps of Jack McLean's wagon, a hand once again concealing the weapon behind her waist. Her other arm was crossed over her chest, gripping against the cold. Her face looked washed away.

One of the freaks stepped forward and pointed. "He shot Scales."

The rest murmured.

Roy tapped the iron ring on the butt of Paul's old revolver as he walked out into the camp's center, allowing the freaks to encircle him. He suddenly drew the weapon, but none of the faces flinched. Somehow this pleased him. He tossed the gun outside the circle.

The freaks drew closer. Their clothes were drenched with rain. Roy wasn't sure if they'd embrace him as a brother or tear him apart as the murderer they had already executed. He slapped both hands on his chest, making sure they saw their vile word.

Jesse came down. She pushed between two of the freaks and entered the circle with Roy. She revealed her snub-nosed pistol, extended her arm and aimed the gun. Above and behind her the rain clouds began to separate.

Roy stepped toward her. He stopped when he felt the gun's cold barrel against his sternum, against their word. She'd already sentenced him at the Corktown Inn, and now his stay of execution was over. He spread his arms and tilted back his head. He could see through the twisted canopy of trees. He could see past the clouds to find the moonlit sky full of twinkling stars. He could see the foundation of Heaven, and he found it beautiful.

43

Paul heard the gunshot and knew its meaning. He pushed the pain aside. Sandy's bleeding had stopped, but the wound was bad, potentially fatal if she wasn't helped soon. He lifted her into his arms and kicked open the wagon door. The performer's stood before him in a half-circle. The illustrated woman was standing above Roy's body with a pistol in her hand.

"She needs help," Paul said, gesturing with his head toward the girl in his arms.

The illustrated woman came toward Paul. She showed him the gun she'd just used on his friend. "You'll die here now, lest you leave."

"I'll take him with me," Paul said.

"And I'll take that," the woman said, nodding at the ornate Dragoon on Paul's waist.

"Can you stand?" Paul said to Sandy.

The girl nodded slowly, but didn't open her eyes. Paul set her down on her feet. She stayed upright, but unsteady. Paul removed the Dragoon slowly and handed it to the woman, hilt first. The woman took the gun, stepped aside, and gestured toward Roy's body.

Paul picked up Roy's body and slung him over his shoulder. He came back to Sandy and took her hand.

The illustrated woman stopped him as he turned to leave. She picked up Paul's father's revolver from where Roy had tossed it, opened the chamber, and dumped the empty shells. She plugged the gun into the holster on Paul's hip.

Paul walked back up the midway with Roy over his shoulder and Sandy at his side. The rain had stopped and the cloud cover was sporadic. The circus tents rippled in the wind. They made their way back to Pine Street and started back toward the city center.

Sandy stumbled as she walked. She was growing weaker.

"Come on, now," Paul said. "You can do it. It's a short walk back."

She stumbled again and fell to her knees.

Paul reached down with one arm and lifted her off the ground, up on to his hip. He clutched her there and began to run, balancing Roy on his opposite shoulder. "Stay with me now."

Sandy murmured. She was fading.

"I'll tell you a story," Paul said. He was breathless, but he continued. "This is one about little Tommy... Tommy was a naughty young boy." He ran several more yards with weakening legs. He steeled his spine, re-hefted Roy's weight, and kept on. "Now, everyone knew Tommy was a foul-mouthed boy-"

A distant sound slowed Paul's pace. A song. He looked down Pine Street to see the silhouette of a man walking up the road. The man was whistling a spirited version of *Camptown Races*.

Paul kept moving. Close enough now to see, he hardly recognized a refreshed and invigorated Frank Ledger. The insomniac look had abated. His face was flush and his eyes were bright. The bastard was damn near skipping down the lane.

Despite himself, Paul's face burst into a smile to match Ledger's. New blood poured from the split in his lip where Roy had punched him. Had Ledger eaten? No. He had rested. The seizure had taken him down hard. The serving woman must have taken him to the hospital, as she said she would. No doubt they supplied him with a dose of Laudanum to put him out, at least for an hour or so. The short sleep must have felt like a week's worth to the restless man.

Paul dropped down to his knees, set Roy down at one side, and stood back up with Sandy still in his arms.

Ledger stopped in front of Paul, and at the sight of Roy's dead body, he stopped whistling. He knelt down and placed a hand on Roy's chest, over the word carved into Roy's diamond skin, over the bullet hole.

Without looking up, Ledger said, "I ought to end you for that story you told. You knew what it would do to me."

"She needs a hospital," Paul said.

Ledger nodded toward Roy's wound. "Your doing?"

"No."

"Was it just?"

"Does it matter?"

Ledger removed his hand from Roy's chest and examined it. There was blood on his palm, his fingers. He rubbed it in like oil, and for a moment just stared as his blood-covered hand. It wasn't trembling, but perfectly still. "Rush Street," he said, "a few blocks down from the Fisherman's. You won't miss it. I'll see this man to the sexton."

Paul holstered his gun and started down the street, moving faster now without Roy's weight on his shoulder. "Hale County," he called back. "Have him sent to the law office of Delmont Graves."

"I know that lawyer well," Frank Ledger said, "you have my word."

Paul glanced back to see Frank Ledger now standing over Roy's body. His head was bowed and his bowler hat was in his hand, held over his heart.

Epilogue

Paul knelt in front of Roy's freshly dug grave, Jacob at one side, Sandy at the other. The headstone simply read *Roy*. Jacob played with the wooden pop-gun his grandfather had given him while Paul was gone. The boy's lips and tongue were green from the rock candy Paul had gifted him after he'd helped dig.

Jacob pulled back the pop-gun's handle and shot it forward. A cork shot off the end and then hung loosely by the thread keeping it attached to the barrel.

Paul's wife had consumed a nearly lethal combination of alcohol and opium. One of Delmont's hands had come to get clothes for the boy and found her facedown in the kitchen, faintly breathing.

Gloria survived the ordeal. Currently she was in the back bedroom, resting. She'd been there since Paul had come home, though she had awakened for a moment when he arrived, had clutched his hand and squeezed it. In that touch he felt more for her than he had in years. He kissed her forehead and told her he was sorry. He vowed to be a better husband to her, a better father to their son and to their adopted daughter. Gloria's tired eyes found Sandy in the room. A faint smile moved across her lips before she closed her eyes again.

The warden informed Paul he was no longer a prison guard. Paul supposed he'd known it all along. Delmont offered him the clerk's job and he took it. He would start next week.

Again Jacob took aim with his popgun. It looked like he was going for a lone dandelion out near the road. The handle shot forward and the cork popped free. "Pow," he said.

"Did you get him?" Paul said.

Jacob nodded. He watched the dandelion for a moment and then slid the wooden gun into the small holster at his side. He looked up at his father. "Tell me again, dad, where'd you go?"

"To the big city," Paul said. He picked Jacob up on his hip. "Chicago." He breathed the city's name and drew it out to give it mystique.

Jacob reached a hand up to his father's face. He touched Paul's lips while touching his own, as if comparing the injury to undamaged skin. The boy's touch tickled and stung.

"Why?" Jacob said.

Paul thought on his son's question. There were many answers. Some he understood, others he didn't. The easy thing would be to say he was just doing his job, but that would be a lie. He recalled the way his body felt after he'd sprinted to the Lincoln Park fairgrounds with Sandy in his arms. He'd been happily exhausted. It was a feeling he hadn't felt since youth. He couldn't quite define it, but he knew the answer was somewhere in that feeling, somewhere in the abandon of it. It was somewhere in the Bayou Rouge, hidden in an old bloodhound's grave. And it was somewhere in the stitched wound above his lip—one of the marks his friend left on him, ensuring he would always have a story to tell.

Printed in Poland
by Amazon Fulfillment
Poland Sp. z o.o., Wrocław